Johnnie &
the Tempest

DS WHITAKER

ISBN: 978-1954794-07-8 (EB)
ISBN: 978-1954794-06-1 (TP)
Library of Congress Control Number: 2024900150

Author photo by Diana Lang
Cover Design by DS Whitaker

To Tim for his love and support

To Nancy and Dad for beta reading

To the Reston Writers for your wonderful insights and friendship

Prologue

Something wasn't right.

Something big was going to happen.

The feathered residents of Stumpy's beach also must have sensed this. Under the dim moonlight, a conclave of seagulls huddled on the sand to his left, chatting fiercely about something. He had never seen so many gulls on his beach and never past dark. Their cacophony caused his shortened tail to twitch with displeasure.

[Leave, you filthy birds!] Stumpy ran toward them, hoping to bite one on the leg. To show them that this was his domain. Because, as the Iguana King and self-appointed ruler of Hawksnest Beach, he needed to set decisive boundaries.

The gulls flapped their wings at his approach, but did not budge.

Stumpy cried, [How dare you! Begone!]

The largest gull, mostly gray with black markings on its shoulders, flew at him and pecked at his dorsal crests. It hurt.

If he had his rightful tail, he would have slapped the intruding foe with all his might. But he had lost his magnificent striped tail many moons ago to another enemy; a large creature encased in metal, rolling at speed and spewing nasty smoke.

Stumpy swiped at the gull with his front claws and lunged to bite. But his enemy flew up and away, only to dive bomb him from behind. He couldn't find an advantageous position.

This was not a fair fight.

Retreat was his only option. Yet he was still curious about this bizarre assembly. He climbed to the top of his favorite palm tree and listened.

None of their chatter made sense.

The seagull leader squawked above the din, gaining his group's attention.

With a burst, the flock took to the air, flapping in unison toward the direction of the earlier sunset.

Where were they going?

Unable to devise an answer, yet happy at their departure, Stumpy closed his eyes to sleep.

After a short time, he noticed the absence of all bird sounds.

Something bad was coming.

And soon.

He knew he'd need to find shelter over the next few hours.

But first, when the sun rose again, he would warn his best friend, the human with the round eyes who called himself Johnnie.

Chapter 1

The otherwise blissful Sunday night on the hillside above Calabash Boom was interrupted by the rhythmic whistling and honks echoing off the concrete block walls of the small garage-conversion apartment. Johnnie pressed the ends of his pillow to his ears.

The high-pitched snorting was unbearable. Johnnie's best friend and 75-year-old new roommate, Cud, was enjoying a deep, albeit noisy, slumber on his sofa just ten feet away.

Johnnie reached for his wire-rimmed round glasses and sat up in bed. The moonlight streamed through his window in the otherwise dark room. He fumbled in the drawer of his side table to pull out his diary and his book light. If he couldn't sleep, he could catch up on his long overdue journaling.

He tapped a pen against his lips, wondering where to begin. It had been several weeks since his last entry. After his girlfriend Greta had found and read his diary during their trip to Miami, just holding the damned leather-bound object made his heart ache. But his psychiatrist insisted that routinely documenting his feelings was important. Surviving a traumatic brain injury five years ago had changed his life and his moods in countless ways. Not that he could remember his moods before.

He ran his hand over the cover, wondering if he would ever feel normal, whatever the hell that was.

Another loud snore and a flutter from his elder friend distracted him from his self-pity.

Johnnie shook his head. It was time to man-up and write in the stupid thing. The worst had already happened. *There was nothing left to lose.*

Dear Diary,

Sorry for not writing sooner. Doctor Lou says I should just put down whatever I'm thinking about and don't worry about it making sense. So here goes.

I'm having trouble sleeping most nights. Cud snores like a congested moose, but that's not the actual reason.

I don't think Greta will ever forgive me, but I keep trying to think of what I can do. She left for the mainland today and will be gone for weeks. She accepted my offer to take her to the airport, but it felt super awkward because we aren't really dating since my blowup in Miami. I can't remember precisely what I said to her back then, but I know I was a complete jerk. Yeah, I know...probably should have journaled that shit. Anyway, I asked her if we could ever go back to the way things were. She said she needs more time. It's been a month and I've been telling her I love her and I'm sorry. Maybe sorry isn't enough. But letting her go can't be an option. It just can't.

Johnnie sucked in his breath. He blinked the water from his eyes and moved onto a different subject.

In other news, Cud's been staying with me for thirteen days since he left the hospital, and yes, I'm counting. He's my best friend, but I'm sick of him singing all the time. He keeps asking Alexa to play Bob Marley or Beatles songs. I didn't mind at first, but if I hear "Yellow Submarine" one more time, I'm going to murder someone.

Okay, not murder. But I'm going to lose my shit and it won't be cool.

Part of me wishes Cud would move out. Although that would make me a hypocrite and an asshole, since I insisted he stay with me. The thing is, I don't think I could live with myself if he went insane again or killed himself. So, I'm stuck.

My landlord Gertie is also driving me nuts. She spies on us like she thinks we can't see her. Today, when I pulled up in the driveway, I saw her hide behind her curtains. She's not fooling anyone.

Jumping Jehoshaphat, it feels like living in one of those cardboard dioramas, being stared at by Cud and Gertie like they expect me to entertain them. Plus, they pretend like they're fine without each other after their break up. But clearly, they have unfinished business and they can leave me the fuck out of it.

My nerves are shot. I just want to be left alone, by myself, to read in peace when I get home. Or to go spear fishing after work instead of running errands for Cud or babysitting him.

But mostly, I want Greta to love me again.

Have a good night diary.

Sweet dreams, Johnnie

* * *

Late again!

In his frantic attempt to dress quickly, Johnnie had already jammed the hem of his undershirt between the zipper teeth of his green cargo pants. It took almost two minutes to work it free.

It made no sense why the alarm on his phone hadn't gone off this morning, since he often double and triple checked it before bedtime. Meaning, Cud must have messed with his phone somehow.

From the sofa, Cudlow stretched his thin wrinkled arms upward and yawned. In a sleepy mumble, he asked, "Did ya gaa ta nahahs a lumba ah nah?" He looked as if he hadn't shaved in weeks; certainly not since he checked himself out of the psychiatric hospital in Grand Bahama. His white hair was longer too, now falling mid-way down his neck. In his newly awakened state, his hair resembled a matted lion's mane.

Johnnie shoved his arms through the sleeves of his Park Service shirt. Cud's question barely registered as he focused on suppressing his current state of panic. "What?"

Cud, rubbing his eyes, spoke slowly, reverting to his native British accent. "The nails and lumber I need for my project! Did you get them yesterday?"

Where Cud used to speak primarily in an American accent up until several months ago, he now spoke in a mix of British and American, which

Johnnie found disconcerting and very annoying. He often wanted to scream, "Just pick one!" But yelling at a recent mental patient would not be helpful, as he knew from his own experience.

"Oh. No. Um, I took Greta to the airport yesterday and must have forgotten."

"Where did she go again?" Cud—wearing only blue boxers with a tiny embroidered frog pattern—ambled to the kitchenette and retrieved the gallon container of milk from the refrigerator.

Johnnie matched up the last button of his shirt, found it correct, and then hunted for his boots. "She's visiting her dad in Pennsylvania. Hey, don't drink all the milk again."

Cud poured himself a tall glass. "Oh, right." He chugged about half of it. "I'm at a standstill without more lumber."

Johnnie looked out the window toward Cud's project in the darkened yard. The sun hadn't come up yet, but he could make out the wonky outline. While his new roommate had been a real estate investment genius in his earlier life, construction was not his strong suit, evidenced by the leaning, oddly spaced posts with screen fabric draped over them haphazardly. "Are you sure I can't help you? I mean, do you even have measurements?"

Cud rifled through the upper kitchen cabinets. "I'm using my creative talents. My sleeping shelter only needs to keep out most of the bugs. Somehow, after my hospital stay, the biting ants won't leave me alone. Johnnie, do you have any more of that powdered chocolate mix?"

Johnnie wanted to tell him ants would most likely get through his ridiculous attempt to construct a shelter, but kept this to himself. "No, you used up all the chocolate. Your shelter, it has to keep out rain also, correct?"

"Precisely. I was thinking about using a tarp. Could you grab me one of those also?" Cud finished his glass of milk with an exaggerated "Ah!" and wiped his beard.

Johnnie donned his round, wire-framed glasses with their flip-up tinted lenses. His phone showed six-thirty and he gasped. *Soooo late.* "Send a text to remind me, okay?"

In his attempt at domestication, Cud had a new phone. "Dratted thing. I don't know how to retrieve my messages. I press buttons and then realize I've called Mo for the hundredth time. He says he understands, but I imagine he's getting cross with me."

"Sorry, I have to get to work. Ask Gertie to help you with your phone. She's retired." He finished tying the laces of his brown ankle-high work boots.

"I'll do no such thing. I told you about my vow."

"Jumpin' Jesus. I said *talk* to her. You can keep your chastity vow."

"I don't know. She's so ravishing. And she's been wearing such seductive clothing lately. I have to avert my eyes whenever she's in the backyard gardening."

Johnnie chuckled. Gertie, his landlord, was seventy years old and, while she was moderately attractive for her age, wasn't exactly ravishing. In fact, she often wore a baggy cotton house-coat while she weeded her vegetable beds. Gertie was often covered in dirt from her frequent gardening. But maybe that was considered seductive for folks over sixty. "Fine. I'll help you with your phone when I get home."

"Thanks, Johnnie. You are tops!" Cud placed his glass on the counter and swished his boxer-clad hips like a hula dancer.

It was time to leave. Johnnie reached for the front door knob, looking forward to some time alone during his drive to work.

"Johnnie! Wait."

He turned. "What?"

"Can I use your laptop this afternoon? I'm having one of those video meetings with Mo to go over the details of Nature Wonderland, you know, the new adventure park."

"Sure, I don't care." He twisted the doorknob and pulled.

Before he got a foot outside, Cud quipped, "What do you mean? Everyone cares about nature. Mo has such great ideas. Like trees that converse with you and a butterfly ride simulation through the Amazon. Mo says hello, by the way. Says you should visit him. Oh, and almost forgot, is it all right if I have a visitor come by?"

He stepped back inside and gestured to the fridge. "Sure…whatever. Just don't drink all the milk."

Cud raced towards him and pointed to the wall calendar by the door. "Don't you want to know WHO my visitor will be?"

Johnnie shook his head, fixated on leaving. Yet, his curiosity won out. He flipped up the round tinted sunglasses over his prescription lenses to read the calendar. A woman's name prominently depicted in black marker under today's date. He closed the door, now completely shaken to his core, and pointed to the entry. "Cud, THIS is your visitor?"

"Yes."

His jaw dropped. "Why is Mildred Johannsen coming here?"

"She's my new architect." Cud jogged over to the coffee table and picked up a worn square cardboard coaster and brought it over to him. "I met her at the Calabash Market. Stunning woman and smart as a whip. I told her about my plan to build an ocean-front cottage." He held up the coaster with his scrawled line-drawing of a house, but it looked like any three-year-old could have done a better job. "She's coming by for an initial consult."

"Hold on…we're talking about the same person, right? The woman who paddleboards around the island every day?" Johnnie furrowed his brow. Mildred, also known as Lilly, was in her mid-to-late forties and looked like a fitness supermodel. Johnnie had been so enthralled with the tall, elusive blonde—watching her from a distance every day as she paddled across the glistening water—that he had nicknamed her The Goddess.

Cudlow beamed. "Yes, which is why I recognized her at the store. She's designed many high-end homes across the Virgin Islands. Her website has exquisite photos."

The Goddess had a website? Did he dare? How could he not check it out? "Yeah? What's the web address?"

"Ocean Vista Architecture STJ dot com. No spaces."

Johnnie entered the website on his phone's browser. He secretly hoped for a picture of the Goddess herself, but found only pictures of houses. Most of them were expensive looking estates, with infinity pools and clean lines. A photo caught his attention; the house overlooking his favorite fishing spot at John's Folly Beach was, in fact, one of her designs. It had been a house he had lusted over. The sort of house that only a bona fide movie star, like George Clooney, would own.

"Hey, I know this one." He held up the picture for Cud to see. "Do you think she could give me a tour?"

Cud stared at the photo. "Johnnie, I don't know. But I'll ask. Hmm. It is very nice. I didn't take you for a fan of modernism."

"I don't know what I'm a fan of. But that house is incredible."

"Yes, I can see its appeal, given its panoramic ocean views. But it has too many walls for me." Cud opened the refrigerator again, wrinkled his nose, and shut it again.

Johnnie shook his head. "Cud, a house is *supposed* to have walls. Otherwise, it isn't a house." As he said this, he noticed that Cud hadn't closed the refrigerator properly, leaving an inch gap, allowing cold air to escape.

His elder friend waved a hand in dismissal as he leaned against the Formica counter. "Pish posh. Anything can be a house if you call it a home. To drift asleep under a constellation of stars is all one really needs. Oh, and the gentle whoosh of the ocean lapping against the shore…makes you feel as if you are a teeny tiny fetus snug in a womb. A house or a home is wherever you are happiest."

Johnnie imagined Cud as a fetus. Finding the thought repulsive, he shuddered and brushed Cud aside to close the fridge properly. "Ha! Like your old tarp and boogie board?"

"Absolutely. I would go back and live at the beach, but people might get *concerned* again." He added air quotes around the word concerned. "And I'm afraid we can't have that."

"Damn straight. Look, I'm really glad you're living with me, but I think we could use more space." He glanced around his square-shaped studio apartment. "You could rent a frickin' mansion for us both until your new place is built." *A mansion with thick walls and doors to block the snoring...*

"Hmm, well, you know how I don't like a fussy home. Plus, it would be too expensive."

Johnnie huffed. "You're a billionaire, remember?"

"Oh, I didn't tell you. My company is fully in my grandson Jackson's hands now, although I'm consulting on our latest theme park project for the mere joy of it. He sends me a stipend for food and basics and will fund my new cottage as long as the price is below three million dollars."

"Jumping Jesus. Three million? That's not a beach cottage!"

Cud chuckled. "Johnnie, the land alone could be upwards of two million. Beachfront is expensive."

"Damn. But still…we could rent a bigger place. Somewhere where you won't have to hide from Gertie. We could each have our own bedroom and bathroom." He gestured to the sofa where Cud had slept since his return. Cud's cotton blanket was on the floor. Johnnie resisted the urge to walk over, to fold it and put it away properly.

"Perhaps more space would be nice…but I don't want Gertie to think I'm afraid to be near her." Cud rummaged through the kitchen cabinets, leaving all the doors ajar.

Johnnie pocketed his phone and shook his head in disbelief. "But you are!"

"Well, yes, but it would be *dreadfully* rude to tell her that. Besides, there are many wonderful native fruits to collect in this area."

"Coward. Whatever. Have it your way." Johnnie turned toward the door, determined to leave.

"You should come with me on my scavenger hunts. Wild mangoes are the stuff of gods!"

Johnnie gripped the door knob and grunted, "Fruit is for the birds."

Cud tsked and plucked a box of vanilla cookies from an upper cabinet. "Speaking of, the birds seemed agitated last night. I barely slept."

Barely slept? Johnnie wanted to say something snarky, but held his tongue. "Right."

"I fear something is coming. Birds can sense things."

He was afraid to ask, but did anyway. "What things?"

Cud mumbled as he crunched a cookie in his mouth. "I'm not sure yet. But I suspect it won't be very good."

Chapter 2

"John!"

Johnnie stomped on the brake of his blue Jeep Compass. *Not even out of the driveway.* He slammed his palm on the steering wheel.

He lowered the passenger side window to greet his landlord. She was wearing her pink terry bathrobe and her hair was in an orange and white floral silk wrap. "Gertie, I'm really in a rush." The sun was up now, casting a glow against the tree line.

Gertie tiptoed across the concrete path to the edge of the stone driveway. "It won't take long. Would you and Cudlow like to come for dinner tonight? I'm making lemon chicken and mashed potatoes. And a cherry pie for dessert. Six o'clock."

"Sorry, maybe another time." He rolled up his window, released the brake and the car rolled backward.

Gertie ventured into the driveway and slapped the hood of his car. "Wait! Why? I heard Greta is out of town. Surely, you must be free for dinner."

He lowered his window again. "It's too soon."

"What do you mean?" Her wide-set brown eyes looked perplexed, but Johnnie considered it inconceivable that she didn't know what he was talking about.

Johnnie whispered, "I don't think it's a good idea. What if he has another…breakdown?"

She whispered back. "Cudlow seems fine. It's only dinner. Can't we be friends?"

This logic threw him as he considered his own breakup. Greta had been keeping him in the friend category for weeks and while he understood her hesitancy to take him back as a lover, it pained him to mask his true feelings. Gertie had left Cud at the altar just two months ago, ultimately causing Cud to be institutionalized for a month. "Look, you two need to talk and leave me out of this, okay?"

"Yes. Yes, of course. I don't mean to put you in the middle. Before you go, do you have a sledge hammer?"

Johnnie blinked, taken aback at this odd question. He flipped up the yellow tinted sunglass lenses to get a better look at her face. "What do you need a sledge hammer for?"

"I may do some remodeling. I hate my tile countertops. Many of the tiles are cracked and the grout is disgusting, no matter how much I scrub. Lord, I've had to deal with those awful things since I first moved here. I've finally decided to treat myself to some fancy quartz ones…you know, the kind that are white and shiny and look like marble." She grinned broadly; her teeth beamed against her caramel complexion.

Johnnie closed his eyes. "I think there's a sledge hammer in the shed. Be careful, okay?"

She grinned. "Thanks. Have a nice day at work."

"Yep. Have a nice day." He raised the window and backed his Jeep down the driveway, determined to ignore any further attempts to delay his departure.

Once he was on the road, he sighed, wondering if he should warn Cud. The clock on the dash showed he was already forty-five minutes late for work, which meant he'd probably need to skip lunch if he wanted to get to the hardware store before they closed.

It wasn't fair he had to turn down Gertie's mashed potatoes to preserve Cud's paranoid chastity vow; Gertie's potatoes were legendary. Buttery with the skins mixed in. Often, her potatoes were the best part of his week, or month, making him forget about loathing his life in general for just a few minutes. Moments of pure, simple joy.

But accepting her invitation would be a dick move.

He also wondered why Gertie wanted to remove her countertops herself, possibly creating a colossal mess. Gertie's hobbies were baking, gardening, and needlepoint. Demolition and construction seemed far outside her wheelhouse. Was Gertie considering some kind of Misery kidnapping to make

Cud fall in love with her again? Johnnie shook off that visual. Sometimes she could be pushy or meddling or ill-tempered, but she definitely wasn't a psychopath.

But it occurred to him that both Gertie and Cud were taking on projects to distract themselves from the other, which didn't seem a lasting solution.

Johnnie arrived at Hawksnest Bay and parked his Jeep next to a white Park Service pickup truck. His boss, Superintendent Kemper Snow, was rummaging through the pickup's rear bed. Her uniform hung on her as if she were a scarecrow. Her straight blond hair, beneath her flat cap, looked like straw. Johnnie often wondered how she remained so unnaturally pale while living in the Caribbean. Even his own Irish freckles on his typically pink skin spread over time to form a semblance of a tan.

He exited his car. "Good morning, Kemper. What brings you here so early?"

She turned her attention to him. "Merv—I mean Ranger Hartley—called out sick and I'm taking his shift today. A park guest called the main office to report broken glass. The pavilion is littered with smashed beer bottles. Help me sweep up?"

Johnnie flipped up his sunglasses. Under the large wood park entrance sign to his right—the sign that plainly states the park rules, including the one that no glass containers were allowed—sat a cardboard Corona beer six-pack with a lone empty green bottle.

"Geez, I'm sorry. I should have been here an hour ago, but Cud is driving me crazy. I mean, I'm glad he's staying with me and all." Not wanting to bother her with a frustration-laden rant, Johnnie allowed his voice to trail off as he headed toward the tool shed and unlocked it.

He said, "Look, I'll take care of it. I'm sure you have more important things to do."

Kemper removed her ranger hat and gripped its wide brim, not making eye contact, as if she was uneasy for some reason. "I don't mind a little manual labor. I have some reports to submit later and I could use a break from my computer."

It made no sense that a superintendent would choose to sweep glass with a lowly maintenance worker like himself. Yet, he chose not to argue, because she was his superior after all. Instead, he retrieved two brooms and a dust pan from the tool shed. After handing her a broom, they walked to the pavilion. The sheer amount of glass, in all shades from clear to green to brown, was incredible. Clearly, there had been a large hell-raising last night. They began sweeping. As they swept, the glass made sharp sounds across the concrete, like a high-pitched bicycle bell.

Without looking up from her task, Kemper asked, "Johnnie, do you enjoy your job?"

His throat tightened. The question seemed like a trap. Was this about him being late today? He couldn't say he loved being a maintenance worker, but he didn't hate it either. "It's fine. I mean, I get to work outside. Cleaning toilets isn't great, but I don't have to talk to anyone." These were all accurate statements, but after he uttered them, he realized the last part made him sound like an antisocial jerk. "I mean, I like the quiet."

"I asked because I need an assistant. The pay scale would be similar. Would you want to apply?"

This question really sounded like a trap. If he said no, it might hurt her feelings. If he said 'maybe' or 'yes', she would expect him to apply. He rubbed the back of his neck. "Boss, you know…I'm not good at stuff that requires remembering things."

"Well, I understand." She continued her sweeping. "But I deal with all kinds of real-time issues. Mostly, the job would involve making calls and answering the phone. You may need to follow up on projects from time to time, but even I use electronic reminders for that. I really need the help. Since my last assistant left, my brain can't handle everything. Sometimes I feel completely braindead."

He knew what braindead felt like, and he was sure Kemper was exaggerating. But he paused and nodded, darting his eyes upward. More for a polite show that he was considering what she was saying, when really there was no question in his mind. "Sorry, Kemper. I think I enjoy working outside."

"Okay. Just forget I asked." Her dejected look switched to one of shock; her jaw dropped and eyes widened. In a sincere tone, she added, "Oh! No. I didn't mean it like that. You know that, right?"

"No worries." He chuckled to put her at ease. "I probably *will* forget." He grabbed the dust pan and, in a reflex move, used his free hand to scoop up the pile she had just made. An immediately painful and very dumb move.

His palm had caught a shard that punctured his skin. "Ow!" He stood and inspected his hand. A bright red blob oozed and the wound throbbed like a bee sting.

Kemper dropped her broom. "Give me your hand."

He did as he was told.

With her slender fingers, she turned his palm upwards. "Oh, that's bad."

On closer inspection, he had a cut about a quarter-inch long. Blood dripped from his wound now and it flooded the cuff of his tan shirt.

He couldn't look any more.

"You might need stitches."

"No, it's fine."

"I'll grab the first aid kit. Take a seat." She pulled him over toward a picnic bench. "Keep it elevated."

He kept his hand upright as crimson streams ran down like water. His stomach felt queasy and he wondered if could keep down the stale granola bar from the glove compartment he'd had for breakfast.

Kemper patted his shoulder and left to get the first aid kit. A minute later, she sat next to him and wrapped gauze and tape around his hand. "Keep pressure on it. How do you feel?"

"I've been better."

She held his bandaged hand, her fingertips caressed his life line, and they locked eyes. Hers were a pale blue, like a Siberian Husky's and just as sweet; her pupils swept back and forth as if she sought a deeper connection.

A connection he had given little thought to before. But eerily, his hearing stopped and he felt oddly outside his own body, as if he were sucked into those eyes, like falling into a crystalline mountain lake. Time slowed and his mind blanked.

In a different life, under different circumstances, he might have leaned in for a kiss. Not because he loved her, but because it seemed the *required thing to do* in the moment. As if he was instantly transformed into the no-name male lead in a very compelling Hallmark Valentines movie.

But he still loved Greta.

Alarm bells sounded inside his brain. He turned away and barked, "Boss, stop fussing. I've got this. Go do supervisor stuff."

She shifted backwards on the bench. "Right. Right. I'll be going." She tucked the roll of gauze and the tape back into the first aid tin and snapped it shut. "Have a good day." Kemper rose and strode in the direction of the parking lot.

Had he read too much into Kemper's look of concern? Was he being a dick-toad to someone who was simply showing basic human decency?

Out of the corner of his eye, Johnnie spotted Stumpy, his short-tailed, wild iguana friend.

The reptile waddled towards him. [Hey, Johnnie. Yum time?]

"Hey, sorry, I forgot to bring cheese puffs. Stay away from the glass." He rose from the picnic bench and picked up his broom. Johnnie glanced side to side to see if anyone was watching their conversation. Because to him, it was perfectly reasonable. But sometimes tourists gave him dirty looks—like he was off his rocker—and he wasn't in the mood to explain himself. Luckily, they were alone.

[Where's Merv?]

"Why do you care?"

[Where's Cud?]

"I told you. He's staying at my place."

Stumpy ran at him and bit the bottom of his pant leg and tugged. *An unusual move.*

Johnnie shook his leg to free himself. "What's gotten into you? Stop it."

The iguana rose on its hind legs and leapt up vertically; a move Johnnie had never seen before.

He chuckled at this foolish dance. "What is it, Lassie? Is Timmy in a well?"

The iguana cocked his head and blinked, then lunged again. Stumpy's sharp teeth sunk into his leg above his boot, ripping a dime-sized hole in the hem of Johnnie's pants.

"Jumping Jackass! Goddamn it. Ow!" Johnnie kicked at Stumpy to get free. When that didn't work, he hit him with the broom's bristles. "Stumpy! Fuck you. Go away!"

Stumpy backed up toward a pile of glass, and Johnnie steered him toward safety with another tap of his broom. The iguana evidently took this as a hostile action; Stumpy gave him an open-mouthed look of perceived hate before he slithered back beneath the underbrush.

His hand and now his ankle throbbed in pain; mixed with the other frustrations of the morning, he muttered under his breath.

"No more fuckin' cheese puffs for you! Punk-ass lazy green bastard. Go bite yourself in the dick." As he continued sweeping, he wondered if iguanas carried rabies. Had he looked that up before? He couldn't remember. He scowled and continued muttering with twists of sarcasm mixed in. "Fucking late to work…boss thinks I'm a raging asshole…Greta wants time to think because I AM human garbage…Cud won't stop singing…shit heads breaking glass…oh yeah, I DO want some mashed potatoes…Goddamned right I do…drinks all the milk and guess who has to go to the fucking store again…can't catch a frickin' break…ha! (in a mimicking British accent) Don't forget my lumber! (back to a growl) Fuck your dumb shelter…"

Johnnie was preoccupied with his heated rage when a woman screamed like she was being murdered.

"AAAG! My foot! Help!"

Johnnie dropped his broom and raced toward the sound. The scream came from the ladies restroom.

A heavy-set middle-aged woman in a navy one-piece bathing suit hobbled out on her bare heels, her foot bleeding, leaving a track. "Help me! Help me!" She lunged for his shoulder with both hands.

He hadn't expected her weight to shift onto him and he teetered back, catching them both by quickly bracing a foot behind him. "Whoa! You need to sit. Let me help you."

"OOOW! I'm…a…bleed to death!" She panted, speaking through gasps. "The glass is still in there."

"Okay, lean on me. Just over to that bench." He motioned to where he had sat with Kemper fifteen feet away. "Take it slow."

"I can't. I CAN'T!" She clung to him but wouldn't move her feet.

He couldn't hold on to her much longer without them both falling. "Look at me. You're going to be all right. Take a deep breath. What's your name?"

"I'm Asia. Like the continent."

"Now, Asia." He met her eyes and spoke with purpose to get her full attention. "You can do this. I can't get the glass out until you sit. But you have to breathe. It helps, trust me. Count with me. Breathe in, one, two, three…"

She inhaled, shakily, as tears streamed down her face.

"Now exhale, one, two, three. You got it? In…out."

After a few more breaths, Asia's face relaxed. Although her false eyelashes were still laden with droplets.

He took her arm and said, "Good. Now, I'll hold on to you. Stay on your heels and we'll sit you down over there on the edge of the concrete. Just four steps. Okay? I have a first aid kit."

Once sitting, he lifted her injured foot. A jagged clear nugget of glass, about a quarter-inch long was embedded in the pad near her big toe. He wanted to gag. "It's in there good. Sit here and don't move. I'll be right back. Keep breathing!"

She wiped her eyes. "Don't leave me here!"

He nodded and returned to the picnic table where he had left the first aid kit. As he grabbed it, another scream rang out. This time, from a young boy, perhaps a toddler. Crying and shrieking as if his hand were on a hot stove. "MOMMMMMY! Blood!"

It *had to be* another victim of broken glass. This time, near the water's edge. Thankful for his own thick-soled boots, Johnnie ran toward the next victim. The boy, sitting with his mother on a beach blanket, wailed; shockingly bright red blood had soaked a circular ring on the otherwise white towel.

Johnnie knelt next to the mom. "What happened?"

The mother, a woman in her twenties with a brown pony tail, held her palm against the boy's foot. "He cut his heel running in the sand."

"Can I see?"

She held up her son's foot. Despite the flow of blood, the wound was evident. A gash almost an inch long had sliced the heel of the boy's foot leaving a thick, pale flap.

Johnnie's stomach flipped and another surge of adrenaline caused a shiver up his neck. "Yes, keep pressure. I'm calling 9-1-1." He tossed the first aid kit onto the woman's beach blanket and stepped away a few yards and dialed. As it rang, he looked across the tranquil bay at the moored sailboats. Normally, the bay would be a soothing view. But the whimpers and cries of the boy overwhelmed the rhythmic sound of the waves.

"9-1-1. What is the nature of your emergency?"

Johnnie instantly recognized the voice. Through gasping breaths, he said, "Janice! Shit! It's me. Johnnie Crosswell. I'm at Hawksnest Beach. Multiple injuries. Send medical help. NOW! Fuck!"

"Hey, Johnnie. I'll send a truck right away. What happened? Was there a knife fight? Do you need law enforcement?"

"No. Fucking glass. Some assholes broke beer bottles all over the place last night."

"Understood. Do you want to stay on the line?"

"Um. I don't…" He looked around, hoping the right answer would come to him. "No…I don't know."

"Johnnie, sit tight. Take a deep breath. It will all be okay."

As he exhaled, the answer came to him. "I need to call Kemper."

"Good idea. Call her. Help is now on the way. Keep breathing. Have a blessed day. Bye, Johnnie."

A group of four beach visitors surrounded him. "Mister, what kind of beach is this? How could you let this happen?"

In his dizzy state, he couldn't make out their faces. He put out his hands defensively. "First aid is on the way. Put on your shoes or flip-flops. It isn't safe to move around."

The group dispersed, cursing him under their breath.

He called Kemper.

"Yes, Johnnie?"

"I…I need you."

"What?"

He walked in a circle, staring at the sand. "The whole beach is a minefield of glass. Several injuries. First aid is coming. Call everyone. We need a full sweep."

"Got it. Stay calm. I'll be there in five minutes."

Johnnie dropped to his knees on the sand and held his head. More screams and wails erupted from every direction. He wanted to vomit. Clasping his hands to his ears, images flooded back from his time in the Marines—five years ago—when he had barely survived the vehicle crash and bullet to his skull, and was transported to the field hospital outside Kabul.

All the blood. Thick red sticky ooze covered his eyes. The urgency in the medic's voices as they hoisted him on the gurney. The man pushing him down the long hall kept repeating, "Stay with me. You'll be all right." He recalled his skull had felt oddly exposed to cool air in a way that didn't seem plausible. And in his disassociated state, he imagined he looked like a hollow chocolate Easter Bunny with its ear and half its head bitten off. Lying face up, overhead lights streamed past, blurring into a solid line, making him wonder if he was still alive or racing toward a different sort of white light…

A hand touched his shoulder.

"Sir? Mr. Crosswell?"

He looked up. Two EMTs, a woman and man wearing similar white and gray cotton uniforms, stood behind him.

Johnnie pointed. "Over there. The little boy needs you most."

The EMTs left and Johnnie cursed himself, knowing this was all his fault. If he had arrived on time this morning, he could have noticed and removed all the glass before these folks arrived.

Maybe Cud needed his own place.

Part of him hoped that Cud and Gertie to get back together because it would solve everything. But then again, that could spell further disaster. Nothing about their relationship had gone well so far, culminating in a failed wedding on a cruise ship and Cud's downward spiral where he nearly jumped from a twenty-story balcony in Miami.

Either way, he needed to apologize to Kemper for dismissing her so rudely earlier.

And he needed a quick solution to his roommate problem.

Chapter 3

Senator Robin Crosswell—St. John's representative in the state legislature—brushed back her wavy shoulder-length black hair and read her email again. Her opponent in the next election a week from now was the Chief of Police, Joseph Tobias. She had expected to run unopposed; but at the last minute, Tobias entered the race. Their last run-in may have prompted him to seek her office, after she taunted him when he wrongfully arrested her younger brother Johnnie without any cause for two homicides.

The most recent polling data, as shown in her email, was not looking good.

She called over to her assistant in the next room. "Dottie!"

Dottie was a petite woman, in her early 50s, well-attired in a cream sheath dress, with perfect arched eyebrows, wearing a chunky gold-tone necklace and pointy-toe electric-blue suede heels. "Good morning, Robin. What do you need?"

"Tobias is kicking my can. Look at this poll. A whole twelve points. Does that seem right?" She turned her secondary monitor towards Dottie.

"I can do some independent polling this morning."

Robin chuckled. Dottie, a social butterfly, knew almost everyone on the island of St. John, particularly the long-time residents. With a constituency of roughly four-thousand residents, not an easy feat.

"Yes, could you ask around? My agenda pushing green energy hasn't gone over very well. And I haven't been able to move the finance committee on the social services budget. I don't know what to do. Meanwhile, Tobias is making promises I know he can't keep." Robin scoffed, "He says he'll bring manufacturing jobs and we know that's ridiculous. We just don't have the infrastructure." She picked up her keyboard and hit it against the edge of her desk three times in disgust. "Fuck! Fuck! Fuck!"

Dottie came around her desk, disconnected the keyboard from her laptop USB port, and set it on the credenza to her right. "Look at me. Destroying more keyboards is *not* the answer." She muttered, "Third one this month…"

Robin pressed her hands to her forehead and took a deep breath. "Sorry. I don't know what to do."

"You could let me help."

"Help? How?"

"Robin, you are an amazing Senator and policy-maker. That's the reason I backed you for the legislature after Irmaria." Dottie leaned her butt on the edge of the credenza. "We were fucked after those hurricanes and we needed someone with your legal experience to cut through the lame-ass posturing bullshit. But we both know self-promotion is *not* your strong-suit. You need a campaign manager and I know just the person." She tapped her knuckles on Robin's desk to punctuate her words.

Robin rose from her seat, reached past Dottie to grab the keyboard, and placed it back in its original spot on her desk. "Sounds expensive."

"Could be. But hear him out, okay?"

"Who is it?" She plugged the keyboard into her laptop and tested the keys on a new blank email. Robin typed, 'The quick brown fox jumped' and found that the shift key and letter 'q' weren't working. Plus, the F9 key was completely missing and the space bar was cracked.

"Someone you've met before. I'll set up the meeting." Dottie gestured to the keyboard. "Is it working?"

"It's fucked. Add another one to the requisition list."

With a sparkle in her eyes and a grin, Dottie reached out. "Hand it here. I'll swap it out with Commissioner Wayne's keyboard. He hasn't typed anything in years."

"Thanks." Her cell phone vibrated. "It's Johnnie. I should take this."

Dot hugged the keyboard, gave her a wink, and headed out. With her hand on the door knob, she asked, "Open or closed?"

"Closed."

After Dot exited, Robin accepted the call from her younger brother. "Johnnie, good morning. How are you?" Robin glanced at the wall clock. It was 8:19.

"Good morning. I'm good, sis. No. The truth is, I really screwed up this morning. The EMTs just left."

"Oh, good grief. Did you find another dead person washed up on the beach?"

"Ha, ha. Sooooo funny. No, folks got hurt from broken glass. See, the thing is…Cud is driving me nuts. I should have gotten to work earlier and taken care of it, but he just talks and talks in the mornings. And I don't want to be rude. So, I was wondering, could I stay with you for a few days?"

She gulped. Not what she expected and not a great idea. "Oh."

"Yeah, I hate to ask, but I might lose my cool and that wouldn't be good for him."

"I thought the idea was you would keep an eye on him…make sure he's taking care of himself. And, you know," she whispered the last part, "not suicidal anymore."

"Yes." Johnnie sighed. "But he's doing well. Jumping Jesus, he sings all the fucking time and he's building this lopsided outdoor shelter thing. I'm just not used to having a roommate or taking care of someone else."

"Why don't you stay with Greta?"

"We broke up, remember? And she's away visiting her dad for a few weeks."

She hesitated, trying to find a nice way to rebuff his idea to stay with her. "Right. My place has only one bedroom. And I would stay at Arturo's, but his damn parrot doesn't shut up at night. I can't get any sleep there." As much as she loved her boyfriend—the sweet, sexy police officer Arturo— she couldn't stand Trixie, his Hyacinth Macaw. He had come by the bird during a drug raid two years ago and adopted it when its owner went to prison. Arturo's sense of decency ran deep, and Robin couldn't persuade him to get rid of it.

"I'd be happy to sleep on the floor."

"Why don't you stay at your landlord's house? Doesn't Gertie have an extra bedroom?"

"I can't. She's acting weird. Staring at me all the time."

Robin huffed, wondering what he meant. "Fine, I'll ask. *Why* is she staring?"

"Fuck if I know. She's spying on me and Cud. She's probably lonely.

23

Anyway, that's not an option."

A knock on her door told Robin it was time to go. "I have to run to a meeting on St. Thomas. I'll call you tonight."

Dottie opened the door, pointed to her delicate gold wristwatch, and mouthed, "Get to the ferry."

Robin didn't wait for Johnnie to answer. "Bye." She ended the call.

To Dot, she said, "I'm going. Ask Jupiter to hold the ferry for me, okay?" She stuffed her planner and some marked-up legislative proposals in her shoulder bag.

"Absolutely. What did Johnnie want?"

Robin gave her a death stare that meant, "None of your damned business."

Dot nodded. "I set up a meeting for you first thing tomorrow morning with the campaign strategist I mentioned. Okay?"

With no time to argue, she changed into her sneakers and threw her dress shoes into a separate canvas tote. "Fine. But he better not waste my time."

Dottie nodded and held open the door for her.

Robin strode out with the two bags slung on her narrow shoulders. Making her way down to the dock three blocks away took little time.

Sure enough, the ferry was still there, with the operator, Jupiter—a tall older man with an unlit cigar in his mouth and wearing a straw hat— standing by the aluminum retractable gangplank.

He tipped his hat, "Good morning, Senator."

"Good morning, Jupiter. Thanks for waiting."

He extended his hand to help her down the steps onto the deck. "I assume you'll be working on the ferry surcharge issue we talked about with the PSC?"

She readjusted the strap of her canvas bag. "I've brought it up, but they aren't budging." Jupiter had been asking her for months to sway the Public Service Commission to authorize a rate hike. Fuel prices had surged and the ferry operators were losing money.

Jupiter handed her his cigar and pulled in the gangplank with an irritating screech of metal on metal. Over his shoulder, he said, "Chief Tobias says he can get it done."

She held his damp cigar between two fingers at arms-length and waited for the clanging noise to cease. "Well, Joe says a lot of things."

He fastened a safety rope across the entrance, then took his cigar back. "Maybe we need fresh ideas."

"Look, he's a decent chief of police. But he can't legislate by barking orders. It doesn't work like that."

"Hmm-mm. Well, at least he's a fighter." He tapped his ear with his index finger. "People listen when he talks."

Robin felt heat rise to her face, and she couldn't take it any longer. In a biting tone she tried to avoid with her constituents, she retorted, "Macho bully tactics won't get him very far! You know what I do all day? Read reams of legislation that I know will never get enacted, try to decipher budgets that...Stephen fucking Hawking couldn't even comprehend, and spend hours in meetings so dull you'd prefer to peel your damn skin off. Oh! Not to mention, every evening spent catching up on a hundred emails to prepare for the next day. He has no idea in holy hell what he's signing up for." As she stopped raving, she realized she had been waving her hands in the air like a lunatic the whole time. She crossed her arms, glanced around for onlookers, and relaxed her muscles to regain composure.

"Hmm. Well, Ms. Senator, the next time I see him, I'll send along your warning." His wide-set eyes gleamed with mischief.

She punched him half-heartedly in his muscled shoulder. "You do that, Joop. Would fucking make my day."

Jupiter smiled so broadly his teeth took up half his face. His gold-enameled lower canine tooth flashed in the sun. "Ha! Smile. You know only I'm playin' wit ya."

Robin sighed. "Yes, I know. Now let's shove off. I have one of those awful meetings to get to. Might just claw off my face and come back looking like Freddy Krueger."

"Yes, ma'am. But don't you bleed all over my beautiful white deck now, ya hear?" He tipped his hat to her and bounded inside to the captain's helm room.

She smiled and pulled open the door to the inside seating area.

Having Tobias as a representative would be entertaining, she thought. Entertaining in terms of the satisfaction of watching him fail miserably. But helping the people was more important. And she was damn good at her job.

No one would take this away from her while she still had breath in her lungs and flesh on her face.

* * *

With hammer in-hand, Cudlow stepped back to assess his work. The sun overhead seared his neck and sweat soaked the back of his T-shirt. His shelter's two-by-four walls leaned outward at an unintended angle. He'd need to correct that. *If I only had a laser level thingy...*

A sultry and familiar voice startled him. "That is *some* project."

He turned. Gertie stood twenty feet away, wearing a white cotton eyelet blouse and tight-fitting electric blue yoga capris. Her hair was pulled back into a tight bun; her fuchsia lipstick made his heart leap.

Returning his focus to his structure, he admired it. "Yes, I suppose it is."

She beamed. "Would you and Johnnie like to come over for supper tonight? I'm going to renovate my kitchen and this will be the last home cooked meal I'll be making for quite a while."

Cud chewed on his free thumb. "Oh. Dinner. I...I don't want to put you to any trouble."

"You know I love to cook." In a crooning tone, she added, "I've made a cherry pie."

He dropped his hammer. "I do love your pies." He squinted to read her aura. It was blue, like the first time they kissed those many weeks ago. The regrettable truth was he loved more than just her pies. Yet, she could never know. "But I'm afraid that wouldn't be wise."

"Do you dislike me that much?" She closed the distance between them. "I wouldn't blame you after what I did."

"My dear, none of it was your fault." These words brought an inner stillness. Deep down, he meant it. "I told you. I was an old fool."

"Cudlow, I still care about you, and I want us to be friends." She came closer and placed her hand on his cheek.

Rockets went off in his chest. Every instinct in his body told him to take her into his arms and stop this foolishness. But would he go insane again? After all the progress he made at the hospital, being near her was far too risky. He took her hand and gave it a brotherly squeeze. "I would like that as well."

"Great, so I'll see you at six?"

"Oh...I...er...yes."

"Wonderful." She smiled and returned to the other side of the back yard.

He stood transfixed as she opened the drawer to her potting bench and pulled on floral-print canvas gloves.

"Gertie, are you going to be gardening?"

"Yes, will I be disturbing you?"

"No…go ahead. Let me know if my hammering bothers you." He picked up his hammer and pulled a two-inch framing nail from his pocket. As he held the nail in place, he glanced her way.

Kneeling next to a stalk of tomatoes, Gertie chuckled. "Ha, you still owe me a new garden gnome."

"Pardon me?"

"You and Johnnie took my garden gnome to Miami. Remember?"

He furrowed his brow, drawing a blank. "Sorry, no. I don't remember much of that time."

She pulled a yellow dandelion and dusted off a wad of soil from its roots. "Probably for the best. I was so scared for you. And I was just kidding about replacing the gnome." With a far off look she said, "You know, my mother had gotten it for me before she passed away."

He dropped his hammer on the ground and walked over to her. Kneeling at her side, he said, "I'm sorry. I once knew a bloke in Scotland who makes the most stunning garden sculptures. I'll have a new one made for you."

Her eyes turned sad. In a soft voice, she said, "Hey, I'm sorry about your mom passing."

He smiled to put her at ease. "Well, Camille and I had a strange relationship. She insisted she saw my father's ghost for decades. Now that she's with Albert, I'm sure she is *much* happier."

They locked eyes. The pools of her large brown irises were deep enough for him to swim in, and he longed to stay in their embrace.

"Gertie…"

She placed her gloved hand on his knee. "Yes?"

He had a decision to make, and he winced. He could so easily kiss her, yet his muscles seized, frightened by the potential consequences.

THWACK!

A sudden blur and a sharp pain to his forehead sent him reeling backward. A large bird had evidently swooped down and pecked him on his forehead above his left eye. Cud, on his back like a turtle, swatted at the air in defense. "Aaagh. What in blue blazes?"

Gertie leaned over him. "I've never seen a bird attack someone like that before. I'll get some ice."

He glanced around, his arms still covering his face, wondering if it was safe. Not seeing any danger, he pushed himself off the ground and stood like a boxer, ready to fend off the next attack. "Where did it go?"

"I don't know. It looked like a seagull."

"A seagull?" He recalled the time right before he checked into the mental hospital, when he tried to dive off a Miami high-rise balcony, thinking he could fly because a seagull told him he could. Obviously, he was in severe emotional distress back then. But a seagull attack had to *mean* something. And he needed the safety of Johnnie's apartment to further assess.

"Gertie, I'm feeling a bit tired. I think a nap would do me well. Have a nice day. Enjoy your gardening." He dusted off his knees and headed toward Johnnie's apartment.

From a few feet behind, he heard Gertie call out, "Oh. I understand. Are you sure you don't want some ice? It's no trouble."

He didn't look back to respond, yet glanced upward to the sky in case of another attack. "No. Thank you. I'm fine." Cud race-walked away, entered the apartment, and shut the door behind him with the full weight of his body. *A close call.* What if the seagull was divine intervention to save him from his misplaced love for Gertie? There could be no other explanation.

Cud ambled to the refrigerator and drank the last of the milk directly from the jug.

With the lights off, the corner of the room by Johnnie's bed was dark. A flicker of an eerie lime green aura appeared and vanished. The vision was unmistakable.

Could it be?

"Mama?" The image of a woman with short silver waves in her hair and high cheekbones looked remarkably like his recently deceased mother. Her eyes twinkled with a knowing look, like they had during his childhood.

"Mama, if that is you, please stay away. I can't deal with you now."

Talking to a figment. But he couldn't discount what he saw.

"If you ever loved me, please don't haunt this place. I beg you. I want to be sane."

There was no response. No noise. No aura. He waited for a full minute, frozen in place, staring at the now empty corner for signs of light or movement.

Seeing none, he voiced, "Thank you."

Cud sought respite on the sofa. Wiping his brow of sweat, he perceived a bump on his forehead where the bird had left its mark. He held his fingers up and saw a touch of blood.

He headed to the bathroom to find antiseptic. After cleaning the wound, he located some adhesive bandages, ones with SpongeBob characters, and affixed one to his forehead.

As he smoothed the strip along his brow, the discarded plastic tabs leapt off the edge of the sink on their own accord, rising five inches and hovering before fluttering down to the floor.

"Aaaa! I mean it. Stop! I won't have this!"

Squeezing his eyes shut, he held his breath, wishing for normalcy. When he opened his eyes, the bathroom was still and appeared as usual.

Yes, I'm going mad, he thought. *Ghosts aren't real. Can't be real.*

He returned to the security of the sofa and drew a sheet over his head. Perhaps his lack of sleep from the bird noise last night, or a bit of sunstroke from his labors, was causing him hallucinations.

A quick nap before his appointment with his new architect would surely bring back his senses.

Chapter 4

Dougie Biffman, WSTJ news meteorologist, straightened his red tie as he inspected his handsome mug in the dressing room mirror. Medium height, deep tan, broad shoulders…he often thought of himself as a slightly older Channing Tatum type, but with long, silky golden hair.

But he couldn't spend time admiring his looks this morning as he recited his daily affirmations in the brightly lit mirror. The moon had been full last night and his morning horoscope assured him that today—with Mercury in retrograde—was the best time to ask for a raise in salary.

As a diligent employee for over two years, he deserved this raise. Many of his colleagues—the other on-air talent—had received pay increases recently. Yet, his producer kept avoiding the topic when he approached her.

He combed his champagne-colored locks from his face and added some mousse along his temples to keep his mane in place. Letters from his fans dotted the wall above his vanity table. Surely his boss knew how much the public adored him.

Just to be sure, Dougie opened an app on his phone for a quick online tarot reading for his astrological sign to confirm his next move. It read, "Prosperity will be around the corner for Capricorns this week."

At the corner of his eye, the news producer, Andréa, walked by. It had to be another good sign.

"Andréa," he called, "do you have a minute?"

His boss was a short but stout woman in her thirties who always wore black T-shirts and black jeans. She never wore makeup, which would not have been his choice given the large splotches of light pink discoloration on her otherwise brown complexion. But he appreciated the fact that not everyone could have his impeccable skin. Andréa also gave no attention to her hair, which was always pulled back by a stretchy head band.

"Aren't you on in four minutes?" Andréa tapped her wristwatch.

"Yes. It will only take thirty seconds."

She placed her hand over her headset mic. "Shoot."

"I'm a valued asset to the station, right?"

Andréa shook her head and huffed. "What do you want?"

"I need a ten percent raise. My contract is up for renewal."

"Dougie, this isn't the right time."

"You always say that!"

"You should be glad I didn't fire you last month."

"Are you still angry about that?"

Andréa gritted her teeth. "Dougie! You claimed that global warming is caused by erupting volcanos and that drilling for oil in the ocean helps reduce sea level rise."

"I still stand by that."

"I don't pay you for your opinions. And what about when you said tsunamis usually occurred when the moons of Saturn are in Uranus…? Whatever the fuck that means!"

"Astrometeorology is a genuine science. It originated over four thousand years ago!"

She took in a deep breath and stared at the hall ceiling. "And now we have satellite imaging and pressure readings…just get your hiney on the set, for fuck's sake." Into her mic, she called out, "Ninety seconds!"

He glanced at the set, noticing the news anchor, Vivia, was already in place. "Wait, I made some…"

Andréa had vanished.

He went back inside his dressing room and scanned the images on his desk. The National Oceanographic and Atmospheric Administration, or NOAA for short, came out with a storm prediction model the night before. A tropical depression had emerged off the coast of Brazil. Only one model of ten, the European algorithm, showed any potential for a storm to intensify and take a turn toward the Virgin Islands. It had to be some type of math error. The other models showed a high-pressure zone near Trinidad that would weaken the depression and send the storm limping off to die in the middle of the Atlantic.

Checking the position of celestial bodies to make sure, and finding the alignment of the moon, sun and Mars to be conducive to good weather, he had contacted the graphics department last night to omit any visuals of the potential storm and re-wrote the copy himself.

With a minute before his on-air appearance, he jumped up and down while throwing his fists in the air to pump himself up. Then, smoothing his hair and tie once more, he jogged to the set. Andréa counted down on her fingers: ten, nine, eight…

In front of the green screen, Dougie presented his biggest smile. On cue, he sang out, "Good afternoon, Virgin Islands from your Mystic Meteorologist with the most! Today will be a nearly perfect day for sun bathing and catching the surf. There may be some clouds tomorrow, but those will quickly blow through. Overnight drizzle is possible. Highs will be in the mid-eighties with an overnight low around seventy-five. This weekend is the music festival on St. Thomas. Bring a hat and some sunscreen, because there will be nothing but sunny skies." He clasped his hands together and looked over at the main news desk to Vivia. "Hey, Viv, will you be going to the festival this weekend? I hear they will have some talented performers. Rumor is, Drake may be coming! I hear the ladies love Drake. Viv, are you a big Drake fan?"

Vivia looked at him with knitted brows, then back at her notes, then back at the teleprompter as if stunned. Probably, he surmised, because Andréa always discouraged his banter with the newscasters. But he risked her wrath in order to further endear himself to his growing following. If he was lucky, increased popularity would bode well for his raise.

Behind the camera operator, Andréa gave him an annoyed look and wound her hands in a circle motion, meaning 'wrap it up'.

Vivia said, "Thanks, Dougie. Now onto a breaking story in Puerto Rico, where a drug cartel kingpin was just captured by the Coast Guard."

The monitors showed he was out of view. Andréa stalked over and grabbed his elbow.

He couldn't argue, not while recording, so he allowed her to lead him to the control room.

Once inside the dark soundproof rectangular space, she closed the door and put her hands on her hips. "What the fuck was that?"

"Just friendly chit-chat. The fans…"

"What fans?"

"I get letters. I can show you..."

"Just read what is on the prompter. Nothing else! Mystic fucker shit-brains…what the actual fuck?"

"The other newscasters get to—"

"For crying out loud…" Andréa pointed to the door. "Go home."

"I have another spot in two hours."

"You just said the weather was fine. We'll edit your last segment and run it again. Now go, before I consider firing you again."

He huffed. "Fine. But you need to calm down, because all this negative energy will send your chakras out of whack. And you don't want that! Believe me!"

Dougie didn't wait for a response and strode to his dressing room. Before long, he was back in his street clothes—cargo shorts, a Billabong T-shirt, and green Crocs. While he didn't negotiate his raise, he was jazzed about receiving a few hours off. Once seated in his 1985 khaki Jeep, he turned the ignition, then pumped the gas to rev the engine, causing a puff of black smoke out the tailpipe. But instead of putting the vehicle directly into gear, he first texted his girlfriend Lilly, "I'm heading home." Dougie added a thunderbolt emoji.

He hoped they could smoke some weed and he could give his beautiful blond lover a sensual tantric massage.

As he drove away, his mind wandered. He wondered if Lilly had some type of mystic power over him. Not that he was complaining. She was the most beautiful woman on the island. It didn't matter that she didn't love him…a fact she repeated often.

Not that he was her man-slave, but even if he was, he reasoned there were certainly worse things in life. Just being with Lilly made him feel special. The look of jealousy on other men's faces was priceless and never got old. In this sense, their arrangement was a fair trade.

There would be a full moon tomorrow night, meaning a surge in cosmic energy. She always insisted on making love outdoors under the full moon, surrounded by candles and drinking a strange liquid from an ornate cup. Very groovy.

Occasionally, she liked to prick his finger with a small dagger and sip drops of his blood during their ritual. He never told his friends or family about that part. While it hurt a little at the beginning, it eventually became the climax of their ecstasy. Now, a year into their liaisons, sometimes he would give himself small paper cuts at the office for a quick rush of sweet endorphins.

As he drove toward Lilly's house, he inspected his right palm. The healed paper-cut lines were shallow but easily distinguishable.

A message came up on his Bluetooth. He played a reply text from Lilly.

"I'm out meeting a client. Can you clean the bathrooms?"

Dang. Not the afternoon he hoped for.

Dougie reduced the car's speed. Maybe he needed to reevaluate his life with Lilly. Take charge. Be a man and stop taking orders.

A wave of defeat and the churn of his stomach disavowed him of these notions. He pulled over and texted back,

"Yes, no problem sweetheart."

* * *

Johnnie pulled a couple of the twelve wood studs from the back of his Jeep. The back yard was quiet. No hammering, so he assumed Cud had come to a standstill with his project.

"Cud! Help me unload!" He walked to the backyard and dropped the two-by-fours next to his friend's half-built, chicken-coop-looking eyesore.

He entered the apartment. It was dark and Cud was asleep on the sofa, mouth open but not snoring.

"Cud! Wake up!"

Cud startled. "Who…what?"

He huffed. "I got your lumber. Help me unload." At the kitchen window, Johnnie pulled open the blind. The room flooded with golden light.

Cud's eyes widened. His white hair stuck straight up in the back. "Oh, sorry. What time is it?"

"It's 5:30. Come on." Johnnie spun and strode to the door.

Cud was in his boxers and a light blue T-shirt. He scratched his knobby knees. "Oh my. I didn't mean to sleep this long."

Johnnie stopped in the doorway. "Hurry up. I'm going fishing as soon as we unload."

His friend ambled toward him, wringing his hands. "John, I may have…accepted Gertie's dinner invitation. For both of us."

"You did?

"She cornered me. I couldn't refuse."

"Hey, what's with the bandage above your eye? Did you hurt yourself building your shelter?" Johnnie recalled Gertie's request for a sledgehammer earlier that morning. "Or did Gertie do something to you?"

"No. Heavens. After I accepted the invitation, a bird attacked me."

"Ha! I think you'll survive."

Cud got dressed and joined him outside. They moved all the lumber to the project area.

After the Jeep was emptied, Cud dusted his hands. "John, can I tell you something?"

"Sure."

Cud grabbed Johnnie's elbow. "I'm *not* crazy. But you might think I am. And I really need you to believe me. I don't need to go back to…you know where."

His friend obviously meant the psychiatric hospital in Nassau, Bahamas. Johnnie flipped up his sunglasses to study Cud's eyes; they looked steady and clear. "Sure. What is it?"

"I saw Camille earlier today."

"Your mom? Here? She died a few weeks ago."

"I've never seen a ghost before. Auras of living people, yes, all the time. But it was *her*. As sure as you are standing here now."

Johnnie wondered if Cud was still on meds and having an adverse reaction. He needed more information and paused to consider what his own therapist would do in this situation. The answer was simple. *Ask questions. Lots of questions.* "Huh. Um…what did she want?"

"Want? Why would she want something?"

"Don't ghosts haunt places because they are upset about something? Like, stuck between worlds or some shit?"

"I don't know. Mama used to see my departed father every day…at least, that is what she told everyone. I thought she just missed him. It was odd, maybe eccentric, but very sweet." Cud rubbed his face and groaned. "But I can't have a ghost here. I need to be sane."

"So…what do we do? An exorcism? Scatter some chicken bones? What the fuck?"

"I'm only telling you to be honest. If you see Mama Loughton or items floating around, please tell me immediately. Now, let's wash up for dinner, and we won't speak of this, correct?"

Johnnie chuckled. "I won't say anything."

A few minutes later, Cud and Johnnie took their seats at Gertie's dining table. Yet, instead of delighting on the bounty in front of him, Johnnie fixated on his landlord's polished appearance. She was wearing her orange wrap-dress with a long full skirt, her hair looked professionally styled in loose curls, and she wore bright lipstick. In Johnnie's opinion, her makeup and outfit screamed of desperation; a desperation to flirt with Cud. And that was the last thing they all needed.

But he couldn't do much about that, so he turned his focus on the generous bowl of steaming white spuds in front of him. "Gertie, this looks amazing. Thanks for inviting us."

Gertie glided over and placed the remaining item on the table—a baked chicken with a perfectly golden-brown skin and an aroma of lemon and pepper that made Johnnie's mouth water.

"I'm glad you both accepted. Tomorrow I'm busting up those awful counters."

Cudlow placed his blue linen napkin on his lap. "I could help you with that...if you'd like."

Johnnie gave Cud a glare. Where was Cud's professed fear of Gertie? What was going on?

Gertie took her seat. "Yes, that would be wonderful. Let's say grace." She reached across for Johnnie's right hand and Cud's left.

They bowed their heads and Gertie began. "Lord, thank you for your bounty and for close friends. May all be fed. May all be healed. May all be loved. Amen."

Gertie had placed emphasis on the word loved. *Not exactly subtle.*

Johnnie opened his eyes. Gertie and Cud seemed to be locked in a gaze that didn't seem appropriate. But he had more important priorities at the moment than helping with Cud's chastity vow. "Amen!" He grabbed the serving spoon and quickly added three large dollops of potatoes on his plate. The hints of golden skins in the mixture made his anticipation skyrocket. "Cud, pass the butter." After a couple of moments, there was still no response. "Earth to Cud!"

Cud blinked and passed the butter. "Gertie, I saw a spirit today. A first for me. Camille appeared. Initially, I thought I was merely dehydrated and mistaken. But she was there, clear as day."

Gertie placed her hand on Cud's wrist. "Really? So interesting. Did she look…at peace?" She looked away and then spooned some green beans on Johnnie's plate, as if she were his mother.

"I can't really say. Have you ever been visited by the departed before?"

She clucked her tongue as if thinking. "Can't say I have. But Dottie said she saw a *presence* at church last year. She was beside herself. Hmm. Said it looked just like black Jesus but wearing silk pajamas. She only saw him the one time. In fairness, the air conditioning wasn't working and it was particularly hot inside. One person fainted, but most likely from heat stress; *not* from seeing Jesus."

"You don't say? Well, I have sternly asked mother to leave. But, in case she is stubborn, does your pastor do exorcisms?"

Gertie rose from the table and picked up her phone from its charger on the kitchen counter. "I'll text Dottie. She would know."

While she was typing on her phone. Johnnie whispered to Cud. "I thought you wanted to keep this a secret?"

Cud grimaced and poked at his chicken with a fork. "I didn't want to trouble you, but Camille threw my razor on the floor while I was combing my hair a few minutes ago."

"How do you know it was her? Maybe you knocked it over?"

"Johnnie…" He sighed. "I just *know*. I'm sorry. Perhaps I need to move out. I don't want her to bother you. I mean, you didn't sign up for *two* new roommates."

Gertie put down her phone. "Sent. Now, let's talk about something else. Cudlow, what are your long-term plans?"

Cud blinked. "Plans?"

"You know, where you plan to live. How long do you think you'll be living with Johnnie?"

"I don't know. If it is a matter of extra rent, I could surely assist—"

"No! Nothing like that. I was just curious. Oh! Your architect stopped by. When you didn't answer the door, she knocked on mine. Ms. Johannsen said she would email you to reschedule."

"Oh my stars! I completely forgot."

Gertie turned her attention to Johnnie. "And what about you? How are things with Greta? Did you kiss and make up before she left?"

Johnnie had jammed his mouth with potatoes and masticated with deliberate speed to allow an answer. "Um. Muh," He cleared his throat. "I acted like a jerk in Miami. She said I scared her. Makes sense. Shit, I scare myself sometimes."

Gertie cocked her head. "What did you do exactly?"

"Before we met, I had written some stuff in my diary about another woman I was sort of infatuated with. And unfortunately, I brought my diary with me to Miami and Greta found it. I can't blame her for being upset. But when she left for a new hotel and stopped returning my calls, I made things a thousand times worse by confronting her and causing a scene at the Librarian Conference. I was a real jackass."

His face felt warm thinking about how idiotic it was for him to bring the bar of Irish Spring soap with him to Miami. When he had learned the Goddess smelled of this brand of soap, he had taken up the stupid habit of sleeping with a bar under his pillow at night. No wonder Greta had freaked out when she made that connection with his diary entries.

Gertie said, "Oh, well, we all make mistakes. I acted awfully in Paris. And obviously over-reacted on the cruise—"

Johnnie's heart stopped. Was Gertie actually bringing up the failed wedding to a clearly fragile Cud? He had to change the subject. "Gertie, what should I do to get her back?"

Gertie stabbed her green beans with her fork. "Did you call her last night?"

"No. I figured I'd give her some space. She said she wanted time."

She hit the table with her palm. "There! That's completely wrong. Distance is death to love. You need to call her *every* night. Even just a brief call to say you are thinking of her and ask about her day."

"Really?" Johnnie nudged his potatoes with his fork, forming them into a circular pool filled with liquid butter. "Sounds...stalky."

"Only if she tells you not to call. Did she say not to?"

"No. Not in so many words..."

"There you go! Call her tonight. None of that texting business. No one ever fell in love over a text."

A knock on the door interrupted the conversation before Johnnie could think of a response.

Gertie pushed her chair back. "I wonder who that—?"

The front door opened.

Dottie strode inside, followed by a tall older gentleman wearing a suit. She sang out, "Good evening, all!" as if she were a famous performer entering a Vegas stage. She was wearing a cocktail dress of pink chiffon and her sparkly sandals. Her hair was slicked into a tight bun with silver combs on the side.

"Dot! What are you doing here?"

"Y'all texted me about a ghost. And me and Reverend Hamilton—you remember, he's visiting from San Juan, he gave the sermon last Sunday while Pastor Lillian is on vacation—we were in the neighborhood. Figured we could help with Cud's problem."

Gertie smiled and extended a handshake. "Good evening, Reverend."

The reverend waved to Johnnie and Cud.

Johnnie stared at the Reverend. He was tall, dressed all in black with the typical white collar, but had he physique of Denzel Washington; good posture, broad shoulders, gleaming teeth. In contrast, Cud looked like a grizzled hobbit compared to this guy.

In a smooth dripping voice that sounded a bit like a television evangelist, the Rev pronounced, "Blessed evening to you all. My, that smells good. I hope we aren't interrupting. Mr. Loughton, I must say I'm intrigued by your visit from the departed."

Cud got up and greeted the reverend. "So nice to meet you. Yes, I'm seeing my dead mother. She gave me quite a fright…"

Gertie took Dot aside and began whispering to her.

Johnnie felt like a deer in headlights, wanting to hear both conversations, but the whispers from the women's discussion intrigued him. He angled his good ear toward them and cupped the other to drown out the reverend.

"Dot, I don't understand. I messaged you literally five minutes ago."

Dot whispered back, "You told me this morning you were cooking. And so, I thought…why not bring this tall, Idris-looking, and AVAILABLE man of the cloth around to sample your wares?"

Gertie glared. "I clearly already have company—"

Dot grinned and continued her whisper. "And Cud is sweet and all but he needs to realize there is a *line* of hot as fuck—sorry Jesus—men waiting for someone with your culinary gifts and your excellent *bedunk-a-dunk*."

Gertie gasped and peered over her shoulder. "Shh."

Hamilton's voice boomed. "...no, please call me Greg. Mr. Loughton, I read your biography all those years ago. Can't say I remember much of it except I found it an enjoyable read. I'm always fascinating to learn of folks' humble beginnings. Now, I heard through Dottie that your mother passed recently? Losing a parent is never easy, even at our advanced age." Elevating his voice to the rest of the room, he announced, "You know, that chicken smells heavenly. I believe it's easier to expel a ghost on a full stomach. Gertie, would you mind if Dottie and I joined you all for dinner?"

Dottie strode to the kitchen. "She always makes enough for an army. I'll get some extra plates."

And it was decided.

With no hint at subtlety, Dot wedged the Reverend's chair between Gertie's and Cud's.

Johnnie remained in his seat, gawking like a five-year-old at their first circus, as the others joined him at the table.

The Reverend offered a new saying of grace before they resumed dinner.

Dottie dominated the conversation by relaying all the church gossip, including a story about a woman who stole ten bottles of communion wine from the storage room. Of course, Dottie had solved the crime effortlessly by driving around the island and inspecting all the parishioner's recycling bins just prior to the regular Wednesday collection.

All Johnnie could do was to eat slowly and avoid eye contact. Church stories made him feel like a complete heathen, as he gave up on all religion long ago. Advertising his disdain for God would not go over well with this group.

But as much as he paced his food consumption by constructing odd shapes from his food, he cleared his plate well ahead of the rest. Because cold potatoes and chicken were simply gross. He sat on his hands, staring at the chicken bones on his plate until a funny idea came to him. "I saw the ghost," he exclaimed.

The chatter ceased and all eight eyes trained themselves in his direction.

"Yeah," he continued, "she was old and looked like Camille. I mean, I never met her, except at the funeral—and it was a closed casket—but I saw her picture. Anyway, the ghost, I mean, Camille, told me that we—Cud and I—should find another place to live. Temporarily. Like, near the beach, or near town. With a pool and a dishwasher, two bedrooms, and…a…um…walk-in closets."

Cud wrinkled his brow. "She spoke? And said those very things?"

Johnnie nodded.

Reverend Greg laughed. "Now, that is a spirit I would like to meet! How about we go take a look now and have dessert later?"

The overall consensus was an enthusiastic 'yes'.

As they left the table to head to Johnnie's apartment, he hung back, feeling foolish for lying to them so blatantly. Yet it got him away from a boring conversation about church. Before he exited Gertie's, he dashed back and grabbed the chicken bones from everyone's plates and stuffed them in his pocket.

Because, if the ghost was real, it might take some actual voodoo witchcraft to undo this mess.

Chapter 5

Dear Diary,

Cud just fell asleep watching a rerun of The Ghost and Mrs. Muir. The Reverend, Dottie, and Gertie left an hour ago. I think the Rev must have scared off Camille, or maybe bored her to a second death with his recitation of scripture. We waited for an hour for her to appear, but no dice.

This makes me wonder if Cud has lost his marbles again. At least he isn't seeing floating cookies that talk and he isn't acting like a garden gnome like he did in Miami.

I really want to tell Greta about this crazy evening. She would laugh so hard. God, I miss her laugh.

Johnnie yawned. He wasn't accustomed to so much social interaction and people talking around him. It was exhausting. Pretending to listen. Trying to nod on cue. The worst was the smiling. Smiling made his brain hurt. He began to wonder what Greta would have said if she had been there. She'd probably would have enjoyed the weird gathering. And she probably could have rattled off all kinds of cool facts about ghosts.

It always amazed Johnnie how Greta knew everything about everything. Watching the Quiz Show Challenge game show with Greta had been one of his favorite things. The way her eyes lit up calling out the answers, the way she thumbed an imaginary button.

Her skin was so beautiful. Kissing her made him feel alive; like anything was possible. And the way she looked at him—before Miami—gave him so much hope for the future.

Johnnie rubbed his eyes, trying to think of anything else; to push these memories out of his mind. Inside, he chastised himself.

Stupid, stupid, stupid!

It was late and time to sleep. Johnnie put his journal in the nightstand drawer, then took off his glasses and placed them by his lamp. He pulled the sheet up to his chest and curled onto his side. His thoughts drifted, wondering what Greta saw in him in the first place.

After a spell of tossing and turning in the dark, Johnnie reached for his phone and called Greta's cell.

She answered on the third ring. "Hi." Her voice sounded a mix of caution and deflation. Not a good start.

"Hi. Is it okay that I called?"

"Sure."

Her one-word answer was not promising. "Good. Because I miss you." With a pit in his throat, he waited to see if she would say she missed him back.

"Uh huh."

"And...I...um, how are things in Pennsylvania. What's the town again?"

"Pottsville."

"Yeah, how are things there?"

"Okay, I guess. Dad is starting chemo in two days. I may need to stay for a few weeks to make sure he goes to all his appointments and eats well. When I arrived, his pantry was bare and all he eats is frozen junk. Sooo many Hot Pockets..."

"He must really appreciate you coming home to help."

"You would think...but mostly he's cranky. Pushes back on *everything*."

"Well, if you ever want to talk, I'm a good listener." He wasn't sure if this was true; that he was a good listener. Often his mind wandered when he listened for long stretches and he lost his place in most conversations. But this was the kind of thing good boyfriends say.

"No. It's okay. He's just scared but won't admit it. Doesn't like relying on anyone."

He debated telling her about the ghost and the dinner, but he wasn't sure he could tell the story well enough. Instead, his brain bypassed all that and he asked the precise thing he shouldn't, unable to sustain the *not knowing*.

"Greta…I know you are dealing with a lot right now. But I need to know…have you forgiven me? Like…is there a chance? Because I love you."

"I can't really think about this right now."

"That's my point. Don't *think*. What does your *heart* say?"

"I think that—in my mid-thirties—I'm too old to make important decisions without *thinking* about them first."

The cutting way she said this made his stomach clench. "Oh. Shit. Yeah."

In the background, he heard a gruff man's voice yell something about a giraffe ringing the doorbell.

That's strange, Johnnie thought.

Greta said, "John, I need to go. Oh, hey, I need a favor. Could you ask Chief Tobias if he could board up the windows at the library? Ms. Teller is too old—"

"What? What's wrong with the windows?"

"The storm! It's hitting St. John tomorrow night. Winds up to a 100 miles per hour."

"Huh? I haven't heard anything about a storm."

"Check the weather service. I received a weather alert on my phone …hey, I've really got to go. Be safe."

"Greta?"

No answer. She had hung up.

Johnnie put his glasses back on and opened the weather app on his phone. Sure enough, there was a storm map showing St. John in the path of a tropical depression.

Out of the corner of his eye, he spotted something.

His heart pounded, sure that Camille manifested her image in the kitchen.

But no, it was just the way the shadows cast themselves at a strange angle from the empty milk container Cud had left on the counter.

Johnnie sighed and wondered if he was also losing his mind.

It had been a long evening, and in his heart, he knew Greta probably didn't love him anymore.

But he would do the one thing she asked.

Tomorrow morning, he would get up early and board up the library windows himself.

* * *

Johnnie opened his eyes to the sound of his phone's alarm. Oddly, his glasses were still on his face and his journal was on the bed next to him. The time was five o'clock in the morning and the room was quiet and dark. Except he could hear Cud breathing. For a moment, he hoped it was Cud and not some mouth-breathing ghost.

Hugging his pillow, not yet ready to face the day, he wondered, do ghosts sleep? And what do ghosts do when no one is awake to haunt? That was the problem with the notion that spirits were real. No one could ever explain how they spent their time.

In any event, he recalled an odd dream he had last night. Odd, first, because he remembered most of it. And odd, second, because Camille was in it. Not that she looked like Camille. She appeared in a gray form with a bright yellow center and introduced herself as Camille Elizabeth Tyler Loughton. Then she yelled at him, calling him a putz while she drank the last drops from his carton of milk. When he asked her *why* he was a putz, she simply hit him with a cane and kept insisting a storm was coming. She used the word imperative several times, ordering him to warn others to seek shelter by midnight.

As he blinked his eyes awake, something nagged at him. Something he was supposed to remember. He picked up his journal and it came back to him. He was supposed to do something for Greta.

Something…something about the library?

A storm! Greta wanted the windows boarded at the library. Now the dream with Camille made sense. His subconscious must have blended all of yesterday's events.

He stumbled past Cud—who was still asleep on the sofa—toward the bathroom to take a shower. The warm water seemed to cleanse away any questioning whether ghosts existed. He liked to believe in only things that were verifiable. The pending storm, however, should be easy to confirm. All he needed to do was check the weather on his phone.

Toweling off, rubbing his hair vigorously to reduce the dampness, he heard a blood-curdling shriek. Like someone being murdered, or a stray cat having its temperature taken.

Cud!

He wrapped the towel around his middle and dashed into the center of the room.

His white-haired friend, visible in profile from the indirect light from the bathroom, was clutching his pillow, sitting bolt upright.

"Johnnie! She was here!"

Johnnie walked to the wall switch and turned on the center ceiling light. He scanned the room. "Come on, bro. Look. She's NOT here."

Cud rubbed his eyes. "Oh. Must have been a bad dream. The worst dream."

"Geez, Cud. You need to relax. You scared the shit out of me."

"I'm terribly sorry. I'm a bit tense. The last two months have been rather difficult."

"I'll say." Johnnie returned to the bathroom and brushed his teeth.

In an elevated voice, Cud asked, "What do you have planned today? Can I help with your chores? You know, like old times? I could use a change of scenery…get thoughts of phantoms and Gertie off my mind."

"Sure. But first, I'm doing an errand this morning." He spat out toothpaste into the sink and swished it down the drain by turning on the water.

"What sort of errand?"

"I called Greta last night. She asked me if I would board up the library windows."

There was silence.

"Cud?"

His friend appeared in the bathroom door frame. "My! What happened to your leg?"

Johnnie glanced down at his ankle, the fang marks bright red with purple circles around them. "Stumpy attacked me. The rat bastard…"

"So why?"

"Why…?"

"Why board up the windows?"

Johnnie gestured for Cud to turn around so he could put on his underwear. "Greta said a storm was coming. She saw an alert on her phone yesterday."

Cud turned to face Johnnie and clasped his hand over his mouth. "No…no…no…"

Johnnie headed to his clothing rack and grabbed his uniform pants and shirt. "What's wrong?"

"That's what mother warned me about in my dream. She showed me the storm…horrible."

Johnnie squinted at Cud, noticing the fear in his friend's eyes. "We have storms all the time. No big deal." As he said these words, a flash of memory came back from his dream with Camille. Was it possible? Dreams weren't real. Couldn't be.

Cud shook his head. "No! It's a very big deal. She warned me that Gertie could die unless…"

"Oh shit." Johnnie waved his arms. "Cud…unless what?"

"Unless we go to a storm shelter by—"

Johnnie's eyes lit up as he finished the sentence. "Midnight?"

Cud stepped back. "YES! But how did you…?"

"Shit." Johnnie grimaced. "I had a similar dream. Your mom said I needed to warn people about the storm or they would die."

"Oh, dear God!" The blood drained from Cud's face.

"Damn. We need some facts." Johnnie brushed past Cud and strode to his bedside table. He retrieved his glasses and disconnected his phone from its charger. They needed to look at the weather forecast. With luck, the storm had tapered off or changed direction. With a few clicks, he located his weather app. Radar showed no storms in the Caribbean.

"Fuck."

Cud came up beside him. "Show me!"

He handed the phone to Cud. "I can't find anything. I saw the storm track on my phone last night. At least I think I did. In the dream, your mom called me a putz and hit me."

"Yes, sounds like her. Toward the end, she hit people with her cane often. I must have mentioned this before?" Cud handed the phone back.

He shrugged. "I don't recall that."

Cud rocked from foot to foot. "Tell me more."

Johnnie told him what he remembered, the details slipping away like grains in a broken hour-glass. "She introduced herself kind of formally. With four names."

"What were they?"

"Um…Camille…something…something Loughton."

"Was it Tyler-Loughton?"

"YES! Tyler!"

"It had to be her then. What do we do? How do I save Gertie?"

"I don't know. Just tell Gertie to go somewhere safe tonight."

Johnnie refreshed the weather app again, but still couldn't find any verification of a storm coming. He pocketed his phone and crossed the room to retrieve his shirt and boots. "Shoot. I can't find any proof of a storm, but Greta wouldn't lie to me and I promised her I'd protect the library."

Cud sighed. "We need something solid. There is no possible way Gertie will listen to me. I can't tell her about the dream. She'll truly think I'm mad."

"Come on, we have hours to figure this out. Help me at the library. Hey, can we use some of your lumber?"

Cudlow dashed to the sofa and pulled a pair of ratty green shorts from the floor. The belt of his shorts held his trusty pocketknife he used for his fruit scavenger hunts. Speaking rapidly as he dressed, he said, "If a storm is coming, my shelter will end up in splinters anyway. I'll help you at the library, then we can visit Chief Tobias to ask him to issue an alert."

Johnnie sighed. Chief Tobias hated Johnnie's guts and the feeling was mutual. Just looking at Tobias askance could result in his arrest. In fact, Tobias arrested him wrongfully for two homicides just a few months ago without even an iota of evidence. "The Chief won't listen to me. It's probably better if you ask him without me around."

Cud slipped his feet into flip-flops with red plastic straps. "Understandable."

Once outside, they took Cud's shelter apart. With very few nails keeping it together, the job was easy. Soon enough, they loaded Johnnie's Jeep with all the intact lumber. Looking back, the shelter looked like a tumbleweed of twine and plastic mesh, accompanied by the five cinderblocks Cud scavenged from the roadside. In short, his deconstructed shelter didn't look much different than before.

Driving west, the sun rose in Johnnie's vehicle rear window. Much of the world was still asleep, evidenced by the empty roads and abundance of chickens acting like they owned the island's transportation network, nonchalantly wandering the road with no concern for safety.

About twenty minutes later, they pulled up into the library's parking lot. Johnnie gazed at the concrete steps leading up to the entrance and immediately his heart felt pain thinking of Greta and the idea of losing her forever. His eyes fixed to the spot where he poured out his love for her the day after he got back from Miami. How she seemed to forgive him and his feeling of elation. But now, he was losing hope.

The building was a bright yellow stucco punctuated with white trim and a contrasting red steel roof; its windows had thick wooden operational dark green shutters. Dating back to the 1700s, the building was the epitome of early Virgin Islands architecture. But what struck Johnnie was how simple it would be to close the shutters and nail a board across them. *Easy peasy.*

His phone showed 6:45. The library wouldn't open for roughly three hours and perhaps, if this went quickly, he could report to Hawksnest Beach to begin his chores by seven thirty.

Johnnie parked his Jeep and he and Cud exited.

"What's the game plan?" Cud asked.

"Let's start on this side, then go around to the front." He grabbed a handful of nails and shoved them in his pants pocket, then picked up a two-by-four, before heading up the steps.

The swivel mechanisms of the shutters were rusty and it took all his body weight to pull them into a fully closed position.

"Hold this for me," Johnnie hefted the first timber up against the shutters.

Cud held it in place and Johnnie put the first nail through. Bam. Bam. Bam. Bam.

In the courtyard created by the adjacent buildings, the noise ricocheted, amplified by the hard surfaces. Except for a passing garbage truck, Johnnie's nailing was the most pronounced noise in the area. With every swing, he cringed inside, hoping he didn't disturb sleeping residents.

When they finished the third window, a black SUV flew around the corner of the parking lot and slammed on its brakes, coming to a dramatic sliding stop beside Johnnie's jeep.

The emergency light bar on top of the arriving SUV told Johnnie everything he needed to know.

Cudlow ducked behind the low stucco wall lining the terrace.

A stench of overpowering cologne exited the vehicle, otherwise known as Police Chief Tobias. Johnnie's muscles froze in a mix of frustration and panic.

Tobias was on his phone as he stared up at Johnnie. In his usual booming tone, he said, "I've got it covered Miss Teller…oh, don't you worry. I'll make sure his ass goes to jail." He ended his call and stood there with his hands on his wide hips, a stance not unlike the Jolly Green Giant. Johnnie half-expected the Chief to shout out, "Ho, ho, Ho." But no, Tobias never laughed.

Instead, Tobias just waved two fingers towards himself in a gesture that meant 'stop what you are doing and get down here NOW'.

Johnnie left the hammer on the ground and whispered to Cud, "Go get out of here. I don't think he's seen you yet. I don't want you to go to jail because of my shit."

Cud nodded and whispered back. "I'll get reinforcements." He stayed low and exited around the side of the building where trees shielded the walkway.

Johnnie took a deep breath. With his hands in the air, palms out, he walked down the staircase toward Tobias. He wasn't sure if he should start explaining himself or just stay mum. With Tobias, anything he said could land him in trouble. The Chief was not easily swayed by words or explanations.

Tobias smirked. "I don't even *want* to know."

"Know what?" Johnnie was now within ten feet of the Chief, but didn't dare stand closer. Tobias was a tree trunk of a man, with an equivalent level of intellect and reasoning. The kind of guy who smiles only when he sucker-punches you.

"Put your hands behind your back. I'm placing you under arrest."

"What else is new?" Johnnie hadn't intended his reply to be so snarky, but exasperation and the assault of the Chief's stupid pungent body spray got the better of him. With an internal sigh, he asked calmly, "I mean, can you tell me the charges?"

"Destroying state-owned property, criminal trespass, violating the noise ordinance…I'm sure I'll come up with more." Tobias unhitched his handcuffs and twirled his finger, asking Johnnie to turn around to be cuffed.

"Is this really necessary? Besides, I'm doing a public service. Greta, I mean, Ms. Hobbs, the assistant librarian, asked me to board up the windows to protect the building from the storm." Johnnie hoped mentioning Greta would soften the Chief. Apparently, those two got on famously…if not mysteriously. The Chief would read to groups of school children at the library from time to time. Which seemed wildly incongruous and Johnnie wondered how two vastly different personalities could reside within this cyborg-acting dick-munch. In hopes of sympathy, Johnnie added, "It would suck if all the books got ruined and you couldn't read to the kindergarten class." He tried a smile, but it felt fake, which it was, so he stopped.

"What storm?"

"Jesus, fucking...the STORM! Greta said she got an alert. It's supposed to hit at midnight." Johnnie swallowed hard, knowing there was no objective proof of the storm currently on the internet. But Greta wouldn't lie to him. Mentioning the ghost's warning in his dream would really set off the Chief.

Tobias' eyebrows protruded and eyes narrowed. "Are you off your meds again? Ha! I KNEW it!

"Sir, I am not off my medication. I am perfectly fine. If you would just listen..."

"Turn around. I'll check the weather when we get back to the station, but even if there was a storm, that doesn't excuse vandalism. Ms. Teller assured me in no uncertain terms that you were *not* authorized—"

"Shit. I told you. Greta asked me to...hey, let me call her. She'll tell you herself." Johnnie reached into his back pocket for his phone.

Tobias' reaction was swift and precise. "Put your hands where I can see them!"

Johnnie froze. Tobias' trained his gun on his chest at close range and he didn't want to die over some stupid shutters.

"Get on the ground now, hands out!"

He did as he was told. Chest down, his chin on the jagged blue rock, he could sense the heat of Tobias' gloating and felt the sharp pain of the nails in his front pants pocket digging into his nut sack. He shifted his hips to drag the nails away from his groin, but the movement only made the situation worse. *Ouch.*

"Lucky for you it's an election year. I would smoke your ass if..."

"If what?" a female voice asked.

Johnnie's hopes soared. *Robin!*

He didn't dare lift his head, so he kept his chin down and just listened.

In an argument with Robin, Tobias didn't stand a chance.

Chapter 6

Cud, not having his phone with him, raced along the sidewalk and through the traffic circle straight toward the Legislative Annex, located only a couple of blocks away. It was still early, but he hoped Dottie or Robin would be at their office.

He felt the plastic band of his left flip-flop break free and he stubbed his toes on the concrete. Bending to inspect the situation, Cud concluded his footwear was clearly unfixable. He kicked the other sandal off and continued jogging barefoot.

Thirty seconds later, huffing from the exertion, he pulled on the entrance door.

Locked.

No security guard was evident. He pounded on the glass and yelled, "Dot! Dot! Are you there?"

A second-floor window opened and Dot poked her head out. "Shush! You'll wake the dead. Give me a sec. I'll come down."

In short order, Dot unlocked the door and ushered him into the lobby. "Calm down. Don't worry, honey. She knows."

"Pardon me?"

Dottie looked like she's been awake for hours, with a polished appearance, and wearing an expensive-looking teal pant-suit with suede flats. "You came to tell me about the police call to the library, right? Robin is on her way."

Cud scratched his head. "How did you know?"

"Sweetie, you are cute. My bestie Janice, who works the police switchboard, told me after the 9-1-1 noise complaint came in. The resident who reported it said the man with the hammer was wearing a Park Service uniform. So, we connected the dots…so to speak." She giggled at her own pun.

But her smile quickly turned into a frown and a pointed stare. "What in heavens were you doing at the library? Is this some sort of retribution for Greta breaking up with Johnnie? Cause if it is, I'm gonna have words with him."

"No, nothing like that. We were only trying to help." Cud sighed. "It's a long story."

She nodded. "Hmm, mm. My fav."

"Pardon?"

"I love me a long story. Don't get me wrong, I like all stories, but long stories are usually the best. Come on up. I've made some English tea. Do you like cream or sugar?"

He followed her up the wide curved staircase to the second floor. He had never been inside the Legislative Annex before, although he had passed it several times. Living as a homeless person over the last decade, he preferred not to put himself on the government's radar. He counted himself lucky that the police never arrested him for vagrancy and that they simply looked the other way. Now, barefoot and wearing ratty shorts in this official building, he felt self-conscious to the point of longing for retreat.

At the top of the stairs, they turned right. Dottie strode into her office, which sat right outside the Senators'. Being so early, he expected no other persons in the building. But a thin man—borderline gaunt with his sunken eyes and pronounced cheekbones—likely in his forties and wearing a navy suit and a purple bowtie, sat legs crossed in Dottie's guest chair, sipping from a flowered teacup.

Dottie waved Cudlow in. "This is Mr. Jacque Lords, former Tourism Minister of the British Virgin Islands. He's a political consultant now. Jacque, this is Cudlow Loughton."

Mr. Lords placed his teacup on Dottie's desk and rose to shake Cud's hand, but offered more of a side grip than a firm handshake. "So nice to meet you, Mr. Loughton. My, I've always wanted to meet you. I'm sure you've heard this a zillion times, but I am quite a fan. And don't think I don't know about your latest endeavor! Nature Wonderland sounds exquisite." He waved jazz hands to accentuate his glee. "Where are you building this glorious theme park?"

Cud shook his head. "A fan? Well, I just pursue projects that bring me joy…what matters in life. What have you heard?" For a moment, he worried that his new project manager, Mo Zaidi, had spilled the beans on some of the park's special features and attractions. The rainforest canopy ride and the beehive simulator were both top-secret. Only a handful of people in the organization were privy to the design details.

Dottie cut in. "Never mind that right now. You can both geek out about saving the earth later. I want to know what you all were doing just now at the library!"

Cudlow took the open seat next to Mr. Lords, but directed his words to Dottie. "Greta asked Johnnie to protect the library's windows from the storm. Also, do you remember me telling you about my mother's ghost last evening?"

Dottie, sitting behind her desk, leaned forward with her chin resting on her palms. "Honey, it's all I've thought about."

"Yes, um, she appeared to both myself and John in our dreams last night. The SAME dream. More of a nightmare. With a very dire warning."

"No!"

"Yes!"

"Well, keep going…"

"Camille also said a storm is coming. A terrible one. High winds…people may die." Cud decided it best not to mention the prediction of Gertie's demise.

Dottie turned to her computer screen and tapped fiercely on her keyboard, showing off her white-tip French manicure. Cud remembered this term, as his former wife wore her nails like this and explained the process at length to him on a flight to Canada twenty years ago. This memory caused a pang in his heart, as he also remembered how he had paid so little attention to his wife, keeping his sole attention on stock quotes and legal papers during their vacation.

A few seconds later, Dot announced, "Not seeing anything on the radar on the NOAA website. Are you sure there's a storm?"

Cud leaned over her desk to see for himself. Plain as day, the radar showed some spots of rain around the region but no clear storm system. "Oh dear." He closed his eyes and sighed. "Yes, you can see our dilemma."

"Well, no one said the government was perfect. The site says the federal government shut down at midnight. No continuing resolution. However, NOAA says it will continue to provide critical weather information."

Dottie clicked some more and she hit the keys with lightning speed. After half a minute, she looked up. "There are other international weather services. But most of them rely on the US for this region. Caribbean governments are cheap-ass bitches. There's a dust storm off of Africa. Not much else."

"I see." Cud pinched the bridge of his nose, wondering if anyone could believe them now. "Dottie, do you think we are both mad?"

"Hmm. I don't mess with spirits. If a spirit tells you something, you best believe it. That's what I think. Mmm hmm." Dottie brightened. "It's not all bad, though. The government shutdown means the Park Service is likely shut down. Johnnie should have the day off. If Tobias doesn't lock him up." Her cell phone rang and she picked up. "Hi, I can't talk right now…say what? Jesus…mmm hmmm…oh good. Thanks for the heads up." Dottie ended the call and placed her cell phone face down. "Janice said Tobias had called the station for backup. That can't be good. But she sent Arturo over. No way Artie is arresting his girlfriend's brother. That should help."

Jacque placed his hand on Cud's arm and gave him a coy look, batting his eyelashes and shimmying his shoulders. "Well, seems like we have ample time to chat, Mr. Billionaire Mogul Financial Genius! Please, tell me everything about Nature Wonderland. As a former tourism minister, I've kept up with all the news, but your company has been teasing the public…not giving the details…but I get it…smart! A four-hundred-million-dollar theme park with five ecosystems represented? Will it be a franchise? Or a single location? You must tell me." Jacque crossed his heart. "I can keep a secret."

It didn't seem right to be sitting here talking about his theme park when his friend was in trouble. "I'd love to chat, but I should really go back and help Johnnie. I can help explain to Chief Tobias…maybe not the dream part…"

Dottie shook her head. "Don't. Robin and Artie have this. Another spectator will only make Tobias see red."

"Oh. I see." He trusted Dottie's advice. Because she certainly had better insights into police dynamics—actually all dynamics—on the island. Cud sighed. "I suppose I'll get the play-by-play regardless, given your network."

She grinned. "Stick with me honey, and you'll know everything the *instant* it happens."

* * *

~15 minutes earlier~

Not an encouraging start to the day.

Robin threw on her cotton drawstring joggers and a tank top, shoved her feet into her white canvas sneakers, and grabbed her overstuffed shoulder bag.

Out the door in under ninety seconds, she jogged four blocks to the library, not looking both ways before crossing the street. In her fury, she felt like she could repel cars with her sheer strength of will, like Storm from X-Men. Not logical, but she dared fate to fuck with her.

Later she wouldn't remember her trip to the library—her brain buzzing, trying to decide whom she was angrier with: the Chief or her butt-head brother. In any event, she was prepared to tear them both new assholes.

The scene upon her arrival was bad. Johnnie was face down on the ground. Tobias, aiming his gun on his back, bragging about wanting to 'smoke him'.

She approached cautiously, not wanting to startle Tobias. "If what?" She paused until Tobias looked up. And his expression was priceless—his upper lip curled back in shock and extreme distaste, resembling the look of a pissed off cat that just sniffed a banana. "You know, shooting an unarmed man would not be good publicity for your senate campaign. So, tell me, what the HELL is going on?"

Tobias lowered his weapon. "Ma'am, I suggest you don't interfere. You can see him after processing."

Robin took a few steps forward, her arms wide. "Is this *really* necessary? What did he do?"

Johnnie, still face down, said, "Chief thinks I was vandalizing the library. But I was only trying to protect it."

She shook her head. "Chief, can I speak with Johnnie for one minute?"

Tobias snorted like a bull, then holstered his weapon. "Fine. Mr.

Crosswell, you can get up. But don't try anything funny."

She helped Johnnie to his feet and they huddled with their backs to the Chief.

Robin whispered, "Go."

Johnnie snuck a look over his shoulder and then whispered back. "Greta asked me to board up the windows because of the big storm coming tonight. Chief won't listen. Said I'm damaging government property and trespassing. Ms. Teller wants me in jail." He shifted his weight from side to side, dug into his pocket and pulled out a handful of nails. "Here, take these."

She took the nails and tossed them into her handbag, not exactly sure why, but there were more pressing matters at hand. "I see. When did you hear about a storm?"

"Last night. Greta saw it from the weather service. Winds over a hundred miles per hour. Oh, and Cud's dead mom also warned both of us about it last night in some kind of mind-melding dream."

Her throat tightened and she squeezed her eyelids tight to process this last portion. "PLEASE. Do NOT mention that part to the Chief." She sighed, then hit her brother on the shoulder with a balled fist. "Really? In an election cycle? Tobias is already eating my lunch and I DON'T need this craziness. Just apologize to Ms. Teller and have Greta explain to the Chief. Okay?"

"Not really up to me."

Robin chewed her thumbnail as she considered their options. "True. Let me do the talking." She broke their huddle and walked up to the Chief, who stood like a stone colossus with his burly arms crossed. "John is sorry for trespassing and if you could call Ms. Hobbs, I'm sure she will verify his story."

Another vehicle pulled into the lot. With glee, she saw it was Officer Arturo Bell, her boyfriend, and mentally thanked the heavens.

Artie exited his cruiser and nodded to Tobias. "You wanted backup, Chief?" He grinned at Robin broadly with his gleaming teeth and cute dimples. "Hey, babe. I mean, good morning to you, Senator Crosswell."

She loved Artie's playfulness and sly sense of humor and immediately wanted to run up and plant a kiss on him. But that could wait until later tonight, when she could thank him in better ways. Donning on a serious, more official-sounding tone, she said, "Good morning, Officer Bell. I think there has been a small misunderstanding concerning my brother."

Tobias narrowed his eyes, looking like a camel ready to spit. His dark complexion reddened. He glanced at Robin, then to Johnnie, then Arturo, and scrunched his face into a pout, as if he was internally figuring out some kind of math problem. He strode to his SUV and slammed his fist on the roof. *BAM!*

He pulled out his phone and dialed. Tapping his foot and with his eyes skyward, he seemed to be on hold. After a few moments, he spoke a message which was clearly meant for Greta. "Ms. Hobbs, Officer Tobias. I need you to confirm some information for me. Call me back as soon as you get this message." He ended the call and slammed his fist on the car roof again. "Officer Bell, tell Mr. Crosswell if I see him near the library again, he will live to regret it." Tobias got into his vehicle, slammed the door shut, and sped off.

After the dust settled, Robin grinned at Artie. "I could kiss you."

Arturo closed the distance and brushed her hair off her shoulder. "Not with that breath. Looks like you just woke up." He leaned in to sniff her neck. "You'd better go shower or you'll be late to work. Hey, I'll see you at five. Remember, it's double pepperoni night!"

She hit him playfully on the chest and blew a kiss. "I'll see you later." Her mood shifted as she faced her brother. "You heard Tobias. Don't you dare—"

Johnnie dusted off the front of his green trousers. "Don't worry. I'm not coming back here. Arturo, did you see Cud on your way over?"

Robin looked at her phone. Artie was right. She had to go. Dottie had set an early appointment with the new election strategist. "Bye! John, stay the fuck out of trouble."

With that out of the way, she wondered if there really was a sizable storm heading their way. Because if John's story was true, the island could be in a world of hurt. As she retreated to her apartment, she called Dottie.

"Dot, crisis averted. Tobias let Johnnie go. Please tell Mr. Lords I'll be a few minutes late. And check the weather. My brother is a butt-head, but best to warn folks if a storm is really coming."

Dot replied in her sing-song fashion. "Got it. Mr. Lords is already here, but take your time. We are having a wonderful conversation. Oh, and the federal government shut down. And I checked; weather sites don't show any storms."

Stunned, Robin slowed her strides. "For fuck's sake."

"Don't worry. I'll make some calls just to be sure."

"Thanks." Robin furrowed her brow, searching her memory for who Dot might know in the forecast business, but given Dot's range of contacts—and her contacts' contacts—anything was possible. She recalled the time she told Dottie she was looking for new recipes for French onion soup. Within ten minutes, Dot handed her the phone number for Oprah's personal chef.

As she walked into her apartment building, Robin wondered if losing the election would really be all that bad. She could shed all her work headaches, maybe take up yoga, eat better, travel, and spend more quality time with Arturo.

But it was the quiet moments in life that always irked her. Stress was her jet fuel.

She just needed to keep Johnnie out of trouble long enough to get re-elected.

Chapter 7

Still at Senator Crosswell's office, Cud sat on the edge of his chair as Dot took another call. "Any word on Johnnie?"

She grinned. "Not arrested. See, I knew they could handle it." To Jacque, she said, "Robin will be in shortly."

Cud excused himself. "I should go. Thanks for your help. Mr. Lords, nice meeting you." He high-tailed it out of the office, still self-conscious of his lack of footwear. Once back on the sidewalk, he considered buying some trainers. But most of the businesses were still closed because of the early hour.

At the library parking lot, Johnnie was conversing with Officer Bell. He waved a greeting.

Arturo waved back. "Good morning, Mr. Loughton!"

Cud came closer until the three were in a huddle. "I heard the Chief came to his senses."

Artie chuckled. "Well, I won't comment on that."

Johnnie clapped Cud on the shoulder. "Where did you go?"

"I was with Dottie. She told me everything. By the way, did you know the Federal government shut down last night?"

Johnnie checked his phone. "Oh. Wait. I think my boss Kemper said that was a possibility last week. I'm supposed to report to her office and sign something…I better call her."

The radio in Artie's vehicle blared with a call to respond to an ATM break-in. Arturo said, "I need to go. You both better leave this area before the Chief changes his mind." With that warning, he got in his police car and drove away.

Cud sighed."No one can locate information about a storm in our region. How are we going to convince anyone to listen to us?"

"I don't know. Hey, come with me to Kemper's office. She might have some ideas. She used to work for FEMA or some shit."

"Jolly good. Let's go."

"What happened to your flip-flops?"

"They broke."

"I have another pair of boots in my Jeep. Want to borrow them? There's a clean pair of socks also."

"What size?"

"Eleven."

"Hmm. I'm a ten. I could give them a go."

During the ride to the Park Service Administration Building, Cud put on the extra socks and ankle-high tan leather boots. Despite being a size larger, they felt heavy and constrictive. But these boots had steel toes, which he had never experienced before. He brought a foot up and knocked on the reinforced fronts with his knuckles. "Very interesting!" He tapped out the tune "Shave and a Haircut" and giggled. Excited by the sturdiness of these boots, he couldn't wait to find some objects to kick, to test the shoe's abilities. After living barefoot for so long, the boots made his feet seem somewhat bionic, like Steve Austin in the Million Dollar Man.

Johnnie sighed loudly, with a long exhale, his eyes fixed on the road, his shoulders tense.

Cud sensed his companion was not having a very good day. Upon reflection, he considered how silly he must seem to Johnnie. Seeing ghosts, bad footwear, hiding from Gertie, sleeping on his sofa. Not to mention all that commotion last month in Miami. With a grimace, Cud broke the silence. "Do you enjoy having me as a housemate? I know I'm not the easiest person to live with. If I've outstayed my welcome, please let me know. I won't take offense."

Johnnie stared ahead at the road. After a pregnant pause, he asked, "Why do you ask that?"

"I brought a ghost to your home. No one deserves that. And you've lived alone for so many years. Very much like myself. I was just thinking, maybe you prefer to be alone. I would more than understand."

His friend continued staring ahead. "I don't know what I want. With Greta, I was excited about the thought of moving in with her. I began thinking that being alone isn't how people are supposed to be. Part of me likes the quiet of living by myself. But I also want to feel normal. Whatever that is."

"I'm afraid I haven't felt normal for a long time either. Happy? Yes, at times, but definitely not normal."

Johnnie sighed. "I would settle for happy."

Cud choked back emotion, suddenly envisioning all the chances of happiness he had thrown away. First with his wife Winifred, now deceased, and more recently with Gertie. "Me too."

Johnnie asked, "Are you crying?"

"No." He considered how to explain. "Just melancholy. Too many regrets. That sort of thing. And you?" He glanced at Johnnie's side profile, noticing he was blinking rapidly.

Johnnie lifted his glasses and wiped his eyes with the back of his hand. "I'm fine." He slowed the vehicle and turned into a parking lot down by the waterfront. "We're here."

They parked on the curb next to the yellow stucco Visitor Center.

The sight of neatly arranged Park Service vehicles instantly validated the government shutdown. It was close to 7:30 according to the Jeep's clock and normally the lot would be mostly empty as the Rangers and other staff went about their normal duties.

Johnnie parked his Jeep in the closest handicapped spot. Cud felt instantly uneasy with this clearly unethical parking choice, but given the government shutdown, the building was closed to visitors, handicapped or not. The sun was hidden behind clouds and there should have been some interior lights visible through the windows, meaning the place was clearly closed. As they approached the main entrance, he could see chains around the door handles.

Cud asked, "Now what?"

Another car, a green four-door sedan, pulled up. The woman behind the wheel had a round face with ruddy cheeks, but a smile so buoyant with enthusiasm that Cud couldn't help but smile back. Cud had seen her before around Cruz Bay, but didn't know her name.

Johnnie waved, "Hi, Candace."

She leaned through her car window and grinned, "Look at you all dressed for work. Didn't you get the memo? Are you here to sign the acknowledgement?"

"Yeah, sure, I guess."

"Cool beans. Kemper's email said to go to the side entrance to the right and take the stairs up to her office. Wait, I'll park and walk up with you."

As they waited for her to park, Cud kicked the concrete curb a few times and asked, "What does Candace do?"

"She works at the visitor desk. You know, answers all the questions and books the ranger-led hikes. Why are you kicking the curb?"

"The steel toes. They do the job, don't they?" He stepped on the toes of Johnnie's boots for emphasis.

Johnnie backed away. "Really? You've never worn these before? Didn't you own a construction business?"

Cud shook his head. "My position was more on the investment side. And I had a staff of site inspectors for my development projects."

"Well, stop it. Don't embarrass me."

"Oh, you mean like this?" Cud did a little dance and kicked Johnnie's toes again.

"Jesus, Cud. Enough. She's coming."

Cud chuckled and stopped his jig. "Hello, Candace. Have you ever worn steel-toed boots? I feel invincible."

She was wearing sneakers. "Yes, I can see. So, Johnnie…is this your first shut-down? Doesn't happen often, but man, it's chaos. A few years back during a shut-down, Ranger Hartley was placing cones across the entrance at Maho Bay and a guy attacked him with a long spatula. Something about ruining his family's picnic."

They followed Candace to the unlocked entrance and up the stairs that sported a sign, "Employees Only." At the end of the upstairs hall, Kemper's office had a line of two individuals leaning against the wall just outside.

Candace explained to Cud, "We have to report in and sign a furlough notice before we are formally dismissed for the day. I heard Congress is trying to pass a funding bill, but who knows? But I tell ya, I could use a week off. Ain't never been a time we didn't get back pay. Furloughs can be sweeeeeet!"

Johnnie took a place in line behind Candace. "Um, so…didn't Kemper work for FEMA before this?"

She chuckled. "No. Not that I'm aware of. I think it was the Bureau of Land Management out in Nevada."

Johnnie huffed. "Damn, I mean. Um. Do you know anyone who's ever worked for the weather service?"

The line moved up one space and another employee rounded the corner out of Kemper's office.

Candy scratched her chin. "Nope. But we have a meteorological station in Lameshur Bay. Why?"

Cudlow bounced up and down at this exciting news. "That's wonderful! Is it possible to see the latest data? Like pressure readings? I mean, I can tell you the pressure is low just from the pain in my right hip. But if we could show people some actual numbers…"

The line moved up and Candace was next. Cud and Johnnie crowded the door frame behind her.

Candy beamed, "Hey boss. Where do I sign up for my free vacay?"

Kemper's eyes looked tired. She pointed to a side table with a stack of forms. "Right there. Nice to see you are in a good mood. Other people, not so much."

Candace had a pen in her hand and began scribbling.

Johnnie waved. "Hey Kemper. Candace was saying we have a weather station at Lameshur. Where does the data go?"

She gave him a questioning look. "Well, we *had* a station. But the transmitter and the solar array died last quarter and I don't have anything in the budget this year to cover their replacement. Why do you ask?"

Cud brushed past Johnnie and extended his hand. "I don't think we've met, Ranger Snow. I'm Cudlow."

Kemper smiled and shook his hand. "Yes, I know who you are. Nice to see you. I hope you are feeling better these days?" From behind her desk, she straightened a stack of forms and placed them in a manilla folder.

"Yes, yes, quite better, thank you. Well, we are asking about the weather because we fear a great storm is coming. And with no hard data, we might not be believed. I'm afraid given our history, John and I are not considered the most credible persons."

Candace handed her pen to Johnnie and switched places with him.

Kemper backed up her chair and stood. She removed a heavy keyring from her uniform pants pocket. "Sorry. I wish I could help."

Johnnie finished signing and joined the conversation. "Boss, do you know anyone that knows about weather? Maybe there is something we are missing. What if radar can't detect it?"

Cud nodded and shook his finger at Johnnie. "Yes, precisely. Mother Nature is so unpredictable. I must add a weather-themed attraction to Nature Wonderland. I'm going to write that down." He stole a scrap of paper from Kemper's waste basket and scribbled a note.

A streak of amber light pierced the window behind Kemper, as if the clouds had vanished instantly. Her office brightened tenfold.

She said, "Hmm. It looks okay outside to me."

Johnnie flipped down his round sunglasses and muttered under his breath.

Candance tilted her head with her eyes upward as if thinking. "I don't know. Remember after Maria? We didn't have power or clean water for months."

"True." Kemper nodded. "Tell you what, since we all have the day off, let's fill the tanker truck with potable water. Johnnie, call Merv and see if he'll help you fuel all the park service trucks to the max, plus test the backup generators."

Johnnie handed Kemper his signed acknowledgment form. "Really? Just like that? I mean, it's everyone's day off."

Kemper shooed them out of her office. Once in the hall, she locked her office door. With a heavy sigh, she said, "Honestly, I have nothing else to do today. And better safe than sorry, right?"

Cud clapped in delight. "Jolly good! But, if there is a storm, how do we inform everyone?"

Candy tapped Cud on the shoulder. "Have you considered calling Dottie?"

Cudlow nodded. "Yes, she is aware. But we don't have any way to substantiate the storm. The sun is shining now. Even Dottie wouldn't be able to convince folks to prepare."

Candy chuckled. "Mr. Loughton, never underestimate Dottie McPherson. Ha! She could convince a stray dog to raise a litter of kittens."

* * *

The sledge hammer felt both heavy and good in Gertie's hands. Just one strike and there would be no turning back.

Channeling Miss Piggy, she lifted the hammer above her head and brought it down to smash the counter's edge, yelling an accompanying "HI-YAHH!"

The blue tiles cracked but remained in place. She grasped the hammer and struck again. Four tiles cracked and came loose from the underlying mortar, revealing white adhesive and some of the plywood underlayment. "Yesss!"

Gertie continued pounding away. In a short time, her biceps ached. Working her way clockwise around the U-shaped kitchen, each square foot took at least five minutes of hammering and scraping with a crowbar to remove the decades-old tile and mortar.

The floor below was littered in dust and shards. But she was giddy with destruction and decided she would simply clean up at the end.

An hour into her toils—now on the last two square feet of counter—Gertie's hammer strike exploded on the tile sending a tiny shard into her left eye. "Aaaagh!" She dared not rub it. "Damn, damn, damn!" She cursed herself. Wearing safety glasses would have been the wise choice.

A knock on the front door startled her. She left the hammer on the counter and gingerly navigated the mess, while covering her injured eye protectively, trying not to blink.

Upon opening the door, she froze. Reverend Gregory Hamilton, her dinner guest from last night, greeted her, holding a sizable bunch of paper-wrapped yellow zinnias. In contrast to the suit he wore last night, he was presently wearing chambray shorts with a white polo shirt. The shirt showed off his physique and Gertie couldn't help but stare at his chiseled arms using her one good eye.

Had the Reverend heard her screaming 'damn'?

"Reverend, hello...I...I'm in the middle of...what brings you here today?"

"Gertrude, please call me Gregory. Are you alright?" He pointed to her eye.

"Oh. I got something in it."

"Let me take a look."

She held the door and stepped aside.

He sauntered inside and dropped the flowers on her narrow side table next to the door. "You've been busy I see." He placed his broad hands on either side of her head. "Now, tilt your head back and look at the ceiling."

She did as she was told. He lifted her top eyelid with his index finger and looked closely.

The whole situation made her feel foolish. Like a small child with a splinter in their finger, asking their parent to remove it. Yet, the Reverend had such a calming presence...a steadiness if you will...that she relaxed to his touch.

"Hold still." He brushed her eyelashes with his fingertip a few times. "Got it."

She blinked rapidly to confirm the shard was gone. "Yes. Thank you."

But the Reverend kept his proximity, his body just inches from hers. At nearly a foot taller, she couldn't help but experience a surge of adrenaline as she inhaled his freshly showered scent. However, this moment was fleeting as she realized she was covered in dust and perspiration and was still wearing her flowered pajamas.

It was clear he wanted to make a romantic move as he gazed into her eyes.

But that wouldn't do.

Panicked, Gertie stepped back, creating at least a yard of space between them. "Sorry for the mess. What brings you here again?"

He clasped his hands together. "I just wanted to thank you again for dinner last night. Being away from home, it meant a great deal that you would offer such hospitality." He gathered the flowers by the door and handed them to her. "The least I could do."

The Rev was a subtle as a barn cat in heat. What was she supposed to do? She didn't want to be rude.

Viewing him framed by the front door, the memory of her first 'date' with Cudlow raced back. How just his formal yet shy mention of his intention to court her had sent her into a lust-crazed frenzy where she dropped the lemon squares she made for the church bake sale on the front lawn and lunged at him for a kiss. Plus, all the rest that followed.

Now, a kind, available, and strikingly handsome man stood before her and she could just as easily initiate a new romance.

It would solve the whole Cudlow mess. Let her get on with her life. And Cudlow had never been a good match for her anyway. Sure, Cud was sweet, but their lives and backgrounds were so different. Too different.

Gregory waved a hand. "Gertrude?"

"Sorry. Thank you, the flowers are beautiful. But I should get back to work. As you can see, I'm no sight for company."

He beamed. "Tell you what…how about I come by later and take you out for an early dinner? Give you a well-needed break from your renovation? I'll pick you up at five."

She liked his confidence. Going out in public seemed safe enough. "Yes, I'd like that. See you then." She hugged the flowers. "Where are we going?"

Gregory gave her a wink. "I'm going to surprise you. Nothing too fancy though."

Gertie laughed. "Good idea. Not sure if I'll ever get this dust out of my hair."

He took her free hand, a very sweaty hand, and kissed the top of it. "I'll see myself out."

Through her screen door, she watched the Reverend as he walked to his car. The man was smooth, with a stride like a leopard, his shoulders sleek and powerful. Dot could be onto something. As she located a vase for the flowers, it occurred to her.

She could wait for Cudlow forever. But also, life is short.

And her bedunk-a-dunk could use some regular tending while she's still had some left to work with.

Chapter 8

Robin checked her watch as she took the stairs. She had her laptop bag over one shoulder and canvas sneakers on her feet. It was a sneakers kind of day. After her run-in with Tobias, wearing heels was a non-starter. Because in her gut, she sensed there were more calamities to come. And no one wore heels to a bar fight and expected to win.

At the top of the stairs, she made a right turn toward her office. The dark paneled walls and sixties-era industrial furniture made her office seem like a mail clerk's. In no way did it instill the gravitas of her position, but she hadn't chosen government service for the glamor.

Dottie stood as she arrived and took her shoulder bag. "Senator, you remember Mr. Jacque Lords. Why don't you get settled and buzz me when you are ready for him?"

Jacque, with a teacup in hand, stood and smiled at her.

Robin remembered Jacque and couldn't believe he had the balls to show his face here again. She was certainly in no mood for his jovial demeanor and simply nodded to Dottie. "Coffee. Big."

Dottie grinned. "Of course. Jacque, can I get you more tea? Some cookies?"

Jacque stood and extended a handshake. "Nice to see you again. Take all the time you need."

After shaking his hand and faking a smile, Robin entered her larger adjoining office.

Dottie followed, unpacked her laptop and arranged it on the senator's desk, plugging in the freestanding monitor and external keyboard. She hissed, "You don't look so good. But be nice. Hear him out."

Robin plopped down in her mesh office chair and leaned back, her hands covering her face. "The Chief had his gun on Johnnie. I think he wanted to kill him."

Dot pshaw'd, flicking her wrist in the air. "Tobias is all thunder and no rain. He wouldn't shoot him. Well...not in an election cycle."

"That isn't reassuring. Look, I don't want to talk about it. Coffee."

"Yes. Right away."

A few minutes later, after she finished half the contents of coffee from her large mug with the words 'Keep Calm and Fuck Off', Jacque came in and took the guest chair. His neon purple bowtie with a lavender shirt looked out of place in the otherwise drab office.

"Senator Crosswell. Thank you for seeing me. I love your mug."

Robin sighed. "Dottie got it for me. No offense."

"None taken. As you've probably surmised, I've left my previous position with the British Virgin Islands as Tourism Director. I'm so sorry for bringing that killer Thomas Smith here to your office all those weeks ago. I had no idea he was...well, you remember. My government was very keen on the prospects of the bridge and transportation hub at the time. I hope you will forgive me."

The stack of mail in Robin's in-box glared at her. The time for pleasantries was over. "I don't care about that now. All I want to know is, can you help me win? What is your strategy?"

"Strategy? Well, believe it or not, most voters choose the incumbent. It all goes to name recognition. Actual policies and platforms don't come near to the power of recognition. Oh, and trustworthiness. You know, I did a bit of polling—informal mind you—on my way in today on the ferry. Eighty percent of the residents didn't know your name. My job is the fix that."

"How?"

Jacque beamed at her. "Social media. Print ads, interviews, even TikTok. That is, if you give me a chance."

She glanced at her laptop and resisted the urge to open her email. "What will it cost me?"

Jacque flexed his fingers with excitement. "That is the beauty of my proposal. You see, you'd be my first client. I need to build my business, so I'm willing to work pro bono. My services will be completely free to you.

All I ask is for referrals if I'm successful."

She squinted at him, feeling contempt for this bullshit offer. "Free? Nothing's free."

"You'd be surprised. I had almost no budget in my last job. I know how to stretch a pound. Word of mouth and social media are very effective tools and cost almost nothing."

Robin knew she didn't have many other options with just a week to go and realized any help would be better than none. This guy sure had energy, which is more than she could say for herself. "Fine. You're hired. Now what?"

"Oooh! Excellent! We don't have a moment to lose. But before we proceed, I have some questions. Believe me, from now on, I want to know who I'm doing business with."

Robin glared at him. "Understandable."

Without meeting her eyes, Jacque took a deep breath. "Ahem. I only ask, mind you…"

She pounded her fist on her desk. "Spit it out."

"Madam Senator, could you…um…I need to know if there are any proverbial skeletons in your closet? I mean, actual skeletons would be nice to know as well." He tittered.

Such a loaded question. She played it safe. "Depends."

He gave her a wink. "No murders I hope?"

She smiled. "No. But we should talk."

"Your secrets are safe with me."

"Let's take a walk. The walls have ears."

"Oh. Yes, let's."

Robin grabbed her phone and purse. "We'll go down to the park."

On their way out, Dottie erupted from her desk, her eyes wide with excitement. "Well, how is it going?"

Robin ignored the question. "I'll be back in ten minutes."

Dot asked Jacque, "I hope she didn't scare you off."

He beamed. "I think we'll get on famously. Thank you, Ms. McPherson."

Dottie called after them as they walked down the hall. "Robin, we'll go shopping! Get you some decent shoes instead of those worn-out things! I made you an emergency hair appointment at Miss Sheila's tomorrow! She didn't have time, but I called my friend Penny and she gave up her slot!"

Robin and Jacque exited the Legislative Annex and strolled down the hill toward the bay. They stopped when they reached a small patch of grass with a bench under some leafy trees across the street from the ferry dock. The area seemed secluded enough. They sat beside each other on the bench.

It was time to get serious and impress on this guy that she meant business. "Jacque, there are secrets and then there are SECRETS. Understand?"

"I do." He nodded solemnly.

"You know about my brother, Johnnie?"

"A bit. I remember his arrest. The St. Johnnie Killer…I think that's what the press called him. They fully exonerated him, correct?"

"Yes. But he has challenges. A wounded warrior. Traumatic Brain Injury survivor. He acts…rashly…at times. It's like trouble finds him. You should also know, Chief Tobias tried to arrest him this morning."

Jacque grimaced and clucked his tongue in disapproval. "Yes, I was with Ms. McPherson earlier and she explained what was happening. But this could work for us. Spin it if we need to…something like, Tobias is an irrational man with a grudge. Anything else?"

"Yes." She took a deep breath to prepare for this next part. Sensing no onlookers, she continued. "Several years back, I had an addiction to pills and issues with alcohol. Led to a nasty divorce. But I've been clean for over twelve years."

His face seemed to remain cheerful and unfazed. "Well, we all have things in our past…"

She wasn't sure about the next item either. Though she sensed Jacque could handle it. *Maybe…*

"Also, you should know, my mother went to prison."

"Oh, dear!" He blinked at her, then stared at the ground between his feet. "For what crime?"

"Embezzlement." Now she had him. Some of the color went out of Jacque's cheeks.

"Oh, goodness! Please tell me…could it have been the result of a harmless accounting error?"

"Nope. Half a million. From a homeless charity."

"Oh, my! Did I hear that right? A…*homeless* charity?" He looked up and pursed his lips, his hands fidgety. "Goodness. Ah. How do I…um, is she still in prison?"

"No. She was reported dead after a prison riot. She and some other inmates tried escaping through the sewers. There was a methane explosion. The coroner concluded there were no survivors."

Jacque rubbed his eyes, then pulled a handkerchief from his pants pocket and wiped his brow. "I'm very sorry for your loss. But now I'm afraid to ask. Is that all?" He pinched his eyes shut.

"That's it. What do you think? Are you still on my team?"

He mopped the back of his neck with the handkerchief. "I've dealt with worse."

Robin laughed. "Good."

Jacque rose from the bench. "Thank you for being candid. This will certainly help my research and strategies. I'll get to work right away on ad copy and other materials. Oh, and as you surmised, Ms. McPherson and I thought your image could use a slight…refresh. No offense." He gestured toward her sneakers.

"Yes. Got it." As Robin rose to shake his hand, she noticed the handmade-looking six-by-ten-foot billboard across the street by the dock. It displayed Chief Tobias with the slogan "Joe Tobias will fight for St. John." He stood in a boxer's pose with a skin-tight red, white and blue T-shirt, displaying his sizable biceps. The Chief sported a curled lip and a menacing look that convinced even her. "Good grief."

Jacque chortled, "Yes, I was wondering if you saw that. But don't fret. He's an amateur."

Robin sighed. "I hope so."

* * *

Johnnie and Cud drove along North Shore Road toward Maho Bay. The sky had turned a hazy gray again but there were hints of sun through the broken clouds. When they pulled into the long rectangular parking zone for the beach, Merv was sitting on the tailgate of his Park Service vehicle, staring at his phone.

Johnnie honked his horn with two quick beeps. "Hey, ready? Where's your uniform?"

Merv—dressed in shorts with a bright orange, cheesy-looking Hawaiian shirt—approached his window. "It's in my car. Couldn't wait to get out of the confines of those dull as fuck polyester-blend costume pieces. And, oh, by the way, do you see these ass-wipes? We're supposed to close the damn beach, but it's useless." He gestured to the shore, where there was clearly some kind of gathering, with about two dozen people; several coolers and beach umbrellas punctuated the scene.

Johnnie shook his head. "Don't worry about them. We have to get all the generators filled and tested. Thanks for helping."

Merv grimaced. "Free labor if you ask me. Damn, I needed next week's paycheck! That's why I always say you can't trust the government." He bent over to view Cud through the driver's side window. "Hey there, Mr. Loughton. You wouldn't have 5 G's lying around I could borrow? I'll pay you back…two weeks tops."

Cud laughed. "Oh, I rarely lend money. Causes too many issues. In the words of Polonius, 'neither a borrower nor a lender be'."

"Ha! Yep, I get that." Merv drummed his hands on the side of Johnnie's Jeep. "What's the plan, O Fearless Leader? Why are you driving your own car? We can't be hauling government fuel with this. It's too sketch."

Johnnie didn't know why Merv was being such a dick calling him Fearless Leader. The sarcasm wasn't necessary or helpful. Part of him wanted to ditch his frenemy and continue without him. But Merv had the padlock key to open the fuel station.

"You win. How about we go in your truck?"

"Don't have a choice now, do we? Hey, what's up with this story about a storm? The weather guy on television, Dougie—whatever—said everything looks rosy this weekend."

Cud leaned over Johnnie to view Merv. "We have it on good authority. My deceased mother warned us in our dreams."

Merv chuckled. "Spirits, eh? No shitting?"

Cud grinned. "No shitting? What an interesting turn of phrase."

Johnnie's phone rang. It was Gertie. "Hey, Gertie."

"Johnnie, I'm trying to reach Cudlow. He isn't picking up his calls. His architect friend is here again. Something about an appointment to see a house?"

He handed Cudlow the phone.

Cud pressed it to his ear. "Yes?"

After a pause, Cud said, "Oh. Yes. Of course. I see. I'll call her directly.

Did she leave her number?" To Johnnie, he whispered, "Do you have a pen?" Back to Gertie, there was another pause. "Thank you." He hung up the call.

Johnnie asked, "What was that all about?"

Cud huffed. "Bollocks. I'd forgotten. Lilly made an appointment this morning for us to tour that house at John's Folly. The one you liked. Gertie is texting you Lilly's phone number."

This information took Johnnie's breath away. "What time?"

"In thirty minutes."

"Cud, we HAVE to go."

Merv drummed on the side of the car again as if playing bongos. "Hey! Don't we have to save the island from ruin or some shit?"

With a resolution as calm as the dead, John looked him square in the eyes. "Merv, you don't understand. I NEED to see the inside of this house. For all we know, the storm could destroy it tonight. Cud and I will make it quick."

His tall-fore-headed buddy smirked. "You ain't getting off that easy. If YOU go, I go too. What's so spectacular about this place?"

Johnnie nodded, but couldn't find the words to explain. "Fine. Come with. You can see for yourself."

Merv rounded Johnnie's Jeep and opened the back passenger door to hop in. "Cool. Let's go."

As they drove, Cud turned to face Merv. "You know, Johnnie had quite a crush on my architect Lilly."

Merv chuckled. "Ah, that's right. Lilly…that's Mildred Johannsen? The super-model looking chick with the paddleboard? Is Greta is still icing you out? What the hell did you say to her in Miami?"

Johnnie tried to keep his attention to the narrow winding road, but Merv's comments made his blood boil. He growled, "Shut the fuck up, Merv. It's none of your fucking business." Gritting his teeth, he fought to suppress his urge to reach back and punch Merv.

"Hey, cool down buddy. I was just wondering how things were going. I mean, Lilly is some prime real estate if you get my meaning." To Cud, he said, "Who knows, Johnnie boy could graduate to the big leagues. Nothing against Greta. Sure, Greta is a cool chick, but my dude, Lilly is next level. Even I would give my left nut…"

"SHUT UUUUPPPP!" Johnnie slammed on the brakes. His chest heaved with exasperation. Seething, he huffed and envisioned beating Merv within an inch of his life.

A moment later, the heat in his chest turned to panic quickly when movement in his rearview mirror alerted him to a garbage truck barreling down on them. He stomped the gas pedal to avoid a collision. The truck driver honked repeatedly, adding to his anxiety. Johnnie wrenched the steering wheel to pull over, putting his left tires in a shallow ditch to allow the truck to scream past.

His other passengers were noticeably wide-eyed and stiff from his display of foolishness and the air was thick with tension.

All he could do was drive, take deep breaths, and count backwards in his head to calm himself before they arrived for the house tour. Because he couldn't act like a raving hot-head in front of the Goddess. *One-hundred, ninety-nine, nighty-eight [breath in] nighty-seven, nighty-six [breath out]*...

As they passed Calabash Market, Cudlow whispered, "So Merv, how are things with your bookie? Have you settled up with him?"

Merv didn't take Cudlow's cue to whisper and spoke freely. "Nah, I still owe him five G's. He threatened to saw off my left pinkie finger."

"That's not very nice."

"No. Not nice at all. I have three days."

"Is this why you asked for the loan?"

"Exactomundo."

"Hmm. Johnnie, could we stop by your apartment? I'd like to collect my phone and ask my grandson Jackson to wire Ranger Hartley some funds."

Johnnie nodded, not feeling ready to engage verbally. His cheeks still burned with anger and embarrassment, and he kept counting in his head. He looked forward to a side-trip home to allow him to change out of his uniform and get some beverages. He needed a cold drink after the morning's chaos. *Not that there was any milk left*...

Merv clapped Cud's shoulder over the backrest. "Dude, thanks!"

"Promise, no more gambling or sports betting. Understand? Try to take up another hobby. I collect native fruit. I say, it is quite a treasure hunt and *gamble* to see what one can find. You might enjoy it."

"Fruit, eh? I'm not really a fruit-based guy."

"Or take up woodworking or yoga. There are scores of things in this wide wonderful planet to occupy one's time."

"Ha! Maybe I'll take up stand-up paddle boarding." He gripped Johnnie's shoulder. "Just kidding, bro. Lighten up, okay?"

Johnnie didn't want to lighten up. But he knew he'd have to. Deadpan, he responded, "Merv, you should take up fucking yourself." He gave a half-grin to sell this was a joke, even though he fully meant it.

Merv roared and clapped him hard on the shoulder again. "Ha! Yeah, bro. But I think I'm an expert at that already."

Chapter 9

Johnnie could have driven to the house at John's Folly beach in his sleep. It was next to his favorite spear-fishing spot. It also overlooked the location of his nearly deadly battle with the assassin Thomas Smith only a few months ago. But he couldn't focus on that now.

His heart raced at the idea of seeing the inside of the impressive glass mansion on the hill. Getting a home tour by the Goddess herself was also intriguing, but he needed to keep his guard up and forget his foolish infatuation with the tall blonde if he ever wanted to get Greta back.

After ditching his park uniform back at his apartment for long shorts and a blue T-shirt, Johnnie felt severely underdressed for the fancy surroundings as the pristinely landscaped driveway came into view. Would the Goddess disapprove of the wrinkles in his cotton shorts and the hole in the hem of his shirt?

Flawless rose bushes, stacked-stone low walls and an open wrought-iron gate greeted them. Turning into the property, the driveway dipped at a precarious angle with nothing but some rocks to save his Jeep from plunging into the ocean should the brakes fail. Another car was in the driveway; a tan Jeep with a ragtop—the Goddess' car.

She was standing next to the front door. However, the Goddess wasn't wearing her usual black shorty wetsuit he had become accustomed to seeing her in. Quite the opposite, she wore a professional-looking skirt and jacket, but with a hint of a sexy silk camisole. Her hair was up in a clip with tendrils framing one side of her face. Just how a Goddess would look if they ran a professional consulting business, which she did.

Johnnie brought his car to a stop and applied the parking brake. He hesitated, waiting for Cud to exit first.

Cudlow exited from the passenger side and waved. "Good morning, Ms. Johannsen. Thank you for arranging this indulgence. We were curious to see this impressive work of yours."

She approached to shake Cud's hand. "Happy to oblige, Mr. Loughton. Perhaps you can take some elements as inspiration for your home's design. Please point out any aspects you like or dislike. This will be a chance for me to understand what you are looking for." A breeze blew some strands of hair across her nose and she brushed them back. "I see you brought some friends."

Cud nodded. "Yes, other fans of your work."

Johnnie exited the jeep and stood a few feet behind Cud. Heat rushed to his cheeks. He should have said something. Anything. Even a simple, 'hello' would have been a normal response. But his mouth felt glued shut in her presence.

Merv sprang forward, with the bouncy enthusiasm of Tigger, his hand extended. "Hi, I'm Merv Hartley. *Ranger* Merv Hartley. Nice to meet you, Lilly. I see you on your paddleboard from time to time."

Lilly nodded. "Part of why I branched out on my own. Having my own business allows more time on the water." She turned to the door and pressed a series of numbered buttons on the electronic lock. "The owner is away for another three months, but he gave me the combination."

Cud asked, "Who is the owner? Anyone we might know?"

Lilly's eyes narrowed and her tone was flat, as if she had found the question annoying. "Sorry, I'm not at liberty to say."

Johnnie's curiosity loosened his jaw. "George Clooney?"

She huffed. "No."

This answer only intensified Johnnie's need to know. But before he could think of another guess, the door opened on its own.

A thirty-something short man with messy brown bangs, wearing a sparkly tank top greeted them. "Hello, can I help you?"

Lilly looked visibly shaken. "Oh…I'm sorry. My name is Lilly Johannsen…the architect who designed this home. I was told the house was vacant. I was going to give a tour. Are you a guest of…" she whispered the next part "…Mr. Gervais?"

"Ha! No. But I'm a friend of his plastic surgeon. Oh no, did I say that out loud?" He clasped his hand over his mouth feigning dismay. "Ha! I won't tell if you don't!" He extended his hand, which had several thin stacked gold rings on his fingers. "Hi, Lilly. I'm Renaldo. I'm sort of house-sitting. You know, this isn't really the best time. I have an injured friend here and he needs his beauty rest."

Johnnie's heart sank, fearing he would lose his chance to see inside. "We won't disturb anyone. Hey, do you have storm thingies…you know, that are metal and roll down over the windows?" He turned to Lilly. "Any storm…things?"

She frowned. "You mean aluminum storm shutters?"

Right, shutters. He mentally smacked his forehead. "Yes."

"Given the location, I spec'ed the house with laminated hurricane-glass. They might show cracks under some force but they won't break, even with 200 mile per hour winds."

He nodded. "Ah." His fears of the home being destroyed by the coming storm were allayed.

Cud placed his hand on Johnnie's shoulder. "Sorry, chap. Perchance we'll get that tour another time."

Lilly tapped her foot and sighed heavily with disapproval. "Yes. I'll call to make another appointment." She turned to Renaldo and in a snotty tone asked, "When would be a good time to come back?"

Renaldo drummed his fingers on the door frame. "Hmm. Wait a sec. Let me check with my friend. I'll ask if it's okay for you to come in. Be right back." He shut the door.

The four of them waited. In the uncomfortable silence among them, Johnnie noticed the security camera above the door. And another camera under the eave of the roof. As he scanned the area, he detected three more.

Renaldo opened the door and stood to the side. "You can have ten minutes. But avoid the primary suite. He's having a late breakfast in bed."

Lilly entered first, followed by Cud and Merv. Johnnie hung back to enter last.

The entrance was spectacular. Johnnie's jaw turned slack with his eyes glued upward. A twenty-foot ceiling with a multi-bulb chandelier that looked like modern art. The floors were white and light gray terrazzo that reflected light like a mirror.

The entry opened into a large open floor plan that included a living area, dining area and a sleek high-gloss kitchen. But the star of the show was the floor-to-ceiling glass wall facing the ocean. Roughly forty feet wide and two stories tall. The view he'd admired from below from the beach.

On the side away from the beach, a series of patio doors opened up onto a small private terrace outlined by manicured boxwood hedges, sporting expensive-looking white outdoor sofas.

To Johnnie, just standing in the space was a religious experience—that is, if he were religious. He felt transported, as if in a different dimension. It was a far cry from his own cinderblock studio apartment whose best view consisted of Gertie's stone driveway.

A noise behind them caused him to turn.

A man, tall, wearing a white bathrobe, his arm in a sling and left leg in a soft cast, face bandaged, had entered the kitchen behind them and began pouring coffee into a black mug.

"Sorry," the bandaged man said. "Don't mind me. Enjoy your tour."

Lilly turned her back to him dismissively. "Thank you." She walked toward the living room; Merv and Renaldo followed her close behind.

But the sound of bandage-man's voice had turned Johnnie's skin cold with terror. He tugged on Cud's arm and took him aside. In a whisper, he asked. "Cud, can you see that man's aura?"

Cud blinked and then squinted. "Hmm…orange…sort of reddish. Why do you ask? And why are we whispering?"

He leaned closer. "Cud. Shit. I think that guy is Thomas Smith."

Cud whispered back. "No!"

By now, the bandaged man had finished topping off his mug and had turned down the hallway toward the other end of the home.

Cud called out, donning a deep and stern British accent, "Smith! Stop! Now!"

The man stopped in his tracks, then turned and came back slowly; a cast on his leg and a pronounced limp were evident. He clicked his tongue three times mockingly. "Well done, Mr. Loughton…Mr. Crosswell. We meet again."

Merv turned to Cud. "Hold on, you know this guy?"

Johnnie's nostrils flared in disgust. "Ms. Johannsen, could you and Merv go outside while we catch up with our friends? Please?"

Renaldo pressed his hand to his chest, his face conveyed happy surprise. "Oh, you know Thomas? How nice."

Merv said, "Johnnie, what's the deal? You got a weird look in your eyes."

Ren's face showed surprise. "Wait. You're Johnnie? THE Johnnie? Oh, holy heck."

Keeping Smith squarely in his sights, Johnnie ignored this banter and took a few steps to place himself between Lilly and the killer Smith, in case anything bad went down. Because Smith was a stone-cold maniac and protecting Lilly seemed the gentlemanly thing to do. "Merv, I'm serious. Get out of here. Take Lilly with you."

Thomas appeared to smile under his bandages. "It's okay. We are all friends here. As long as you all respect *our privacy*…" he bared his teeth and his voice turned less cheerful "… if you get my drift." He took a sip of coffee and his sunny tone returned. "I'm going to finish my coffee outside on the patio while you finish your tour. Enjoy."

Johnnie scratched the scar above his right ear, wondering how Thomas Smith could act so nonchalant. He took a deep breath and strode across the living room to follow him outside.

On the patio, they were still plainly visible to the others, given all the windows, but he closed the door and tried to ignore the others staring at them.

"Smith. What the fuck are you doing here? I should call the police."

His evil nemesis eased down on a sofa, keeping his bad leg extended, while cradling his coffee to prevent it from spilling. "Ow." Instead of answering Johnnie's question, he took another sip and seemed to gaze off toward the sea.

"Hey, shit-head, answer me."

Smith shook his head dismissively. "Do what you must. But you are probably wondering if I'm a threat to you. The answer is no. I don't expect you to believe me. Hell, look at me. I can barely move most days. I just want to live a quiet life."

"Jumping Jesus. You killed two people. AND kidnapped Gertie!"

"Did I? I was just carrying out orders from my employer. It was never personal."

Johnnie knew this wasn't true. "I won't let you get away with this."

"Look at me. I'm broken. I may never walk without a limp again. And, if I wanted you dead, you would be dead already. Leave me alone and I'll leave you alone. But if you get any bright ideas and I'm arrested, I'll inform the authorities how Ms. McPherson—your sister's administrative assistant—tried to kill me. I would imagine pushing someone's car off a cliff counts as attempted homicide. And this information wouldn't bode well for your sister's re-election chances."

Johnnie searched his memory but none of this computed. "Wait…what?"

"You didn't know?"

Johnnie tried to process this information, but it didn't seem plausible. "Dottie wouldn't do that."

"She would and she did. The universe knows I deserved it." Smith chuckled and then exclaimed, "Ouch!" He clasped his ribs and took a couple of deep breaths to compose himself. "In any event, after Ren came to my aid, he went back to lift her fingerprints off my mangled car and we kept the evidence. I would also hate to tell Chief Tobias about how you stabbed me and left me to die on that stupid island… and didn't report it to the authorities."

Johnnie stared at the ground. "Fuck."

Smith sipped his coffee. "Finish your tour. I expect we won't see each other again?"

He certainly didn't trust Thomas Smith. But the killer was so immensely calm and rational that he questioned all reality. A metallic taste in his mouth made him want to spit. He clenched his fists. This was so wrong, but he couldn't come up with a better idea. "Someday…"

Smith shook his head. "Someday you'll see that this arrangement is for the best. I'm in a very forgiving mood lately. Now leave me before I change my mind."

Flummoxed, Johnnie turned and went back inside the house. Merv, Cud, Renaldo and Lilly were standing shoulder to shoulder, their eyes piercing him with intense questioning looks.

Cud spoke up first. "What happened?"

"I'll tell you later. We should go."

Renaldo pointed toward the ocean-facing windows. "Look!"

The sunny vista from moments earlier had been replaced with dense dark clouds, turning the sky to a menacing shade of dark green. The ocean also looked deep green with big rolling waves. Johnnie had never seen the sky this color before.

Cud exclaimed, "Oh, Dear Lord! I think this means Mother was right."

Lilly asked, "What's wrong?"

"Right about what?" Merv asked.

Johnnie said, "The immense storm."

Lilly shook her head. "What storm? Dougie said the weather was going to be great this weekend. He's taking me to the music festival tomorrow on St. Thomas."

Johnnie asked, "Who's Dougie?"

"My man-friend. He's the meteorologist at our local news station."

Finally, thought Johnnie. A meteorologist could help his quest to find the truth about the storm. "Cud, we need to go there and talk to him."

But before Cud could respond, Johnnie's phone rang. It was Robin. He stepped a few feet away to take the call.

"Hey, I can't really talk right now."

"Don't hey me!" Robin was nearly shouting. "You lied to the Chief. He just got a call back from Greta. She said she never spoke with you last night."

His jaw dropped and he searched his memory. He'd called Greta last night right before bed. There had to be proof of this on his phone. "No. Why is she lying? I can show you the record..." He looked through his call log and then scrolled through a second time, becoming increasingly confused. But there were no incoming or outgoing calls last night. "Goddamn! Sis, I swear, I didn't...fuck. I'm must be losing my mind."

"Are you taking your meds? Because if you aren't—"

"Stop! I am. I can't explain. Maybe I dreamt the call? Jumping Jesus." In that moment, it came back to him. On the call with Greta, her dad said a giraffe was at the door. This should have been a huge clue the call wasn't real.

Johnnie's head ached. He wanted to crawl into a hole and die. Instead, he hung up on Robin, ran outside and pounded the roof of his new Jeep. BAM, BAM, BAM! His hand throbbed from the force. His throat constricted and he wheezed trying to catch his breath.

Cud strode toward him. "Johnnie! Stop! Who called? What happened?" He grabbed Johnnie's arm.

Red-faced and seething, he turned. "I'm a fucking basket-case, is what. I didn't talk to Greta last night. My idiot brain made up the whole shitty thing."

Cud gasped. After a beat, his demeanor turned serious. "Maybe this was a sign from a higher power. She told you to board up the library because of the storm, right? It could be just like my dream with mother."

Johnnie scowled. Cud wasn't helping. All this nonsense with ghosts and higher powers sounded insane. "You don't get it. I don't even know WHAT is real anymore. Fuck ghosts. Fuck you. Just leave me alone." He got into his car and backed up the steep driveway, accelerating without checking his rear-view mirrors.

Was anything real? Was that really Thomas Smith behind the bandages? He waved his hand in front of his face as he drove toward his apartment. Perhaps he was in the Matrix…or in a deep hallucination?

He needed to go home and check his pill bottle, to count them and make sure he wasn't in the throes of some chemically imbalanced derangement. And then take a cold shower to shake him out of whatever nightmare this was. He didn't want to call his therapist until he had some answers.

After a ten-minute drive, Johnnie arrived at the turn for Gertie's driveway.

But then he had another thought and turned around.

His mission was clear now.

And he drove west.

Chapter 10

Cud went back inside the beach house and scratched his beard. *Where could Johnnie be going?* He hoped his friend wouldn't do anything rash. He took out his phone and scrolled to the number of Dr. Louisa Phillips.

Dr. Lou was Johnnie's psychiatrist and Cud had become her patient in Miami a few weeks ago when he was having his own sanity issues. But perhaps it wasn't his place to intervene. It was possible Johnnie only needed a few minutes alone to cool off. Cud put his phone away and went back inside.

Merv, Lilly, and Renaldo huddled in the wide hall between the foyer and kitchen. Thomas was nowhere to be seen.

Merv chuckled. "Well, I guess the tour is over. What got into his drawers, speeding off like that?"

Cudlow apologized. "I'm sorry Ms. Johannsen. Johnnie has apparently stranded us here. Could we trouble you for a ride…if you are headed our way?"

Lilly pulled her phone from her shoulder bag. "I have an appointment in Cruz Bay with my hairdresser in an hour. Sure, I could drive you. Where are you going?"

Merv turned to Cud. "Are we still fueling the generators? Because, if Johnnie is ditching us, I got better things to do."

"What things?"

"I don't know, Cud. Things."

Renaldo interrupted. "Generators? What were you saying about a storm? The sky looks really strange."

Merv cracked his knuckles. "Something about high winds and evil spirits. Ha! What if the Wicked Witch of the West is headed our way? Sky certainly looks green enough."

Ren smiled. "Yes, those damned witches. I always hated the flying monkeys as a kid. Made my mom fast forward through those parts of the movie. But…um…*is* there a storm coming? Cause it sure looks like it."

Lilly chirped. "Ahem! Dougie said the weather through the weekend will be fabulous. At worst, a possible short afternoon sun-shower." She fished in her sizable shoulder bag, pulled out a set of keys, and headed to her Jeep.

Cudlow noticed Ren's aura against the green sky backdrop—pink with a light blue ring, like a pastel Easter egg. He'd never seen this kind of aura before. With Lilly out of hearing range, he said, "You know Smith killed two people and kidnapped my lady friend. But you seem like a nice bloke. Nice aura and all that. What are you doing with the likes of him?"

"You can see my aura? Wait, you're Cudlow Loughton, right? Thomas told me all about his past deeds. But he's turned over a new leaf. Rarely mentions wanting to murder you and Johnnie lately. And believe me, that was all he used to care about. Did you know he started reading books by the Dalai Lama and practices Buddhism? Heck, he thinks he actually died in the car accident and has been reincarnated or some goofy thing. Anyway, with the blackmail in place, I think we can all go back to being friends. Isn't that great?"

Cud squinted, unsure of what Ren meant about a car accident and blackmail. But the message about being friends seemed genuine. "Hmm, I see. Well, I'm not sure, but I'm not looking for any trouble as long as what you say is true. That Gertie is safe."

"Absolutely. In fact, send her my love. I don't actually know her, but Thomas said her lack of fear impressed him." Ren gave two snaps. "She sounds *fierce*."

Cud chuckled, because this description was truly accurate. And part of the reason he would always love and admire Gertie. "Yes. Yes, she is."

From across the driveway, Lilly jangled her keys to get their attention and shouted. "Let's go."

Merv lifted an abstract white marble statue from the side table by the door and inspected the bottom, as if he were looking for a price tag.

Cud tapped his shoulder. "Merv, are you ready chap?"

Merv placed the object down. "Yep, let's go. Kemper thinks I'm being a big hero helping prepare for this storm, so we might as well make a good show of it."

Cud shook his head and tsked. "It's important, in actuality, to prepare. It would be quite callous not to."

"Yeah. Yeah. Right."

They walked to Lilly's car. Cud took the front seat. "Sorry for all of this bollocked business. I imagine this was not the house tour you expected."

She backed out of the driveway, straining her neck to check the vehicle's alignment on the driveway. In a disgruntled tone, she replied, "Well, it's not the *worst* client meeting I've ever had."

Merv grinned. "No way. What could be worse than a house occupied by an angry mummy and his rainbow sprite boyfriend?"

She K-turned onto the road and replied dead-pan, "Worst? Client wanted a room designed with orange shag carpet and a conversation pit. Can you imagine? With shiplap walls, which made no sense. Talk about a nightmare."

From the back seat, Merv asked, "Yeah? What did you do?"

Still expressionless, she glanced at him in her rear-view mirror. "I burned their house plans and told them to find a new architect."

Merv belly-laughed. "Damn. Really?

"There is nothing worse than poor taste. Like your shirt, Merv. Did you get it from a thrift store or a trash can?"

Cud couldn't discern if Lilly was attempting a joke. There was a coldness that conveyed no sense of humor. And it occurred to him, she didn't have an aura. *Curious…*

Merv chuckled. "Hey, I'm an acquired taste. At least I'm not boring. You know, if you ever need a little spice, call ol' Merv. I can show you a great time. Ha! After I pull the stick out of your fine ass."

Cud froze. Merv appeared to be joking, but that was no way to talk to a woman. Merv had gone too far.

Lilly was quiet for a few seconds.

Cud held his breath, not knowing what to say.

She eased her shoulders and chirped, "In your dreams, *Merv*. Tell me, have you always been a scumbag?" Under her breath, she muttered, "Asshole."

All conversation ceased for the rest of the twenty-minute trip to Maho Bay.

* * *

Cud was grateful for the end of the excruciating and charged silence in Lilly's Jeep. They exited her vehicle after pulling up at Maho Bay next to Merv's Park Service truck.

Cud waved. "Thank you for the ride, Lilly! I'll be in touch next week to discuss designs for my new home."

Merv pulled open the driver's side door of his truck. "Johnnie really dicked us over. I'm going home."

Cud chased after him. "No! We have to fuel the generators."

"Look, man. Thanks for the loan. I appreciate it. But this fueling business…what's in it for me?"

Cud shook his head. "Don't you care about anyone besides yourself?"

"Yeah. I might. So?"

"The universe is watching."

"Ha! Ooh. I'm scared," Merv mocked with a waving of his fingers. "The big bad karmic boogey man is going to get me if I'm a bad person."

Cud tried a different approach. "I suspect so. But, more importantly, I'm asking…as a friend…please help me do this." He kicked the tire of Merv's truck. "If I'm being honest, I'm lost here. I need to save Gertie, and all I can think to do—the *only* thing I can think to do—to get my mind off this horrible nightmare, is to help others. Will fueling generators save Gertie? May bloody well not. But I have to do SOMETHING. Anything to be *useful*. Do you understand? I need to be useful!"

He grabbed Merv by his shirt collar. "I might be going mad. But you see it! The sky was green earlier and the birds have left the island. Listen…do you hear any? No! And that's my point. Something bad is coming. The entire island has an eerie, dark silver aura. Last time I saw this silver? Was right before Hurricane Irma. I swear on my mum's grave. If you don't want to help, fine. But drop me off at Ranger Snow's house. I'm sure she'll help me."

Merv stroked his chin. "Hmm. I'll help if you answer one question. Truthfully."

"Anything."

"At the beach house…was that guy with the bandages and broken leg really Thomas Smith?"

Cud nodded.

Merv whispered, even though they were alone. "Why didn't you call the police?"

Cud felt ashamed and stared at the ground. "I don't get involved."

"Ha! You just said how you want to get involved saving the island. What's the matter? Does Smith have something over you and Johnnie?"

"I'm not exactly sure. His boyfriend said something about blackmail. All I care about is Gertie's safety. Smith doesn't seem to be a threat anymore."

"I bet there is a sizable reward for Smith." Merv bit his finger nail in scheming manner.

Cud shook his head and sighed. "Must everything be weighed in financial terms with you? Believe me, money is not the key to happiness. I've had a vast fortune and I've also been penniless. I prefer being poor."

Merv snorted. "Only a rich person would say that."

"Believe what you want. Now, will you help me?"

"Get in, old man. But afterward? I want you to tell Kemper what I good guy I am."

Cud got into the passenger seat and buckled in. "Ah! Now I see. You are in love with her!"

"Hey. Love is a big term. I just dig her, okay?"

"Ha! See, right there. You are blushing. Your aura turned bright blue just now. You love her!"

"All right. Knock it off. I have a reputation to uphold."

"Have you told her how you feel? Because you should. Never wait when it comes to love. Listen to one who knows."

"Easy for you to say. She's my boss…hell, I could get laughed at *and* fired for harassment."

"Well, I suppose that is an impediment."

"Yeah. My plan is to spend more time with her. Alone. So she can get to know the real me. But not be so obvious about it."

They drove west toward Cruz Bay. "Well, I hope that works out." Cud pulled on his right sock, which had fallen down under the top of his boot. "Blasted socks. I'd forgotten how difficult they can be."

Merv chuckled. "Look, the sky looks completely fine." He pointed off to the west as the road curved around the hill, revealing an unobstructed view of the bay and the horizon. "I'm still not buying this bird-brained island bad aura shit. No offense."

"None taken. I very much appreciate your help."

"Well, since you loaned me the five G's and helping you gives me a chance to impress Kemper, I can give up an afternoon." After a long silence, Merv added. "Hey, so for real, I'm glad you are feeling better these days, man. But I got to ask…are you still in love with Gertie? I mean, she left you at the fucking altar. When a chick ditches you cold like that, it's time to walk away, bro."

Cud stared out the side window, wondering if his belief in the storm was a sign of a deep detachment from reality. The sky was a whitish blue now and the waters surrounding the island appeared calm. The sun beamed with great intensity. But deep down, he was determined to protect Gertie's life over his own sanity. "I still consider her a good friend. But you are right. Perhaps my attachment to her requires further reflection."

"Ha! So, what's your big plan to save her from tonight's non-existent storm?"

Cud pulled on his left sock to fish it above the top of his boot. "Right now? I haven't the foggiest notion."

Chapter 11

Johnnie stopped at the Calabash Market for a soda and a box of vanilla wafers. In the cookie aisle, he held the box and stared at the packaging. The round pale wafers pictured on the front seemed bland and he wondered why he began buying them in the first place. The shelf in front of him sported Oreo's in six flavors, plus chocolate chip cookies and even little fudge covered elves. They all seemed like better, more interesting options. When had his life become so unimaginative and pitiful? He didn't know. But he was done with that bullshit. If a killer like Smith could live like a king in a fucking palace, then maybe he needed to take notes and be more assertive.

He needed answers about the stupid storm. And people were going to listen to him.

Johnnie switched the vanilla wafers for a package of mint Oreo's and headed to the register to pay for his items. At the counter, Johnnie slammed his aluminum soda can down, causing it to dent.

Behind the counter, Mr. Bravos, the store owner, smiled. "Good afternoon, Johnnie. How are you today?" Bravos was a burly man with Italian-looking dark skin. He had a 'Carpe Diem' tattoo along his hairy forearm. Johnnie couldn't remember what that meant. *Fish Day?*

Johnnie pulled a ten-dollar bill from his wallet. Without looking up, he asked, "What's the best route to the television station?"

"Oh! Are you going to be interviewed about the government shutdown? Such a pity. I hope those nitwits in DC get their act together."

Johnnie wasn't prepared for questions. He kept his answer simple. "No. Just visiting."

"Ah. Well, take Centerline Road. It will be on your left near the big antenna. Can't miss it."

"Thanks." He strode off with his change and snacks toward his Jeep. Before he started the engine, his phone rang. It was Cud.

"I'm busy."

"Johnnie, that was very rude leaving us like that. Where are you? Don't you want to help with the fuel?"

"I'm going to get some answers."

Merv's voice came on the line. "Hey, are we getting fuel or not, Johnnie-boy? This was your idea, hotshot."

Johnnie hung up and turned off his phone's ringer. Several incoming text alerts showed up at the top of his phone. Mostly Robin.

He drove up Centerline Road for a couple of miles. Sure enough, a tall red antenna appeared above the trees. He turned into the driveway and came up towards a chain-link fence, but the vehicle gate was open. A concrete, squat single-story building had only one primary entrance door. A news van with the WSTJ logo was parked around the side. This was the place. His watch showed half past noon.

He slammed two cookies into his mouth. He pulled the tab of his soda and it exploded across his chest, streaming liquid down to his crotch. Still, he took a sip to reduce the damage and then threw the can out of the side window while cursing under his breath. He grabbed some napkins from the center console to wipe up the mess. Nothing was going right today.

Johnnie exited the vehicle and stormed to the entrance, kicking blue rock with each step. At the entrance, he pulled the latch and found it unlocked. A surprised-looking receptionist, a young dark-skinned man in his twenties with a short cropped fade, wearing a white short-sleeve dress shirt, greeted him. "Good afternoon. How may I help you?"

"I'd like to see the weather guy."

"You mean Mr. Biffman?"

He didn't know, but went with it. "Sure."

"Do you have an appointment?"

"No."

"Please, take a seat. I'll ring him."

Johnnie took a seat in the shitty lobby, which was not his idea of taking bold decisive action. But he could deal with the guy making one phone call.

Still, he raged inside wanting to punch a wall. He held his shirt away from his mid-section to inspect the dampness and staining from the soda. He'd likely need to buy a replacement.

After the receptionist said a few 'a-huh's' into the phone, he addressed Johnnie. "Mr. Biffman will be right out. He only has ten minutes until his next segment, so you'll have to be quick with the photo."

"Photo?"

"He always makes time for his fans."

Fans? Johnnie wanted to spit. But he played along. Through gritted teeth he added, "Awesome. Yeah, I'm a big fan."

The receptionist whispered, "Do you believe in all his astrological stuff? I mean…I don't get it."

"Astro…what?"

"You know, the 'mystic meteorologist' and all that."

"Huh. No. I don't…he's a scientist, right? Like, he has a degree in weather stuff and shit?"

"Lord, who knows. I heard from the graphics department that he makes his own radar maps. To align with Venus in retrograde or some nonsense. I'm sorry, has that offended you? Being a fan?"

"He makes up his own…? Like, makes up the weather report?"

In a sing-song voice, the receptionist said, "Seems that way. But its weather. Wait ten minutes and it changes, you know?"

"Does his boss know?"

"You mean Andréa? She has to…maybe…but I don't really know. She's always busy. Not a lot of chit chat with her."

"Oh, jumping Johosephat. You are kidding, right?"

"Seriously, I think my cat could give a better forecast." The receptionist's phone rang. He put up a finger for silence and answered it.

Johnnie stared at the floor. All his plans to get answers seemed futile. Like he was in a bad dream. He gazed down to make sure he was wearing pants. Because many of his terrifying dreams involved some shocking revelation of having no pants.

The young man finished his call and cocked his head to the side, peering at Johnnie in a way that made him uneasy. "I'm Benji. I hope you don't think this is rude…but is your name John Crosswell?"

Johnnie's eyes widened at hearing his name uttered by this stranger.

"Um. Yeah. Have we met?" It was always possible they *had* met before and he had forgotten. He saw hundreds of people on the beaches every day, although he rarely interacted with them. Only speaking with people when it couldn't be helped.

Benji rose from his chair and walked around the reception desk, taking the seat next to him. "That was our head of security. He saw you on the camera outside. Recognized you immediately. My goodness, I can't believe you are *actually* here. You're like…a legend!"

"What? What do you mean?"

"You don't know? Well, our news ratings go up…*skyrocket*…with every one of your escapades." Benji appeared giddy, shaking his shoulders. "I mean, first the murders, then lost at sea, then kidnapping an unhinged billionaire? Wait, I *must* tell Andréa you are here. Sit. Stay!" The receptionist burst from his seat and headed to the door next to the desk. But before he passed through, he held the door and looked back. "Johnnie fucking Crosswell. You can't leave without giving me a selfie! Promise!"

Johnnie rubbed his throat, feeling his airway constrict. He wheezed, forcing his lungs to breathe. Did the entire news station know about his misfortunes and thought of him as some kind of side-show freak? They wouldn't be wrong, even so, he wasn't sure he wanted to be gawked at. His mind blanked and he struggled to remember why he was there. He gripped the bottom of the plastic waiting room chair, ready to bolt for the exit.

The door opened. A tall, tan middle-aged man with shoulder-length blond hair and a goofy grin walked toward him.

And it all came back.

Fabio! The Goddess' boyfriend and person who might have weather information. Hopefully *accurate* information from a government source about the storm.

"Hi, nice to meet you. I'm Dougie Biffman." He extended a handshake. "And you are?"

Johnnie rose to meet him in the middle of the waiting area, his hands balled up. *Nuts to pleasantries…* "Just tell me, is there a storm coming tonight?"

Dougie pulled his hand back and, in a cover move, ran his fingers through his thick hair. "Excuse me? Storm?"

Johnnie crossed his arms and planted his feet wide, realizing that the idiot in front of him was a good three inches taller, filling him with self-hate at his own lesser stature. He narrowed his eyes and growled his words. "From the last information you received from the…um…you know." Johnnie winced at his inability to describe the correct source of weather data. He grimaced and spewed, "You know, radar…computer shit. Is a storm heading here?"

"You seem agitated. I didn't catch your name, mister…?"

"My name isn't important. Jumpin'…" He huffed. "GO LOOK OUTSIDE! The sky is fucking GREEN!"

Dougie looked puzzled; he squinted and reared back. "Look, I have an on-air spot in five minutes." He tapped his expensive-looking gold watch; the kind that had a bunch of pretentious dials that no one ever used or understood. "Do you want my autograph or not? Do you have a pen on you?"

"Fuck." Johnnie grabbed the front of Dougie's loud, tropical-themed tie. "DO YOU KNOW IF A STORM IS COMING?!"

Dougie pushed him away.

Johnnie tumbled back and landed on his butt, rolling back like a turtle, the coolness of the floor transferred through his sweat-soaked shirt. His glasses fell off his face and onto his chest.

The red-faced meteorologist glowered at him from above. "HEY! NEVER touch the talent! Got it, buddy?"

Three things occurred to Johnnie in that moment. The first being, that anyone who referred to themselves in the third person as 'the talent' had to be an even worse asshole than himself. Second, that despite the jerk-head's anger, his forehead remained smooth like glass, not displaying any wrinkles one would expect at his age. Johnnie's third and final thought was, 'What did the Goddess see in this guy?'.

As Johnnie rolled to a sitting position on the floor, he weighed his options. Punch the dude in the testes? Or save further embarrassment and retreat? If his opponent hit him in the skull, it might be lights out forever, since the bone graft in his cranium was a weak spot. Dying at the hands of this idiot might not be worth it.

Johnnie placed his glasses back on, with the tinted lenses down. Before he could decide, Dougie's posture changed and he backed away. The meathead smoothed back his hair, then adjusted his tie. In a near whisper, he said, "Namaste. You have a nice day now. Don't come back."

The weatherman spun on his tiny dress shoes and headed back inside the studio. At first, Johnnie just stared in disbelief at the man's feet as they passed through the door. And then a satisfied smile crossed his face. Dougie had child-sized feet for someone over six-foot tall. Freakish really. Not that they were having a dick measuring contest. Not actually. But he took it as a small win.

Johnnie bolted up from the floor. A woman with short pulled-back hair and a blotchy complexion approached him. "Mr. Crosswell, are you all right? I'm the station's producer, Andréa Halley. I'm sorry about Dougie. Do you want to press charges? We don't tolerate violence in the work place."

He shook his head. "I'm fine. I just need to know; do you have the latest weather forecast? I really need to see it."

She cocked her head to the side and blinked. "Weather? Sure. No problem. Come to my office and I'll have my assistant dig it up."

Benji came through the door. "Johnnie, are you okay?"

Andréa waved Benji aside. "Follow me."

Johnnie followed Andréa through the door into a long white corridor with doors on each side. Some doors had signs like "maintenance" and some had names of people. When they passed by Dougie's, the door was open and a security guard appeared to be taking a statement from the weatherman. Which sent a shiver down Johnnie's spine.

At the last door on the right, Andréa opened it and revealed a square office with windows in the back corner and a large wood desk. Her windows looked out onto surrounding trees and native vegetation. A long conference table with cheap looking metal chairs was situated to the left, with an impressive wall of bookcases behind it. More books than at Greta's house, which was a lot. Without thinking, the books pulled him past the conference table like a gravity force and he inspected the titles. Lots of non-fiction about video production, the Golden Age of Television, and lighting and sound design. But on the last bookcase were scores of 1950s-era science fiction and pulp fiction.

He mumbled, "I like books, too."

She sat at her desk, "Have a seat. I'll have the research desk bring up the latest forecast." Her phone rang.

"Uh, huh. I see. Send him in." Andréa hung up the phone and said to Johnnie. "I'm sorry. I have an appointment. Should be just a couple of minutes. I'll have to ask you to wait in the lobby until then. Okay?"

He lifted a book from the shelf, *Revenge of the Smog Monster from Outer Space*. "Could I take this to read in the meantime?"

Andréa smiled. Which made Johnnie realize this was the first time she cracked a smile. "Ha, that's one of my favorites. Yes. But you'll need to return it."

A slender man in a navy suit popped in. "Return what?"

Andréa said, "Mr. Lords, sorry, I was talking with Mr. Crosswell here. Please come in."

The well-dressed guest turned to Johnnie. "Crosswell? Are you the Senator's brother?"

Johnnie clasped the book behind him and studied this new well-dressed person. "Yes. And you are?"

"Oh, how fabulous!" the man exclaimed. He approached to extend a handshake. "I'm Jacque Lords, your sister's new political strategist. So nice to meet you."

Johnnie shook his hand, but only for a second. The man's exuberance made him uncomfortable.

"Oh, well, she hired me just this morning. I can see I've startled you. I'm here to see Ms. Halley about some pricing for television spots. We need to get your sister some much-needed name recognition."

Johnnie tried to hold in his sarcasm, but was unsuccessful as he sighed, "Great." Because his sister's last name was the same as his last name, and by all accounts, most people already knew his name, but not for good reasons.

Jacque continued, "Pray tell, what brings you here today? Does it have to do with your near arrest this morning?"

Andréa's eyes widened. "You were almost arrested? What happened?" She stole a notepad and pen off her desk and walked up to the two, as if she were a new reporter on a hot lead.

Johnnie waved his arms and shouted, "No! Shit. I just want the weather. Leave me the fuck alone."

Jacque backed away. "Sorry, my mistake. Please don't be upset. I'm on your side. In fact, I very much need to hear your version of recent events if

I'm to help the Senator. You do want to help her, don't you?"

Johnnie slipped around Jacque and reached for the door handle. "Leave me out of it." It was time to depart, weather information or no. He held up the smog monster book, realizing he shouldn't leave with it and glanced around looking for a safe place to lay it down. When nothing in arm's reach was available, he tossed it to Jacque and raced out of the room.

He made his way back down the hall. Thankfully, it was empty. Thinking the coast was clear, he race-walked toward the reception area. Behind him, he heard Andréa's office door open and he panicked. He ducked into Dougie's now vacant dressing room and closed the door. Trapped like a low-down dirty animal, he turned off the light and held his breath. Not a smart move, he thought. He should have kept going straight. *Now what?* Would he have to wait until the dark of night to escape? What if Dougie came back and they had to fight?

A light rap on the door told him the jig was up.

The jig was up. He cracked opened the door a few inches.

Jacque stood there with his purple bowtie and perfectly combed salt and pepper hair. "May I come in?"

He turned on the wall switch and opened the door. "Sure, why the hell not?"

Jacque nodded and scurried inside, taking a seat on the small sofa along the rear wall. "John, may I call you John? I made a terrible mistake just now and I'm supremely sorry. Can you forgive me? This is my first time as a political consultant. Have you ever tried to play a part and failed miserably at it? I want you to know that anything you say to me will be completely private and I will only use information in a way that benefits you and your sister. You can understand that, I hope. I mean—"

"STOP TALKING!" Johnnie held his head. "You're making my head hurt." He slumped down on the chair in front of the makeup mirror. Discovering the chair swiveled, he spun around slowly, his hands covering his eyes. In a softer tone, he asked, "What do you want from me?"

"I have some questions. Important questions. You know her best. There are some inconsistencies in things she's told me…"

"Incon…what? Are you saying she lied to you? She isn't a liar. A real pain in the ass sometimes, but she's a straight arrow."

"Like any good political strategist, I've gathered my own opposition research. I like to be quite thorough. Everything she says rings true except for one nagging aspect. And you are the only person who can help me."

"Me? What is it?" He hoped this wasn't related to his sister's past addiction to pills. Robin had gotten past all that and had been sober for years. Well, except for that time a year ago when she and Dottie had a little too much wine on a business trip and had a bizarre battle where they sent bare-assed booty selfies to each other. He hadn't actually seen the photos—which he was glad for—but Dottie had later told him the story in her usual gossipy fashion. *Definitely not Robin's finest hour.*

"Tell me about your mother."

He furrowed his brow. "Shit. She's dead. She went to jail and later died. What the fuck does she have to do with anything? Robin is *nothing* like her."

"May I show you something?" Jacque took a phone from his jacket pocket and tapped the screen a few times outside of Johnnie's line of sight. He turned it around and hit play on a video. "Do you remember this?"

Johnnie's eyes turned to slits and his pulse raced with anger. "Yeah. A few weeks ago. I was an idiot." The images of him and Cud running away from the hospital in Miami, chased by Paparazzi, were not ones he could easily forget. "Turn it off."

"Do you remember the older woman you were with?" He pointed to a still shot of the trio racing into the road across from the hospital to stop a bus. A bus that had allowed for their escape.

"I guess." He remembered she was old and thin and had helped Cud when he wandered off from the hospital. Though he couldn't remember her name or much else.

Jacque pulled up another photo on his phone. A picture of a woman in her thirties with long red hair. "Do you know who this is?"

"No. Get to the point."

"Look at them side by side. I think they are the same person."

"Okay. Could be. So what?"

"John…" He pointed to the younger woman's photo. "This is your mother. Don't you recognize her?"

The sallow-eyed man said this with a sense of authority, without any inflection to denote questioning that Johnnie could latch on to. He peered at the photo. The earlier picture was a tad grainier and muted.

Sometimes he would have flashes of his parents from a time when he was about ten years old. In those flashes, he didn't make out their features, only their general demeanor. His mom was funny yet bored with her life. His dad, also now deceased, was a demanding S-O-B. He remembered his mom's red hair; how she stashed candy bars with yellow packaging in the kitchen cupboard; and her love of shopping. Not much else. "I don't…um. Are you sure?"

"I ran a facial analysis. Even with the deformities your mom received during the prison break explosion, it is a 98 percent match. So, if I can put this together, others could too."

Johnnie shook his head and crossed his arms. "No, can't be. Robin asked me about that lady. Said she reminded her of mom. Maybe it's just a freaky resemblance. Mom is dead. There was a funeral. I couldn't go because I was in the hospital."

"I'm sorry, John. But in truth—and mind you, I looked at the news coverage of the prison riot and called the coroner—they only found one of her teeth in the sorted mess. I suspect the prison authorities were so embarrassed of their security failings, they didn't want to admit the possibility of one of their felons escaping. Now, let's assume she *is* alive, because I strongly suspect she is. If your sister knew your mother was alive and has been helping her evade capture in any way…this would be, eh, um, *difficult* to explain."

Johnnie closed his eyes and ran his hand along the scar above his ear, feeling where they had reconstructed his skull. "Why would Robin lie to me? She doesn't lie to me. Hell, she is always on *my ass* about not lying to *her*." As he said this, a dark realization came. If Robin did know, she would have no choice but to deny any knowledge. As a public figure, she couldn't risk her reputation. Besides, Robin wouldn't rat out their mom.

He looked up. The political consultant's mouth formed a concerned frown, his hands folded in his lap patiently.

After an awkward length of time with neither speaking, Johnnie huffed. "Look, I don't know if she knows. What do you want? You want me to ask her? What good would that do?"

The man straightened his bow tie and cleared his throat. "I don't want to offend her. But would you? I gather the question would be better received from her only brother."

"Oh, jumpin' Joe, she already thinks I'm a nut case. Now I'm supposed to bring her this conspiracy theory? No way."

Jacque stood and walked to the dressing room door. "Just consider it. No pressure. But wouldn't you like to know?"

This must have been a rhetorical question because Jacque handed him a business card with gold lettering and exited the room without waiting for an answer.

Johnnie sat, stunned, staring at himself in the vanity mirror. Which was unusual because he rarely looked at himself. At home, he had the tiniest wall mirror in his living room, with no mirror in his bathroom. It was a choice he made soon after moving to the island. Facing himself in the morning irritated him like sand rubbed on his skin.

How would he ever bring this up to Robin?

Did he have the nerve?

But the man in the bright purple bowtie had a point.

Now he *had* to know.

Chapter 12

Gertie stepped out of the shower and toweled herself off. Bits of ceramic clung to her pajama shirt on the floor. She scooped up the mess of dusty clothes and dumped them in her laundry basket.

Now what to wear?

What did one wear on a semi-date with a man of the cloth?

Sorting through her closet, she pulled out her green Lycra wrap dress. It always hugged her curves best. But no, this was not that kind of date.

Next, she evaluated her floor length orange cotton dress. Wearing it always made her feel light as a feather. As if nothing could ever hurt her. Perhaps it was the color. Or maybe how the sleeves billowed. Whatever it was, this dress was dangerous, imbuing a confidence she didn't think appropriate in this circumstance. She wanted something flattering, but more modest.

The next dress on the rack sent a dagger through her heart. It was the white dress Cudlow had given her; the one she wore at their failed wedding ceremony on the cruise ship. Gertie had washed it several times, attempting to remove the blood stain from when she tripped and fell face first in her haste to get away. Most people wouldn't notice the remaining dim splotch. But her eyes always went right there.

The fact of keeping this dress made her question her own sanity. She had convinced herself that with some tailoring and shortening of the hemline, she could wear it to church events or brunch with the girls. Her eyes watered, feeling the truth within her bones. Keeping the dress meant a small part of her hoped she and Cud would reconcile. She shook her head and put it back in the closet, tucked on the far side, hidden from view.

A strong breeze blew through her half-open bedroom window that rattled her blinds. Shivers ran along her arms. She shut the window. A lone-dark cloud outside dimmed the room.

Probably just a passing shower.

Her phone rang.

"Hello?"

"Good afternoon, Ms. Brown, it's Robin. Sorry to trouble you. I'm trying to get a hold of Johnnie. He isn't answering my texts. Is he home?"

"I haven't seen him since early this morning. He left with Cudlow. I figured he went to work."

"Oh. Well, if you see him, have him call me right away? It's urgent."

"Sure. Anything I can help with?"

"Um…no. Sorry. Bye."

Gertie hung up. She wondered what could be so urgent, but dismissed the thought and went back to her current challenge.

She settled on her pale-yellow linen blouse and a denim knee-length skirt. Gregory had said the restaurant wouldn't be fancy. Clean hair and clothes would have to be enough. For good measure, she pulled her brown wavy hair up in a bun—with some loose strands framing her face—then added gold hoop earrings. *Definitely island casual chic.* Something she would wear to an outing with her girlfriends. In the mirror, she evaluated her face. No makeup yet. On her dresser tray, the green lipstick she had bought in Paris made her giggle. Did she dare? It was definitely *a look.*

What the hell? she thought. She added some pastel pink rouge, black mascara, and last, added the green to her lips.

It might shock the good reverend. But life was too short to play it *completely* safe.

* * *

Still sitting in front of the weatherman's dressing room mirror, Johnnie took out his phone and wrote out a text to Robin.

"I know about mom. What gives?"

He considered whether to hit send. Was this conversation better had in person? Probably. But he needed an answer and sent it.

The dressing room door swung open. A surprised Dougie yelled, "What are *you* doing in here?"

What was he doing here? Experiencing a meltdown and life crisis, certainly. But that wasn't this asshat's business. "Don't worry, I'm leaving."

"I'm in deep shit with my boss because of you. First you assault me and then question my expertise in weather? You aren't qualified to read this data."

Johnnie rose and brushed past Dougie. "Whatever. I never wanted your stupid autograph."

"Are you stealing? Where is my watch? I left it right there!" Dougie grabbed his arm and yelled, "Security! Security!"

"Let go of me!"

Andréa appeared, standing in the hall outside, holding a few loose pieces of paper. "Dougie, leave our guest alone!"

A security guard—tall with a square jaw and bald head—showed up. Despite his height and excessive muscles, there was a gentleness in the guard's facial expression. "What's the matter?"

Dougie didn't let Johnnie go. "Alonzo, this guy stole my watch. It's a vintage Zenith Chronomaster with moonphase display. Eighteen karat gold. Check his pockets. I'm calling the police."

Andréa shook her head. "Alonzo, do *not* allow Dougie to call the police. Help Dougie find his watch. I need to talk to Mr. Crosswell." She directed her next words to the weatherman. "Calm down Dougie. Consider this another warning." Gesturing to Johnnie, "Follow me."

Back in her office, she spread several colorful sheets of paper on the conference table. Andréa explained, "Thank you for staying. These were the last radar maps we received about 24 hours ago. Dougie didn't want to let me have these. You can see here," she pointed to a color map, "that someone, I presume Dougie, crossed out this part before it went to the graphics department."

He examined the page. In yellow highlighter, one of the several predicted storm tracks had been crossed out—the only one showing a track towards the Virgin Islands.

"Whoa. So there IS a potential storm! Ha!" He stomped his foot in vindication.

Andréa looked at him quizzically. She scratched her forehead. "Um, Mr.

Crosswell, read the bottom. This is the radar projection for the next few days. Even if it does hit, which doesn't seem likely, it won't be for another five days. Is this what is concerning you?"

Mouth agape, he squinted at the words in disbelief. But the description on the bottom of the page indicted she was correct. "Shoot."

"What's wrong? If you tell me *why* you are here, I can help."

He thought hard to recall his dream, wondering how he could have misinterpreted it so badly. "You'll think I'm crazy."

"Try me." She put her hands on her wide hips and tilted her head.

Despite her head-to-toe black attire, this producer woman didn't seem evil. Her own pronounced blotchy dark and pink skin—which some might call a kind of deformity—made him think she could understand feeling different, perhaps like an oddity, as he deemed himself. Her taste in books was certainly excellent. Maybe he could trust her. Besides, what did he have to lose? His entire existence was in shambles. Did it matter what anyone thought anymore?

He took a deep breath and expelled his words quickly. "Cud and I each had a dream where his dead mom's ghost warned us about a terrible storm where people could die. She told us to get folks to a shelter by midnight. I thought she meant tonight. Or maybe this was all just a weird coincidence. I don't know what to think anymore."

She sat against the edge of the conference table. "Do you believe in ghosts? Generally speaking?"

"No. But the sky looks really terrifying."

Andréa pointed to her window. "Looks normal to me."

Sure enough, the view was sunny, with a pale blue sky and mere wisps of high clouds.

"No! It was just green! Near the coast. Like as green as...um, green as an iguana."

"An iguana? Huh?" She crossed her arms and blinked at him.

"Not an iguana. But like a weird glow. Really ominous. Only like twenty minutes ago."

"You know, sometimes I have very realistic dreams. They scare the shit out of me, too. Makes me question everything...for days at a time. They feel like premonitions. But then a few weeks go by and nothing happens. But it is sweet that you were concerned enough about your fellow islanders to find out."

Johnnie couldn't make eye contact. "I appreciate you being so nice about this. I should have known better. Cud got me all worked up." He wondered if ghosts understood time. Cud's mom implied the storm was tonight. But maybe spirits didn't own smartphones with calendars.

Andréa smiled. "Speaking of, I would love to interview you about what really happened in Miami. You and Cudlow Loughton. From the footage of your escape in Miami, I can tell you really care about him."

"Yeah, Cud is a good guy. He's driving me nuts right now, but he's my best friend."

"I'd also like to ask you about your arrest for the murders that Thomas Smith committed. It has been a few months since his disappearance, but the public is still very interested in the story. We've reached out to Senator Crosswell several times and she won't comment."

Exasperation boiled in his veins. "No! No interviews!" An interview with the press would be an utter disaster, knowing he could blurt out the wrong thing at any moment. Television reporters were full of Jedi mind tricks to weasel out dark secrets. Right now, he had so many secrets he couldn't recall them all. "Sorry. I'll be going. Thanks for your time." He headed to the door.

She followed. "Are you sure you don't want that book? You could keep it. As a thank you for your service."

"Service?"

"You were a Marine, correct?"

"Yes." He wondered if the offer was a way to butter him up. But on balance, he really wanted something new to read to get his mind off his shitty day. "Sure. Thank you. I'll return it, though."

She reached back to her bookshelf and handed him the paperback. "Benji texted me. Still wants a selfie with you. Would you mind?"

"Um. Sure." He held the paperback and flipped through the yellowed pages. The cover art was phenomenal, with a Godzilla-sized fog monster gripping a retro-looking rocket ship. The premise looked ridiculous, but he appreciated its absurdity.

Johnnie said a quick thank you and left Andréa's office. At the front lobby, Benji was leaning against the reception desk with a cheerful expression.

"Mr. Crosswell, did you find what you were looking for?"

Johnnie frowned. "I confirmed that I'm losing my mind. But I guess it's better to know the truth."

"Aw, sorry to hear that. Hey, can I get that picture?" Benji had a phone in his hand and waved for Johnnie to come stand next to him. "In front of the station logo? Man, my friends are going to be jealous."

Johnnie gripped the paperback in his left hand and inched over to Benji. Smiling was never his strong suit for two reasons. One, his smile revealed mostly his upper gums, and two, it never felt natural. But he attempted to smile. Wanting to appear 'cool', he flipped down his sunglasses.

Benji put his free hand on Johnnie's shoulder and extended the phone in front with his other. "Say cheese!"

The receptionist took photos at different angles and then pronounced them done. "Thank you so much. Here is my card. If you ever need anything, call me."

Johnnie took the card. The man's title was "Media Relations", which may have been a stretch, but Benji seemed so friendly, he didn't ask about it.

"Thanks, bye," Johnnie said. "Have a good afternoon." He fiddled with his car keys in his shorts pocket and approached the exit, his head high, feeling like he could leave all this nonsense behind him. His plan was to go home, enjoy the rest of his forced vacation day, and read this intriguing paperback.

He reached his vehicle and tapped his key fob to unlock it. The sky was still blue as a bird's egg; A pleasant breeze billowed his untucked T-shirt. He shook his head, wondering what could have happened to that green glow from earlier.

A small metal object flew past him and struck the rear panel of his Jeep before hitting the ground. Next to his tire, the item came into focus. A gold-tone watch with fancy dials. *What the hell?*

Johnnie heard charging footsteps behind him. Before he could turn, the unknown assailant had him in a choke hold.

He kicked and struggled, gasping for air.

Until all went black.

Chapter 13

Johnnie woke to a sky as dark as pitch, a downpour, and a howling wind outside his bedroom window. He wasn't sure how many hours had passed or how he had gotten home. The time on his phone showed ten o'clock. If this was the storm, there was little time to save the library or to get folks to safety.

Interestingly, he could now read the small print on his phone without his glasses. *Strange*. He tried calling Cudlow. No answer. Robin: no answer. Gertie: again, no answer. Where was everyone? Did they make it to the shelter after all?

He felt like he was forgetting something. Someone else he had to save.

Sitting on the edge of his bed, he mentally went through his list. Greta was safe in Pennsylvania. His sister Robin was likely busy with emergency coordination stuff. Cudlow and Gertie were probably with each other. Who else mattered?

Stumpy!

He had to save his friend. Because he had no idea how an iguana would survive the storm surge. Johnnie's mission was now clear. Get Stumpy!

He hopped into his Jeep and drove northwest toward Hawksnest Beach. Branches and mud flowed along the pavement. The road was deserted, which was helpful, because the rain made it difficult to see. Water pounded down his windshield like a raging river. Wind buffeted his vehicle. All he could do was hold on to the steering wheel and course-correct with every gust.

After several harrowing minutes of driving, he parked at the beach's empty lot. Dashing into the storm, rain plastered his hair against his forehead.

"Stumpy! Stumpy! Where are you?" he shouted.

Johnnie ran under the shelter of the pavilion roof. He rubbed the water from his face to scan for the iguana. "Stumpy! Come here! Yum time!"

Was it too late?

The palms swayed and bent like springs. The roar of the ocean drowned out all other sounds, even his own shouts.

He sat on the picnic bench to contemplate his next move.

What if he lost Stumpy forever? It was probably dumb for him to have such an attachment to a stupid reptile. But Stumpy was a part of his life; usually the first person to greet him each day at work. And Stumpy never judged him or asked dumb questions. To other people, this relationship probably made no sense, but Stumpy was like family. Like a shorter, greener, and more ornery kid brother.

Johnnie screamed once more, cupping his mouth with both hands. "STUUUMMMPPEEE!"

He felt a nudge on his sneaker. Underneath the table, Stumpy, oddly wearing a sequined bow tie, had placed his front foot on his.

[Yum time?]

"Hey buddy! I'm sooo glad to see you!"

[I tried to warn you earlier.]

"Sorry. I know. I shouldn't have laughed at you. Come on. We need to get to safety."

The iguana blinked at him.

Johnnie chuckled and picked up Stumpy, placing him on his shoulder. "Hold on. We'll run to the car." He kept a hand on Stumpy's back and braced himself to face the tempest's onslaught.

Once inside the Jeep, Johnnie craned his neck to search the backseat and found a dry towel with rainbow colors. He couldn't recall owning such a towel before, but felt lucky to have it at that moment. He dried off his face and wiped down Stumpy for good measure. "Ready boy?"

There was one more thing to save before he headed to the public shelter at the community center.

He had to protect the library, to show Greta how much he cared. To finish what he had started.

No matter what the cost.

A short time later, Johnnie arrived at the library. There were no vehicles or people in the parking lot. Somehow, the lumber and nails he had brought earlier that morning were still on the walkway at the top of the steps. The wind pushed against the two-by-four as he lifted it into place across the shutters. Barely able to see, he swung and missed the first nail head, sending the hammer into the side of his thumb. *Motherfucker*! He whimpered in pain, yet the driving chilly rain numbed the sensation only a few seconds later.

He continued nailing boards. BAM, BAM, BAM. The pounding mimicked the sound of the rolling thunder. Time seemed to slow and he felt like an automaton in a trance, repeating an endless cycle: lift a board, nail, wipe the water from his eyes, on to the next.

Someone tapped his shoulder. He startled.

Johnnie turned to face the librarian, Ms. Teller. She was wearing an all-black Victorian-era dress, unlike her usual pastel polyester pantsuit. Yet, she still wore the same shocking red lipstick and too much rouge. In her hand, an oversized black umbrella.

"Mr. Crosswell. Come with me."

He let the hammer fall to his side. "Ms. Teller, you need to get to the shelter. The storm is dangerous."

She waved her arm and the rain immediately stopped. "What storm?"

The wind died down abruptly. The sky brightened as well. What kind of witchcraft was this?

"I...what? What did you do?"

Her umbrella had disappeared also, like some kind of sorcery. "I didn't do anything. It is YOU who is trespassing. You and that wretched THING!" She pointed to the ground at Stumpy. "Come with me. NOW!"

Johnnie searched his memory, wondering how Stumpy got there. He had assumed he left the iguana in his Jeep. None of this made sense.

He picked up his leathery friend, placed him on his shoulder, and followed Ms. Teller inside.

As they entered the library, the sun came out in full, flooding the sky with a yellow light.

"What time is it?" He scratched his forehead.

She scowled, deepening the lines around her mouth. "A quarter to noon."

"Noon?"

"Are you deaf now?" She continued walking to an unmarked door. "Get inside."

"Why?"

"You want to help? I need a shelf fixed. Leave the animal."

"Look, I only wanted to save the library from the storm. I should go."

"Ha! You wanted to save it for Greta, didn't you? Pathetic. I probably shouldn't tell you, but her fiancé came to visit her last week. He is quite handsome. And a doctor."

Johnnie shook his head. This must be a bad dream. "No. Engaged? Greta? I don't believe you."

"Well, yes, he was her *ex*-fiance, but he wants her back." Her lips formed a gruesome smile, like the Grinch after he stole all the children's toys, but somehow more malevolent. "Miss Hobbs seemed *thrilled* to see him."

"No!"

"Yes, my Johnnie! Now, give me that stupid reptile!" She smiled eerily, her eyes wild. The librarian added a witch's cackle. "Heh heh heh...hmmm."

Stumpy, still on Johnnie's shoulder, leapt into the air directly at Ms. Teller. He dug his outstretched claws into her face.

The hag shrieked and swatted. "HELP! GET IT OFF!"

For a split second, Johnnie enjoyed the sight of Stumpy attacking Ms. Teller like the baby pod alien in that space movie. Before he could grab Stumpy, the iguana leapt to the floor and raced along the wood floors toward a high bookcase, and climbed to the top.

Ms. Teller's face was marred with slashes of blood that matched the color of her lipstick precisely. Johnnie hadn't thought she could look more gruesome, but he was clearly wrong.

She screamed, "JOSEPH!"

Johnnie didn't understand who Joseph was, but he knew he needed to retrieve Stumpy and get out of there. He chased after his friend. A burly arm stopped him in his tracks. The stench of a musk ox filled his lungs.

Chief Tobias' thick fingers clenched onto his arm. "Crosswell! I told you to stay away. I saw the whole thing. Assault with a deadly animal."

Before he could explain, Tobias shoved him into a small room. "I'm going to give aid to Ms. Teller and then finish reading to the school kids downstairs. I'll deal with you after." He shut the door and Johnnie heard a key turn in the lock.

Trapped.

Johnnie yelled, "Don't hurt Stumpy!" although he couldn't be sure they heard him.

The room was a utility closet. A small high window let in bright light. There was a water heater, a bucket and mop, and four brooms. There was something carved into one of the broom handles: the letter W.

Johnnie tried the door knob. It didn't budge. He picked up every item in the small space for anything that could help his situation, as if he were in one of those puzzle rooms with a secret code that opened a trap door.

He sat on the floor and felt a bulge in his back pocket. His phone!

Johnnie considered who to call.

Robin would be pissed. Cud was unpredictable and didn't own a car. Merv would laugh at him. He didn't want to impose on his boss, Kemper.

Regardless of his present circumstances, his mind could not focus on anything but this new revelation of the return of Greta's former fiancé. He called her.

Greta picked up on the first ring. "Johnnie, what's going on?"

"Tobias locked me up at the library. And Stumpy attacked Ms. Teller."

"Holy shit. That's bad. Do you want me to talk to Joseph?"

"Um. Maybe. But that's not why I called."

Greta sighed. "Okay. What is it?"

"Ms. Teller told me about your fiancé. Is it true? Are you back with him?"

"What? Are you feeling okay?"

"Fuck. I'm losing my mind. Listening to ghosts, seeing green skies. Got punched by a stranger. I think it was the weatherman with the small feet. Nothing makes sense. So, no, I'm not fucking okay."

Greta didn't respond.

After an achingly long silence, he took a deep breath. "Shit. You don't deserve this. You know what? Go back to your old boyfriend. Get married. Have super smart genius babies. Live happily ever after. I...I won't bother you again."

He ended the call and threw his phone against the wall.

Breaking up was the right thing to do. Closure for both of them.

His life was falling apart. His sanity and his hopes for the future were completely gone.

Would Ms. Teller have Stumpy put down?

Everything he touched turned to complete shit.

He buried his face in his hands, trying to suppress the wave of sickness in his stomach. How could he let Greta go?

Sobbing never solved anything.

But he did anyway.

Chapter 14

Reverend Greg held the door open for Gertie as she entered the Tuna Bay Café. She was familiar with this place, as it was close to their church and had been in business for as long as she could remember. Although, in Gertie's opinion, calling the place a 'business' was being generous. The café was small, with only six tables, had a history of health violations and was not very popular.

The décor and menu were casual, as Greg had promised. Perhaps a bit too casual for a first date. After seating themselves, Gertie noticed the plastic-coated menus were sticky and the yellow-brown Naugahyde on the metal chairs was torn; only kept intact with swatches of green duct tape. Yet, she made the best of things and continued smiling.

Greg cleared his throat as he examined the menu. "Have you been here before?"

Gertie recalled her first time at this restaurant. It had also been her *last* time because of the cockroaches she witnessed prancing around the cash register. So far, she hadn't noticed any insects or vermin. However, there was a stench of stale vegetable oil that permeated the walls.

"Um…yes. A long while ago." Gertie wasn't feeling particularly hungry anymore and she put her menu down. "What drew you to this restaurant?"

The reverend gave a wide smile. "A parishioner mentioned it to me. Said they had deep-fried fish tacos that were a *religious* experience." He chuckled. "Get it?"

She assumed this was an attempt at humor, but it wasn't even funny in an ironic, dad-joke kind of way. Gertie continued her smile. "Yes. I take it you like fish?" She inwardly cringed at her pathetic attempt to continue the conversation. *Do you like fish?* This was not a good start. And definitely the opposite of romantic flirtation.

Gertie instantly wanted to change the subject. "So…Greg, what types of things do you do in your spare time?" She lifted her palm from the table, found some type of orange sauce on her hand and, not having any napkins, wiped the goo off on the table's edge.

Greg leaned forward. "What is that? Let me find you a napkin." He bounded from his seat toward the server's station. In a flash, he returned with a stack of white paper napkins.

"Thanks." She wiped her hands yet still longed for alcohol wipes or a hazmat suit.

He gazed at her intently. "Now, what was your question?"

"Hobbies. What do you do for fun?"

Greg cracked his knuckles. "I do some carving. Although I'm not very good."

This gave Gertie hope. "What do you carve? Birds? My dad used to carve horses. Not that we ever owned or rode horses."

"I carve crosses for the kids in our Sunday school. Nothing intricate or detailed like birds or horses."

"What about other hobbies?"

He sat back in his chair, eyes upward as if thinking. "I belong to some Facebook groups with other ministers and pastors. Sometimes I create Bible-based crossword puzzles."

Not remotely interesting. Gertie couldn't do anything with this information. "How about exercise or sports?"

"Can't say I exercise much. I often ride my bike to church back in San Juan, but the route is only a few blocks."

Gertie inwardly sighed with defeat. Reverend Greg was the most boring person she'd ever met. Weakly, she tried, "Family? Do you have a lot of family back home?"

A server came over—an older man with a stained apron and a cruddy looking food-service net over his chin that didn't come close to covering his thick bushy beard. "What can I get you?"

Greg gave the man a warm smile. "I'll have your *famous* fish tacos. And some water with lemon. Gertrude, what would you like?"

She chewed her thumbnail. "Do you have salads?"

The server narrowed his eyes. "No. No lettuce."

"Um. Anything *not* fried?"

"Nope."

She glanced at the menu. "I'll have the grilled cheese. And water."

"We don't have cheese today." The waiter crossed his arms, acting annoyed as if she should have known this.

"How about a tomato sandwich? Just bread and sliced tomatoes?"

"Hmmf. Whatever. Weird lips, lady." He grabbed the menus and raced away.

Gertie realized the server was referring to her green lipstick. With an unused clean napkin, she wiped it off.

Greg spread his hands on the table. "Not a very joyful fellow. Are you sure you are okay with just the tomatoes?"

"It's fine. I had a large lunch." She hoped her lie wouldn't show. In fact, she had skipped lunch because she was busy with kitchen demolition and barely had time enough to shower and dress for this date. It was doubtful the tomatoes would be edible. Her stomach ached for sustenance, but absolutely not from this biohazard of a restaurant. Gertie wondered if she could somehow excuse herself to the ladies' room, escape through a back door, buy a snack at the grocery store one block up, and return without Greg being the wiser.

Her phone rang. It was Dottie.

Normally, she wouldn't take a call during a date, but in this situation, she craved a distraction. "Greg, do you mind if I take this? It will only be a minute."

"No. Go ahead." Greg pushed back from his chair. "I'll go hit the little boys' room."

Gertie answered the call as he walked to the back. In a hissing tone, she whispered, "Dottie, I'm kind of in the middle of something."

"How is your date going? He's dreamy, right? So, what do you think? Are you gonna do the nasty tonight with Reverend Make You Come to Jesus?"

"Dottie!"

Dottie donned a cutesy tone. "Oh, don't act so prissy. I'm just teasing ya.

Give me the deets. And why in Hades are you at that disgusting fish cafe?"

"Wait, how…? How do you know where we are? Are you spying on me?"

"I may have put an Airtag in the Rev's car. Fine, you're right. I have no boundaries. Don't judge me."

Gertie slammed her hand on the table and hissed, "What? This is a new low. You can't be spying and tracking folks every minute. It isn't right."

"Sure, what-ev. Just promise me you'll call me in the morning. You know, if I was getting some, I'd call you too. That's what best friends do. By the way, I didn't tell Greg about your husband. The Rev is probably a very forgiving guy and all, but probably best not to chance it."

Gertie whispered, "Shhh! Shut your damn mouth. I'll ring you tomorrow. If I'm still speaking with you after this stupid stunt."

"Oh, come on. I know you love me. Hey, avoid the salad! It'll give you the runs. Bye!"

Dottie had hung up. But the timing was perfect, because Greg had returned. She turned down the ringer volume before tucking her phone into her purse.

He asked, "Anything important?"

"Oh. No. That was just Dottie."

He took his seat and raised an eyebrow. "You don't say. Is everything all right? You look a bit flustered."

"Um. No. Everything is fine. Just some girl talk."

"Ah. I see." Greg cleared his throat. "Well, as I recall, you had asked me about family. I have a sister in Alabama; she's retired now. We don't get together as much as I'd like. And, in case you were wondering, I was never married. But I've always felt my parishioners are my flock, my family. What about yourself?"

His face was handsome and his eyes sincere. Both nice qualities, yet there was little spark. All Gertie could do was to keep the conversation going, hoping for any kind of connection to latch on to. She nodded. "I was a school teacher most of my life. So, in a sense, they were my children."

She recalled some of her favorite and some *not so favorite* students. One in particular that used to spit on her. She didn't regret not having kids. Gertie couldn't bring up her bad marriage in her twenties. That saga needed to remain in the past. "Most of my family are gone now. I have a cousin in

Spain."

Greg beamed. "Spain, eh? Do you visit your cousin often? I travel several times a year with my ministry. But, unfortunately never to Europe. How is it there?"

She straightened in her chair, hoping a mutual love of travel could bring them together; also meaning perhaps he wasn't as dull as he seemed. "The weather and food in Spain are sublime. A few months ago, I visited Paris. It was absolutely beautiful. A place I'd love to visit again, perhaps for a longer spell." She ran her fingers through the loose strands of hair around her face and tilted her head in a flirtatious manner.

Greg chuckled. "Paris may be a bit out of my league! Our ministry travels all over South America. Last year, our church group dug wells in a shanty town in Bolivia. I'll admit it was tough sleeping on the ground, but *so* rewarding. In fact, we have a trip to Belize coming up, to build a footbridge and community gardens. Hey, Dottie tells me you have a green thumb. We could use someone with your gardening knowledge on this trip."

Gertie felt flattered. Yet, he made this invitation seem like a job interview. "Oh. I don't know. How long would this project take?"

"Three months. You'll need your own tent and water purification supplies. Are you current on your vaccinations? Wait. Let me show you some pictures." Greg scrolled through his phone, then turned it to Gertie. "These are from our trip two years ago."

She shifted her chair closer to Greg to view his screen. The photos of Belize painted a dim picture. More of a mud pit than a town. Emaciated dogs lying in the street. Poorly built concrete homes with re-bar sticking out. Children with no shirts or shoes, and dull joyless looks in their eyes. Women with no teeth carrying babies on their chest in filthy slings.

"There was a jaguar roaming the area on our last visit." Greg pointed to a picture with a hillside. "It generally stayed up in those hills, although it walked along the river in town a few times. We called the local animal control office, but they didn't help."

"Jaguars? Sounds dangerous."

"Oh, we were fine. The locals helped us rig up some string and tin cans around our camp." After a pause, Greg reached out and placed his hand over hers. "I'd really enjoy your company."

Perhaps the Reverend was trying to be smooth. Or perhaps he just wanted a new recruit for the free labor. Everything about this Belize trip spelled misery. "Can I get back to you on that?" Gertie tried to think of an excuse. "I have a bit more renovating to do at the house." This seemed plausible enough. She worked her hand free and rearranged her chair to its original position across from Greg.

"Oh, I should also mention the snakes."

"Snakes?"

"They don't bother people often, but there are several species of highly venomous snakes in this region of Belize. Some of our volunteers have panicked. Do you have any snake phobias?"

Gertie gulped. She rearranged her cutlery to occupy her hands. With a weak smile and a soft voice, she replied, "Snakes are not my favorite."

Camping in the mud with jaguars and snakes—surrounded by abject poverty—was not the life she envisioned for herself. Sitting across from the holy Reverend, it felt selfish to want a more glamorous and carefree life. But deep down, this was her truth.

"I only mention it to be completely transparent. I'd be more than happy to inspect your sleeping bag each night, to put your mind at rest. Many of the staff have the same concerns." Greg chuckled. "I often pray to the Lord to protect me from Satan's serpents! So far, the big guy has kept me safe."

Another unsuccessful try at a joke. "Certainly something to think about." *Inspecting sleeping bags?* Gertie cringed inside at this potentially pervy offer.

The waiter returned and plopped their plated dishes in front of them. He'd forgotten about their drinks. When Greg asked about the water, the man shook his head. "Fine. Look, I'll be locking the doors in thirty minutes. I need you to move this along."

"Closing? It's only six. The sign on the door says you are open until nine."

The server grumbled. "Yeah. Well, I'm closing for good. Government shutting me down with all their red tape and health inspections." He pointed to a wall sign with a grade of C minus from the health department. "Called the café a *public risk*...I call what they are doing a damned conspiracy."

Gertie's eyes widened. "You're closing? Will there be a new owner soon?"

"This place is going on the market tomorrow. You know anyone who wants to buy a restaurant?" The anger in the man's voice indicated a verbal attack instead of a question.

She bit her bottom lip, sorry that she'd asked. "Um. No."

"Thought so." The man sneered and stalked off to the kitchen.

Greg said, "I'm sorry, Gertrude. I suppose we'll have to cut our evening short. Unless you'd prefer to go somewhere for dessert afterward?"

Her mind was going a mile a minute, taking visual measurements of the space. Envisioning it with a pastry counter and cute marble-topped tables. With some fresh paint and clean floors, it could be a cozy patisserie, like the ones she adored in Paris. Was she too old to start her own business? Dottie and the other ladies at church were always telling her she needed to sell her baked goods. Not just at the annual charity bake sale, but year-round.

Greg placed his hand over hers and rubbed his thumb tenderly along her wrist. "Did you hear me? Would you like to go somewhere after this?"

She did. But not with him. "Oh. Sorry. I spaced out a bit. Could I get a rain check?"

As if on cue, a heavy drum of rain pounded the pavement outside the restaurant. Visible through the front window, pebbled-sized hail bounced off the sidewalk and roofs of the parked cars lining the street.

Greg's jaw dropped. "Good Lord! Is that normal here? We almost never see hail back home."

"No, not normal at all. We had some hail a couple of months ago. Perhaps it's global warming?" Or perhaps divine intervention to end this date...

"Could be. I'll take you home right after our meal. Not really a night to be outdoors."

Inwardly, Gertie voiced to the heavens, "Thank you, Lord!" She smiled, then bit into her sad-looking sandwich on soggy white bread. As she expected, it tasted like mushy garbage. But she kept chewing, knowing the sooner she finished, the sooner she could go home and plan the next phase of her life. And it would not include purifying drinking water or fending off deadly snakes in Belize.

Chapter 15

Johnnie heard his name called. Groggy and disoriented, he squinted at a bright ceiling-mounted fluorescent light.

"Mr. Crosswell? I need you to answer if you can hear me."

The woman was unfamiliar. The room was white. A clip on his index finger was attached by wires to a monitor. "Where am I? Where's Ms. Teller?"

The nurse was fussing with the knobs on the monitor. "You had us worried. The EMTs brought you in fifteen minutes ago. Can you tell me what happened?"

Johnnie felt his face to see if he was real. To determine if any of this was actually happening. "I was at the library…locked in a closet." He realized he didn't have his glasses.

The nurse held up his chart. "Says here they found you passed out at the television station parking lot."

He furrowed his brow, trying to recall. "I don't remember."

"We spoke with your sister. She's arriving shortly. She said you had a previous head injury? The doctor ordered a cranial CT scan. Should be soon."

Before he could conceive his next question, the nurse drew the curtain around his hospital bed and walked away.

A chill ran through him; the thin hospital blanket offered little warmth. Putting the pieces together, it occurred to him that his ordeal at the library with Ms. Teller was just a dream or delusion in an unconscious state— meaning Greta was likely *not* engaged to a handsome and successful ex-boyfriend. At least, not at the present time. This also meant that Stumpy hadn't actually peeled off Ms. Teller's face like Hannibal Lecter, which was a true pity.

The remote control for the wall-mounted TV was on the table next to him. After his year-long stay in a Miami hospital after coming home from Afghanistan, just the smell of the sterile air made him want to heave. The blank walls and sounds of the medical equipment were equally unsettling. Johnnie turned on the TV, hoping for a distraction. Switching through every channel on the remote, he found a children's station and settled on Blue's Clues.

A voice rang out from behind the curtain. "Knock, knock," said a woman.

"Come in."

It was the television news producer, a welcome sight.

Until Chief Tobias walked in right behind her.

Andréa said, "We heard you were awake. How are you feeling?" She handed him back his missing glasses. The left side prescription lens was cracked down the middle. The metal-framed flip-up tinted lenses were mangled and half-detached.

Johnnie kept his eyes locked on Tobias, wondering why he was there. "I'm okay. Confused, but okay. What happened? How did I get here?" He placed his glasses on the rolling side table.

Tobias stood behind Andréa, like a stone wall, expressionless.

Andréa pulled up a chair next to his bedside. "Our receptionist, Benji, found you unconscious on the ground next to your Jeep. The security cameras didn't pick up on the attacker, but from partial footage, it seems a shadowy man followed you to your car."

Tobias cleared his throat. "AHEM. Mr. Crosswell, can you identify the man who beat you? If so, I assume you'll want to press charges?"

Johnnie looked up at Tobias, seized in a wave of flashback from the morning confrontation at the library—reliving the Chief's gun trained on his forehead. But now Tobias was on his side, which irked him. Until it occurred to him that perhaps Tobias simply loved arresting people and this was an opportunity for the Chief to wield his power on a new target. Unfortunately, Johnnie didn't see his attacker, although he strongly suspected it must have been the douchey weather guy. Johnnie shrugged.

"Sorry, I never got a look at him."

Tobias huffed; his teeth clenched. "Okay then. If you remember anything, call the station." He gave Johnnie a steely look, spun and left the room.

"Hmm." Andréa shook her head. "I think we both know it was probably Dougie. We found his gold watch next to your car. He claims you stole it, but I don't buy his story for a second. Our head of security, Alonzo, found some footage of Dougie wearing it just minutes before we found you. Why didn't you just tell the Chief that he attacked you?"

Johnnie touched the scar along his skull, the one from the former bone graft, but didn't detect any new breaks. "Hell, I know what it's like to be wrongly accused. I can't point a finger when I'm not sure. Besides, with my poor memory, no jury would ever believe me."

Andréa nodded and rose to leave. "Well, I'll let you get some rest. Remember, I still want that interview. Anytime you are up for it. Here's my card. Feel better."

Andréa left and he held her business card. *A. Halley, Producer.*

He doubted he would ever call her. But he might eventually return the paperback he borrowed, if he could remember where it was. Did he leave it in his car? Was his car still at the studio? Before someone attacked him, he recalled there was something he wanted to talk with his sister Robin about.

His clothes were in a plastic bag next to his bed. He eased out of bed, detecting a cold draft up his backside, and took his shorts out of the bag to slip Andréa's card in a cargo pocket. But oddly, there were two other business cards inside: *Mr. Jacque Lords, Political Consultant* and Benji's.

Now he remembered. Mom was alive, and Robin was a hypocritical bunghole.

But his head hurt and he didn't want to think about Robin now and the concept that his mom was still alive. Instead, he continued watching Blue the dog solve a rather easy mystery. *Of course, it was the cat that hid the ball of red twine.*

During a commercial, the curtain parted. He expected it to be the doctor, as in the doctor he'd been waiting for since the nurse left thirty minutes ago. Instead, a red-faced Robin came in, pointing her finger at him like he had been a naughty dog.

"Butthead! What were you thinking? You could have died! Fighting at the television station? What the hell were you up to?"

He considered spitting in her general direction but found his throat dry. Instead, he chose the easier course of returning his attention back to the show, which had resumed after the commercial. With forceful sarcasm, he snarled, "Nice to see you too, sis." Johnnie increased the TV volume.

Robin grabbed the remote from his hand, turned down the volume and chucked it on the floor, where it skittered to the corner. "What is *wrong* with you?"

"Me?"

She stomped her foot. "Yes, YOU!"

"I'm not the one who lied about mom being dead. So fuck you."

In a lowered voice, Robin hissed. "We can talk about that some other time."

Johnnie snorted a laugh. "Ha! There it is! It's true! Damn. What else are you lying to me about? Fuck. Is dad still alive, too? Was the moon landing faked? You're such an asshole. I would never lie to you like that. I mean, yeah, I lie sometimes. But not about important stuff like that. Jumping Jesus, you get on my case ALL the time! Act like you're Miss Perfect and I'm just your idiot, brainless brother. Well fuck off!"

She glowered. "After everything I've done for you, you can't talk to me like that."

"Sure I can. Your consultant with the bowtie showed me *proof* you are full of shit."

Robin's cheeks looked like balloons ready to burst. And not in a fun way. She pulled her dark hair back from her forehead, showing a deep vein protruding above her right eye. "You have no idea what I've had to deal with. All our lives, I've protected you. You don't remember mom and dad fighting all the time. And you left home right after high school and didn't give a shit when mom went to jail and later when Dad got Alzheimer's. I uprooted my whole life to come here to take care of him. Fuck you, little brother. You only ever cared about yourself."

Johnnie's ex-wife Darla had said something similar last month in Miami. Something about how he had always been a selfish jerk. Not that he remembered how he was before his brain injury, but maybe it was true. "That's not fair. You know I don't remember any of that."

"Yeah, well…you remember how I spent every weekend visiting you in the hospital when you came back from overseas? And how I got the charges dropped when you hit that group of people in Miami with your car? Ha! I stopped Tobias from arresting you when you jumped on the ferry naked! Or did you forget that too? For Christ's sake, my constituents still call me the 'naked guy's' sister—"

The pain in Johnnie's head transitioned from a dull ache to a sharp pounding. "Robin, stop trying to save me. I never asked… oh for fuck's sake, just leave me alone. Get OUT!"

"Make me." Robin stood over him with her hands on her hips. "You can't go ONE day without my help. Hell, Tobias wanted to shoot you dead this morning. Or did you *forget* that already, too?"

Johnnie couldn't catch his breath. The adrenaline in his veins boiled with an overwhelming urge to punch her. "Shit. Why won't you leave? Stop being such a fucking bitch all the time! I keep waiting for the day when Arturo sees you for who you truly are and dumps you. Jumping fuck, I have a crushing headache and don't need your shit right now. Robin, if you don't leave this minute, I'll…" He paused to think of what he could do to hurt her the most.

"Hmm? Do what?" She jutted her chin defiantly.

A despicable answer came to him. "I'll tell the police about mom."

Robin slapped him across the face. "Don't you dare!"

It wasn't a hard blow, yet he felt her palm imprinted on his cheek.

"Ow! Shit. Get off me." He tried slapping her back but got tangled in the wire connected to his pulse monitor. The springy plastic clip on his finger flew off in a high arc and bounced off the rear wall. Still in attack mode, he tried again to swat her, now with his left arm free. He swung both arms, like a half-blind cat pawing at a string.

Robin's reflexes were quick and she reared back.

He caught only air, the momentum causing his upper body to fall off the side of the hospital bed, his legs still straight out. With a quick one-handed save, he prevented slamming his head on the ground. Johnnie's sheet and blanket fell to the floor and he realized how thin, nearly transparent, and short his cotton dressing gown was. Most notably, he discovered he had no underwear.

Hitting her to make a point was one thing, but even with potential skull damage, Johnnie knew being naked in front of his sister eliminated any possibility of 'winning'. To preserve whatever dignity he had left, he scrambled his upper body back into the bed, and grabbed the sheet to cover his lumpy nether region. The pulse monitor, now disconnected, made annoying alarm sounds.

Robin rolled her eyes. "Really? You want to punch me? Grow up."

"You hit me first!"

"Yeah? And I'll slap you again if you ever…" Robin whispered the last part, "discuss mom with anyone."

Before he decided on a cutting reply, the nurse rushed in.

"What's going on here?" The nurse's eyes darted to each of them.

In unison, they replied, "Nothing!"

The nurse wrinkled her nose, as if she wasn't believing them. "Miss, you should leave. The orderly is taking him down for his scans in a couple of minutes."

Robin nodded. "Fine. John, we WILL continue this discussion. LATER. AT HOME. Got it?"

Johnnie kept his hands protectively over his groin but elevated a middle finger in response.

Robin grimaced and mouthed the word 'butthead', but in a way that didn't convey her usual sisterly tenderness. She huffed and disappeared past the curtain.

The nurse returned Johnnie's blanket before placing the monitor back on his finger. "Are you all right, Mr. Crosswell? Can I get you anything?"

Every fiber of his being wanted to get out. Out of the hospital. Away from everything and everyone. To find a dark corner and wallow in it.

He knew where he wanted to go. But he had to create a distraction first. "I could use a couple more blankets. Maybe warm them up a bit?" Johnnie affixed what he hoped was an endearing smile.

The nurse smiled back. "Of course."

"And some socks?" he added for good measure.

"I'll see what I can scare up. Be back soon." The nurse picked up the television remote from the floor and returned it to him before she exited, pulling the curtain closed again.

With the nurse gone, Johnnie threw off his blanket and gathered his clothes. He began the difficult feat of dressing himself while still wearing the monitor clip on his hand most of the time until he was ready to go. Once dressed, Johnnie peeked through the curtain, and fortunately, didn't see the nurse. He disconnected from the clip and the monitor made a whining noise. His heart raced, knowing he needed to be quick.

Johnnie glanced around the emergency room ward. There were five other curtained bays. Some closed, some not. The nurse's station in the middle of the room was unstaffed.

Aiming to appear calm, he took relaxed strides, while inspecting the signs on the walls like any bystander would, as he ambled toward the exit. In order, the posters read:

> No smoking.
> Don't leave children unattended.
> No guns.

Then, a very long patient's bill of rights with small print he couldn't read without his glasses. He checked his shorts pocket and found his phone, wallet and car keys. From the other pocket, he took out his broken glasses and ripped off the bent sunglasses attachment before trying them on. The sizable crack in one lens probably made him look ridiculous. But having one good eye was better than none. And perhaps he wouldn't need his glasses where he was going. He put his glasses back in his pocket.

The last sign along his trek to the exit read, 'Your copayment is due at time of service'. He didn't recall if his insurance had a copayment. But he didn't care.

Johnnie pushed a wide swinging door and found himself in the emergency room lobby, where several eyes among those in the waiting room trained themselves on him with a flash of hope, then quickly turned back to their phones, obviously realizing he was not the help they sought.

The motion-activated glass door to the outside was just steps away. He made a bee line.

Cud and Merv intercepted him.

Merv blocked his path. "Hey! Dude! How are you feeling? Dottie called a while back, saying a security guard at the television station found you on the ground unconscious."

Johnnie nodded but continued looking over Merv's shoulder at the exit. "I'm fine. I've got to go."

Cud grabbed Johnnie's shoulder to stop him. Johnnie noticed Cud was still wearing the boots he'd lent him earlier. "We filled all the generators. You wouldn't believe the downpour we just drove through. Seems to be tapering off. Where are you going?"

Johnnie ducked his head and plowed ahead toward the door. "I...I'll see you later." Not looking back, he exited the hospital. He gazed at the parking lot and realized he didn't have any mode of transportation. The asphalt was wet with deep puddles. The sky was dark; a stiff chilly breeze turned his thighs to gooseflesh.

But he needed to go to the place he felt most at peace. Even if he had to walk.

It was not the best plan. In fact, it wasn't even a plan. Just a guiding thought.

Perhaps Cud had the right idea all those years.

Forget society...and family.

The world could leave him the fuck alone.

* * *

Robin entered her one-bedroom apartment and slammed the door behind her. Where did Johnnie get off talking to her like that? But he said that Mr. Lords had proof mom was alive. If a political consultant whom she had known for five minutes discovered the truth, then anyone could. Which meant her political life was likely over.

"Shit!" She threw her shoulder bag across the room. She collapsed across her sofa, face down, and pummeled a throw pillow. "Aaaaagg!"

Her doorbell rang. A muffled voice outside her door asked, "Babe? You all right?"

She climbed off the sofa and smoothed her hair. At the peephole, she confirmed it was Arturo.

He called out, "I got the pizza! Open up. It's chilly out here."

Robin looked at the clock on the wall. It was their usual Wednesday pizza night and, as usual, Arturo was on time. She opened the door and steeled her resolve. Without meeting his eyes, she said softly. "Hey, can we do this another time?"

"Can you believe this cold?" Arturo, dressed in civilian attire, leaned over and kissed her cheek. In her ear, he whispered slyly, "I think I should probably stay over. What do you think?"

Normally, she would nuzzle him back, drop the pie box on the floor and jump his bones. But not tonight. Instead, she backed away. "I have lots of work tonight. Can I see you tomorrow?" She crossed her arms and kept her gaze on the floor.

Arturo tilted his head to read her face. He nodded. "I understand, babe. Here, you take this." He handed her the box. "Are you okay? Is this about Johnnie being in the hospital? How is he? Aunt Dottie knows the nurse on duty; she called a few minutes ago and the nurse she said he's alert and seems fine."

The bottom of the box was very warm. Seemingly more so with the gust of cool air that swept in from outside. "Yes, I just saw Johnnie. He's his usual self." For a moment, she considered coming clean. Telling Arturo about her mother might be liberating. Or his profound respect for the law might drive him away forever. In her bones, she needed some time alone to figure things out. She held her tongue. "Can I see you tomorrow?"

He placed his hands on her waist and kissed her lips. "Sure. Save me a slice, okay babe?"

She sighed. "Of course."

Arturo departed and closed the door behind him. Robin took the pizza box to the kitchen counter and cursed. "Damn!" She now regretted not inviting him in. She could have had one more magical night with him before the news came out. *Before* Arturo knew what a liar she was.

Too late.

Robin headed to her bedroom to put on her warmest clothes—sweatpants and her two decades old Georgetown Law sweatshirt over two layers of thin long sleeve knit shirts. Then she found what she needed in the deep cupboard above the fridge. Way in the back. A half bottle of scotch that had gone untouched for three years. Unscrewing the cap, she inhaled its sweet fumes.

Tomorrow's headlines would read, "Senator at Large Abets Fugitive Mom." Clearly, Tobias would win the election by default. To calm the likely media hysteria, she would have to drop out and take an off-island trip somewhere for a few weeks. Somewhere very far. Unless, of course, the authorities arrested her.

And it was all Johnnie's fault. Why did he have to go to Miami last month? Why did he kidnap Cudlow and evade the police with the help of their estranged mother? In retrospect, the sheer coincidence of him running into their mom defied all logic or statistical possibility. Perhaps the universe was trying to tell her something.

Robin gulped the scotch from the bottle. She hadn't gotten blackout drunk in ages. But now was a good time—no, the perfect time—to drink herself into oblivion.

But first, she rummaged through her handbag on the floor to find her phone. She dialed a number she had hoped she would never have to. To cover her tracks, she labeled it "Dermatologist" on her contacts list. As the number rang, she took one more swig, which landed down the wrong pipe. Coughing, her eyes watery, she struggled to listen for a response on her phone.

A woman answered, "Hello?"

Suppressing her coughs, she croaked, "It's me. Tell her she isn't safe. She has to leave. Now. Tonight."

In a calm voice, the woman stated, "I understand."

The call ended.

Robin sighed with both relief and heart-wrenching despair. Relief, because if the authorities or press couldn't find her mom, they wouldn't be able to verify she was still alive. It was the only chance for them both. Her despair stemmed from the finality of this decision. Now mom would truly be in the wind. No safety net. No way to communicate. And it was all Johnnie's dumb fault.

After another gulp of scotch, Robin wiped her mouth and tried calling her shithead brother. When it went to voicemail, she waited for the tone and screamed, "I hate you! I fucking hate you."

She threw the phone on the floor and sobbed.

I'll never forgive him.

Never.

Chapter 16

Still perplexed by Johnnie's hasty exit from the emergency room, Cudlow kicked Merv's shoe. "We should go after him."

Merv didn't look up from his phone. "What?"

Cud shook Merv with both hands. "Ranger Hartley! We must go after Johnnie. I need his help to save Gertie. I need to convince her to go to the shelter. Without mentioning mother's ghost."

Merv backed away from Cud's grasp and put away his phone. "I just paid Bisbee. That's my bookie. Thanks for the loan." He flexed his pinkie fingers in the air. "Guess I get to keep these guys this week. But man, I just lost big on the Washington Nationals' game. Damn."

"I told you no more gambling!"

"Sure, scout's honor. But I placed a big Nats bet a week ago. Didn't expect them to lose. Got to pay up in five days. Fuck."

Cudlow noticed a commotion at the intake desk. Two medical employees were yelling at each other; another seemed to be on the phone and kept saying, "Security".

A woman with a stethoscope around her neck and white scrubs, called out, "John Crosswell! John Crosswell, return to the emergency room immediately!"

Cud pulled Merv's arm as he crossed the floor toward the doctor. "What's the matter? Our friend Johnnie just left."

The woman's face was red and she clutched a clipboard to her chest. "Are you family?"

"No. Just...I'm his best friend."

"Did you see where he went?"

"He walked out these doors just a minute ago. I thought you had released him."

"No. Not released. He may have a concussion and a fractured skull. He needs a CT scan. Possibly an MRI. Please, call him and ask him to return."

A security officer arrived, a lanky tall man with a light blue shirt with an embroidered tag reading "Island Security". He interrupted. "Did you see which way he went?"

Merv shook his head. "Crosswell just left through those doors; he seemed okay, well, okay for Johnnie."

The officer frowned. "Do you have a physical description?"

"Caucasian, medium height, brown hair, brown eyes." Cud paused, because he wasn't sure how else to describe Johnnie. On reflection, Johnnie didn't have very many distinguishing characteristics. Other than some of his scars, but those weren't always plainly visible. "He's wearing boots like these." He lifted his foot and held it in the air. "Ranger Hartley and I will help to go find him."

The security guard nodded and walked away.

Merv sighed. "Fine. But man, that dude is going to owe me one."

"Does everything have to be a transaction with you? Wait. Don't tell me. We don't have a moment to lose. Come on."

Cud raced to the door and Merv followed. A chilly rain was coming down steadily and Cud hugged himself as he strode to Merv's truck. "Hurry! Open this up!"

Merv hit his key fob and the lights flashed.

Cud got in the passenger side. "Ooh! My it's cold. He couldn't have gotten far in this weather." He wrung his hair over the foot well.

Merv got in and started the engine. He turned up the heat to full blast. "Fuck. This is no night to be out. And now I have to go save an idiot janitor with a broken skull. I SHOULD be with some hottie, getting steamy and sweaty." He put the truck into reverse.

"You have a girlfriend?"

Merv scoffed. "I have what the kids call a fuck buddy. She's a freak, if you get my drift. Into the bondage stuff. Hell, she gets off licking my face. Bleck. But man, she's got a tight one." The Ranger paused at the end of the parking lot. "Which way?"

Cudlow closed his eyes. In his mind, he asked his mother, "Which way? Left or right?"

No voice offered help.

He sighed. "Right?"

"Right." Merv turned and headed down the darkened road.

Cudlow dialed Johnnie's phone, but it went right to voice mail. He left a message. Cud scanned the road and surrounding areas for signs of movement, hoping to spot Johnnie. After an hour of driving in circles, their search seemed hopeless.

They came up to another intersection.

Merv glanced at Cud. "Which way?"

"I don't know. It's too dark. Perhaps he went towards home. Let's head there."

As they drove, the silence became heavy.

Merv cleared his throat. "Hey, can your mom's ghost really tell the future? I mean, not for like sports betting, but like, for my overall future in life?"

"I don't rightly know. Why?"

"You were right before. I think I love Kemper. And if we are going to end up together, I need to know now. See, if it ain't gonna happen, then I can move on. Continue to be an asshole and not worry about it. But if there is a chance with her, I need to do things…differently. I think she is the only person who can save me."

Cudlow contemplated these words in light of Merv's earlier confessions. He liked to think Merv was being sincere, but had genuine doubts. A sign for the Calabash Market came into view, and Cud was thankful for a reprieve from this topic. "We should stop here. Get some snacks and water for ourselves. And Gertie."

"Sure. I'll look for some extra clothes or T-shirts. I'm freezing my balls off."

They parked and ran through the rain to the door.

Once inside, Ranger Merv exclaimed, "Whoo! Mr. Bravos! You got any hot cocoa? Any parkas?"

Mr. Bravos was a rotund man, with thinning dark hair, wearing a green apron with a beach towel around his shoulders like a shawl. He stood at the checkout register and was winding a fresh roll of receipt paper into the machine.

Cudlow wiped the water from his arms and wrung his hair. "Good evening. Have you seen Johnnie Crosswell in here recently?"

Bravos nodded. "I saw him a few hours ago. He asked about the television studio."

Merv scurried down the produce aisle toward a row of vacation-themed T-shirts. "Seriously, any rain-coats or long-sleeved shirts?" He flipped through the hangers, scrunching them to one side after inspecting each item.

Mr. Bravos shook his head. "Trash bags, aisle two in the back. Best I can do. A couple of folks came in a few minutes ago and made ponchos out of them...three layers each."

Cud understood. "Merv, grab a box of large trash bags and a roll of plastic food wrap. Just in case." After spending nearly a decade living on a public beach, he recalled a few cool nights where he scavenged plastic bags to wrap himself in. But on this reflection, a wave of embarrassment caught him, thinking about how odd he must have appeared then. Not that other people really cared. Most of the tourists averted their eyes or discounted his presence all together. Seeming invisible then was a blessing in many ways. But now he wore clean clothes and people noticed him...spoke to him...met his eyes. He intended to keep it that way.

Cud ran through the aisles, picking up whatever food seemed convenient: some canned peaches, a box of cereal, some hot dogs and a six-pack of water. He didn't have time to really think about these purchases. They had to keep going to find Johnnie.

His arms laden, Cud dumped his bounty on the conveyor at the cash register. "Could you put this on my tab?"

Mr. Bravos nodded and rang up the items.

Merv stared at Cud. "What do you mean?" To Mr. Bravos, he demanded, "Hey! How come I don't get a tab?"

Bravos put down the item he was scanning and crossed his arms to address Merv. "I think he's good for it. You, on the other hand, well...do you really want to get into this now?"

Merv huffed and shook his head.

Back inside Merv's truck, Cud explained, "My grandson pays my grocery bill each month. I rarely have cash on me. In fact, I don't own a wallet. Jackson tried to explain methods I can use to pay by phone, but I don't possess a credit card or bank account."

The ranger gripped the steering wheel, not making eye contact. The wipers were at full speed. "Sheesh. How do you go through life without a credit card or bank account? I mean, you aren't a vagrant anymore…um, no offense. It's just not normal."

Cud wiped the rainwater from his face. "You make a very valid point. But I'm not quite ready for all the trappings of indoor life…not yet. My therapist says it may take time. Just owning one of these new-fangled phones makes me feel like I've stepped onto the bridge of the Enterprise. Ha! Beam me up and all that jolly stuff."

"Hey, you don't have to justify your decisions or lifestyle to me. I was just curious."

Cud stared out the side window and said softly, "It understand I'm a bit of an oddity to most."

Merv didn't respond, seeming preoccupied with driving, so Cud left the conversation there. A few minutes later, Cud offered. "Hmm. I used to think true love could save me."

The ranger fiddled with the rear-view mirror as he drove. "Yeah. What happened?"

"I discovered that love can't save you. You must save yourself first. Much like putting on your oxygen mask before helping others on an airplane. At least that is what they said in group therapy. In my case, I had to forgive myself."

"Fuck. That's deep bro."

"Yes, truly."

Merv chuckled. "How's that working out?"

Cudlow laughed. "Not bloody well at all."

Merv slowed the vehicle as they went around a tight bend. "What did you do that needs forgiveness? You seem like a good dude."

Cud opened the box of trash bags and pulled out a couple. "I lost my wife to cancer. But in actuality, I lost her far before that. After her passing, I discovered what an awful husband…awful human being I was. Apparently, my wife Winifred had been in love with someone else for years and had wanted to leave me before her illness. In hindsight, I threw away our chance for happiness by only caring about money. I ruined her life with my careless greed."

"Oh, dude. Sorry."

"Merv, I hope you will take this advice. Try to change now. As of this minute. Strive to be worthy of the love you seek first. And when you are, tell Kemper you love her."

His Ranger friend was quiet for a few moments. Cud examined the side of his face. Merv appeared to be concentrating on the road, yet holding his breath.

When he finally spoke, he muttered, "I don't fucking know how to change."

"Let your conscience guide you."

Merv snorted. "Easy for you to say. I've made deceit and self-hatred a science. Hey, not to change the subject, but I'm still struggling to understand. Why are we not reporting Thomas Smith to the authorities? What if he kills again? Seriously man, I could really use the reward money."

"Please don't. If we go against him, Johnnie and Gertie might be in danger again. Don't misunderstand, I would prefer Smith behind bars. But for now, better to let that sleeping dog lie."

Merv shook his head and grunted. "Yeah. Whatever."

They turned into Gertie's driveway. The lights were on in her house, but Johnnie's apartment was dark. Gertie's car was out front.

"Merv, take my key to Johnnie's place. Get some warm clothes for us both, and some blankets. I'll get Gertie and meet you back here."

Merv asked, "Why don't we just stay here to ride out the storm?"

"We can't. Mother said Gertie can't be here at midnight or she'll die."

"Yeah, but *how* will she die?"

"Mother wasn't specific."

"Okay, but how do you know where we go won't be just as dangerous? In fact, where *are* we going?"

"I suppose the community shelter in Cruz Bay."

"Ugh. That place is gross. I'll drop you both off there, but I'm heading to the bar after."

"Thank you, Merv." He exited the truck and slipped the plastic bag over his chest.

Merv rolled down the window and yelled. "What are you going to tell her?"

The rain dotted his face as the wind howled. "I don't know!"

Cud raced to the door, the wind billowing his plastic bag poncho. He knocked. After a moment with no answer, he knocked again. He recalled her spare key was under the flower pot to the right. He slipped it into the lock and was quickly inside.

The kitchen was a disaster of dust and broken tile. "Gertie! Are you here?" He checked her bedroom. Empty. In her bathroom, her cosmetics were out on the counter, including her mascara and eyeshadow. A pair of blue high heels were on the floor next to the shower and a pile of jewelry was arranged messily on the dresser top. It was apparent she had gotten fixed up for some occasion.

He jogged back through the house and exited. He ran to Johnnie's apartment. Inside, Merv was standing with his back towards him, struggling to fit a thin yellow sweater over his head.

Cud announced, "She wasn't home."

Merv contorted his arms, struggling with the garment like a wild cat trying to get out of a harness. "Do you see this shit? What is this? A child's size small?" He pulled it off, freeing his face, then looked at the tag. "Fuck's sake, this is a woman's sweater. What the hell?"

Cudlow approached. "I think that must be Greta's. I was hoping Johnnie would be here."

Merv grabbed the blanket off of the sofa. "Do we wait? I really want to get home."

"You can go without me. I'll wait for them. We'll use Gertie's car to get to the community center. Mr. Bravos mentioned the television studio. Could you stop by to check for Johnnie? Perhaps he is on his way there to retrieve his car."

"Sure. Whatever. It's on the way." In a heartbeat, Merv wrapped the blanket around his shoulders like a cape. "I'm borrowing this. See ya. Be safe and have fun." He clapped Cud on the back before slamming the door behind him.

Cud removed his trash bag garment and found a dry towel in the bathroom to rub down his soaked hair and beard. He checked his phone; no return call from Johnnie. Opening the fridge, he found the milk carton empty. But Gertie usually had milk on hand for her baking. It was worth a dash in the rain for some refreshment.

Once at her place, he was thankful for his boots as he crunched through the broken tile toward the fridge. Indeed, she had milk and he drank about a quart. Cud wiped his beard. "Ahh."

But this mess wouldn't do. He found her broom in the laundry room and began sweeping up debris. Soon, with that out of the way, he went to her closet to look for a warm jacket or a robe. Gertie's pink terry oversized robe looked comfy, and it was. It fit him surprisingly well. But the deep chill in his bones remained. Her bed looked even more comfortable, and he chuckled to himself that she might find him in her bed like one of the three little bears. Although knowing Gertie, she might mistake his presence in her bedroom as some type of overture. And they had no time for such entanglements.

Instead, he returned to the kitchen and turned on the oven to 300 degrees. He kept the door ajar and let it warm his body. Were there safety issues with warming a house with a stove? He had heard news stories long ago about house fires from such origin. Cud dismissed the notion as an insignificant risk as he savored the warmth.

The day's events had been tiring. Now that he could relax, the pain in his shoulders surfaced from his labors helping to fuel the generators with Merv. The sofa in the living area appeared inviting. He settled lengthwise across the couch and dragged a green crocheted blanket across his legs for a brief rest. Perhaps a rest that might help him devise a plausible reason for Gertie to come with him to the community shelter.

With his right shoulder aching, he shifted his body to rest on his left side, facing the back of the sofa. He adjusted the collar of the robe up around his neck. Before he drifted to sleep, he implored Camille's ghost, wherever she may be. "Please mother, help me save her."

Cud heard the creak of a kitchen cabinet door. An affirmation his mother heard him.

In a whisper, he thanked her. Then settled off to sleep.

Chapter 17

Johnnie's legs ached and his skin pimpled with gooseflesh from the cold damp air. Still the mantra in his head urged him to keep walking through puddles, in the dark of night. Rain drizzled on and off. Cars buzzed past, but he didn't step to the side.

He passed a mile marker. Then another. His soaked shirt nearly reached his knees. Damp socks made his toes blister. Each step sent pain. Pain was good he reasoned. At least he was still alive and not dreaming.

His stomach was empty. What had he eaten today? Just some mint Oreos on the way to the television studio.

Around the next bend in the road, he heard the crash of the ocean waves. His destination was close now.

Hawksnest Beach.

The parking lot was empty, which seemed fitting given the government shutdown and the dismal weather. He found his way to the pavilion and sat at a table. The same table where Kemper had bandaged his hand two days ago.

Had it only been two days?

It seemed a lifetime ago.

He untied his boots and poured water out of them. Stripping off his socks, he wrung water from each, then laid them with care on the table, hoping they would dry by morning. Which didn't seem likely with the cold. He also wrung the bottom of his shirt.

Johnnie checked his phone to look up the temperature. His phone had been in his short's cargo pocket during his trek and was drenched. He pushed the home button, but it didn't light up. Probably fried.

He hunched over the table with his head tucked under his arms. Why would Robin lie to him all these years? Deep down, he knew the answer. Robin didn't *trust* him enough to keep the secret.

No. That wasn't quite right. Robin didn't think he had the *mental capacity* to keep mom's secret. Which made her betrayal far worse.

His sister had always acted superior to him. He had chalked it up to typical sibling rivalry; the kind of playful fighting they did as kids. Not that he remembered much of their childhood. But he remembered their epic feuds when he was around eight. Robin had said something snotty to him and, in retaliation, he pulled off the head of Robin's Skipper doll. The next day, Robin ripped the arms off his GI Joe. Several days of secret physical combat followed, each pushing or punching the other when mom's head was turned.

Finally, mom made them call a truce. To make amends, Johnnie superglued Skipper's head back on, but at a strange angle by mistake, and the glue smeared unavoidably in the doll's hair, making a solid lump. With the best of intentions, he cut out the lumpy parts of Skipper's hair, but soon she was nearly bald. Robin was apoplectic with rage, reinvigorating their feud. The evil deeds continued until GI Joe was a multiple amputee whose fuzzy beard was burned off with matches, and Skipper's eyes were bored out with an electric drill. Mom threw both dolls away with no replacements.

A much simpler time.

Robin, despite being an asshole, was right about a few things. He probably would have been in jail this morning—and countless other times—if she hadn't interceded. The only reason he had his present job was because of her connections. Hell, she had even found his current apartment at Gertie's place when he first arrived on the island. There was nothing of his own. Nothing he had done for himself.

Even his attempt at having a girlfriend had failed completely.

So what was the point of continuing? Everything he touched turned to disaster.

The wind gusted. The temperature seemed to drop. It had to be in the low 50s, which was very cold for St. John. He needed to get out of the wind and find warmth.

The restrooms would have to do. They were enclosed except for some ventilation gaps near the ceiling. He decided on the men's room.

The space was dank and smelled bad. Johnnie flipped the wall switch for the light, but it didn't turn on. Feeling along the wall, he inched toward a corner. He eased down to the cold floor to sit. In his mind, he could hear Robin's mocking laughter. Laughing at his decision to sleep on the floor of a stinky beach rest room. Laughing at his choice to leave the hospital when he might have brain swelling or a broken skull.

Something moved under the sinks. It was coming toward him like a sloth but with lumps along its spine.

Stumpy!

"Hey boy." Johnnie reached his hand out to pet the iguana's head. "How did you find me?"

Stumpy flopped over next to Johnnie's leg, but did not answer.

"Are you okay?"

Johnnie grew concerned. Stumpy never 'flopped'.

Waddled? Yes.

Jumped? Sometimes.

Stared at him relentlessly asking for treats? All the time.

Johnnie stroked the iguana's side. "Hey. Don't feel like talking?"

Still no response. Not even a twitch of his short tail.

He picked up his friend. The iguana was unresponsive—seeming more like a scaly brick than a living creature.

"Oh, shit." Johnnie had seen iguanas paralyzed by the cold once before. That had been in Miami during a freakish cold snap.

"Please don't die. Please. I can't take one more…" Johnnie sobbed as he stroked his friend's belly. "Don't leave me."

"Johnnie?" a woman's voice called.

With the wind, he couldn't tell whose voice it was. But he bet it was Robin. "Just leave me alone! I fucking hate your guts."

A woman opened the door, holding a flashlight. "You need to get back to the hospital. You can hate me all you want, but you can't stay here."

Kemper.

"Damn. Kemper. Sorry. I didn't mean you." Johnnie pushed himself off the floor, cradling Stumpy by wrapping him in the bottom third of his shirt like a hammock. "I'm pissed at Robin. She said some messed up shit to me."

"Merv called me. He said you left the hospital without being released.

Everyone is looking for you."

Kemper held his boots and wet socks, the ones he had left on the picnic table.

"Well, here I am." He leaned against the wall and a wave of dizziness blurred his vision. He closed his eyes, willing himself not to faint. Because hiding in a restroom was embarrassing, but fainting in front of his boss would be doubly so. "Look, don't worry about me. I'm not going back to the hospital. I just need some time to think. Hell, who knows, maybe I'll live here with Stumpy. Yeah. It was good enough for Cud. He lived on the beach for a decade just fine. The world will fucking go on."

Kemper grabbed his arm. "You CAN'T stay in the men's restroom and I forbid you to live on this beach."

Johnnie twisted away from her grasp. "You aren't the boss of me."

Kemper laughed. "Well, technically, I am the boss of you. Unless you plan to file paperwork to quit." She cocked her head. "What's wrong with Stumpy?"

He sighed. "Too cold I guess."

"Johnnie Crosswell, you are soaking wet. Come on, sit with me in my truck. I can't talk to you here like this."

He wasn't sure what other good choices he had. With a huff, he slumped his shoulders and voiced a sarcastic, "Fine." Once inside her truck on the passenger side, he placed Stumpy like a stiff log on top of the dashboard.

She reached under her seat and pulled out a beach towel. "Here."

He ran the towel over his head, then wrapped it across his chest like a blanket. "Why are you being so nice?"

"Is it a crime to be nice?"

Kemper's tone was angry. Upsetting her wasn't his intention. Now with protection from the wind and added warmth of the towel, his body relaxed. She deserved an explanation. He hoped she would understand.

After a deep cleansing breath, he closed his eyes. "Sorry. No, it's just that…Robin treats me like I'm a moron. She always knows the perfect goddamn thing to say to cut me. Cuts me up into little pieces. Like a frickin' GI Joe doll with no arms or legs. How am I supposed to live like this? I know she cares in her own fucked up way. But sometimes I want to smash her smug pointy face. You know?"

Kemper nodded. "You could simply stand up for yourself. *Without* punching anyone."

"Ha! She fucking slapped me at the hospital. Who the hell slaps a person with a potential brain injury? Have you ever had an argument with our esteemed Senator?"

"Hmm. No. I don't think so."

It would take too long to explain. Robin treated arguments like an art form. The kind you had to experience for yourself. So he changed the subject. "Hey, do you have any food? I'm starving."

"I might have some Lifesavers in the glove box."

Johnnie opened the box and saw a small blue velvet case on top of some vehicle manuals. "What's this?" He opened the lid. Inside was a pear-shaped diamond engagement ring.

Kemper sighed. "I've been meaning to return that. But I keep forgetting to go to the post office."

"Oh. Right. I forgot about your fiancé leaving you. That really sucks."

"I don't want to talk about Blake." She grabbed the ring box and tossed it under her seat.

"Got it. And I don't want to talk about Robin."

Kemper reached over to pet Stumpy, who was still comatose on the dashboard. "Poor little guy. I think you were right about the storm. There was hail earlier."

A surge of sideways rain buffeted the car, rocking it like a seesaw. She turned on the ignition and the outside temperature registered on the dash.

Kemper's jaw dropped. "The temperature is…holy cow…forty-five degrees! Do you still think folks need to get to shelter? If this gets worse, it could be dangerous." She put on the heat full blast.

He scoffed. "It's not my problem."

"Johnnie, that's a rotten thing to say! The Johnnie *I know* cares about people."

"Oh yeah? You don't know me. Hell, *I* don't even know me. Robin and my ex-wife both claim I was always a selfish asshole, even before the accident. I wouldn't want to *disappoint* them."

She looked him in the eye. "I see you, Johnnie Crosswell. You may not know who you were. But I know. You are the guy that races into danger to save others. You are a bona fide hero. Remember that. So, explain to me, what did you and Robin argue about? What did she say that made you leave the hospital?"

Johnnie felt a lump in his throat. "She lied to me. Not like a little dumb lie. A BIG one. I'll never forgive her."

Kemper sighed. With a far-off look, she asked, "She's your only family, right?"

"Sort of." He couldn't tell Kemper about the whole 'mom's a homeless fugitive from justice' situation.

"Johnnie, you *have* to forgive her."

"No, I don't. You just said I should stand up for myself."

"Look. Family is never perfect. But they will always be there for you in ways others *never* will. I mean, I thought Blake and I were forever…" She dropped her chin and rubbed her temples. "Never mind. Let me give you an example. My family is *full* of maniacs. We have some *epic* fights. Did I tell you about last Thanksgiving? Our whole family was in Massachusetts at my parent's farm. We had a lovely dinner, but afterward, my cousin and brother got into a crazy drunken fist fight. Long story short, my cousin shot my brother's toe off with a rifle! But they made up the next day. That's how families are. We all stay together, despite all our differences, and love each other."

"Jumping Jesus, your family brings guns to holiday meals?" The air from the vents had finally gone from cold to warm, and his bare legs were regaining feeling.

"That's not the point. John, listen to me. Family matters more than anything. Just be brave. Tell Robin how you feel, and if you need to, agree to disagree. Trust me on this." She turned on the windshield wiper blades to full power, then put the vehicle into reverse. Completing a K-turn in the parking lot, she steered the truck toward the lot's exit.

"Where are we going?"

Kemper drove out of the lot, taking a right on North Shore Road toward Cruz Bay. "Back to the hospital. I will not let you die of a concussion on my watch. Don't even try to argue. Put on your seatbelt."

Johnnie laughed. "I'm not going to die. I'm cold and hungry, that's all."

Kemper scanned right and left, as if struggling to see the road. "Ugh. I hate driving in the rain at night."

The windshield wipers made a rapid 'whomp whomp' noise; Johnnie noticed that rubber on one blade had split off into a loose strand.

He pulled the nylon seatbelt across his lap. "Boss, I'm fine. Don't take me back. Heck, I promise to make up with Robin if you drive me back to my car at the television station."

"Oh no!" Kemper slammed the brakes.

"What?"

"There." She pointed west; the sky illuminated by a distant show of lightning rolling across the clouds.

Unlike typical lightning that flashed for an instant and disappeared, these were a dozen simultaneous bolts like bright razor-wire, crisscrossing horizontally, circling the heavens in a way that seemed like Armageddon. The sort of light in the sky that signals the arrival of a skyscraper-size demon in an overproduced superhero movie.

Still at a complete stop, they watched with mouths open.

"Holy crap." Johnnie couldn't take his eyes off the sky. A cluster of lightning strikes in the distance looked eerily like the outline of Cud's mom's ghost from his dream—including holding her cane. His throat clenched. "Shit...maybe Camille was right." He blinked, still seeing the ghost's image seared in his eyelids.

Kemper gripped the steering wheel hard, revealing all the tendons on the back of her bony hands. "I don't like the look of that."

BOOM! A bolt of light exploded directly in front of them; momentarily lighting up the area like a sunny day.

Kemper, appearing startled and wild-eyed, reversed the truck, heading backwards on the slick road. The tires lost traction. Swerving, trying to gain control, she yelled, "Hang on!"

BAM! In a crunch of metal, the rear tailgate crashed into a low rock wall.

On impact, Stumpy flew off the dash, still comatose, and hit Johnnie squarely in the chest like frozen pork tenderloin.

"Ow!" Johnnie rubbed his sternum. The impact had taken the wind out of his lungs. He took a deep breath and looked over at Kemper. "Are you okay?"

She shook her head and blinked. "That was close. We need to get to safety. Now."

Johnnie wrapped Stumpy in the beach towel and rearranged him like a toddler on his lap. "We need to go to the television station. To warn folks to seek shelter. If it's this bad now, I can't imagine what will happen at midnight."

"Yes. Absolutely. But how do we get them to broadcast a warning?"

Deep down, Johnnie knew the weatherman would never listen to him. He scratched the scar above his ear, understanding what he had to do. He hated the idea of public speaking. With all those eyes on him. Judging him. Sneering at him. But there was no other way. "Can I use your phone? I need to make a call."

Chapter 18

Sitting next to Kemper in her truck, Johnnie squinted at the phone number on the soggy business card through the one good lens of his glasses and dialed his best guess.

An upbeat male voice answered, "W-S-T-J, your source for local news. This is Benji. How may I direct your call?"

"Hi Benji. It's me, Johnnie Crosswell. Could you do me a favor? I need to speak with your boss, Ms. Halley."

"Johnnie! Great to hear from you. I'll connect you right away."

Kemper must have hit something in the road because the truck shook and there was a crunching noise under the tires. She said, "Sorry. There was a vehicle bumper in the road."

Great, thought Johnnie. This was definitely not a sign they would all die tonight. Being on-hold, he shook his head and continued listened to awful background music on the phone. Some stupid ballad about 'rising up' and 'we can move mountains together'. Even listening to Yellow Submarine would be more tolerable.

After a few moments, a woman's voice came on the line. "Good evening Mr. Crosswell. How are you feeling?"

"Um. I'm fine."

"So glad to hear that. Have you reconsidered pressing charges against Dougie?"

"No. But remember how you really wanted an interview? Can we do it tonight? Say in twenty minutes?"

"Oh. Next week is better. How does Wednesday afternoon sound?"

"No. It has to be right now. I want *you* to interview me. No one else. Say yes before I change my mind. And it has to be live."

"Live? Why can't we record it and play it later?"

"I have something important to say that can't wait."

Andréa asked, "Can you give me a hint? Is this about your sister's re-election?"

"Are we doing this or not?"

Andréa whispered something to someone in the background.

Johnnie asked, "Who is that?"

"Sorry, our news manager, Stew, says we don't have room in the schedule tonight."

His face felt warm despite the chilly temperature and his muscles felt paralyzed with defeat. There was no point in arguing. "Fine. Nice knowing you." Johnnie hung up and placed Kemper's phone on the dashboard.

Kemper, wiping fog off the inner windshield, said, "Well? That didn't sound good."

"They don't have room in the schedule."

She drummed her fingers along the steering wheel. "Surely they would pre-empt some commercials for you? If they really want an interview as much as you say they do."

"Yes! That's it!" Johnnie fished for the other business card in his pocket. He dialed Jacque Lords.

After a couple of rings, Jacque answered with an enthusiastic musical tone in his British accent. "Hello, Jacque Lords, political strategist. How may I help you today?"

"Hey, Mr. Lords, it's me, Johnnie Crosswell. Robin's brother."

"Yes, how are you? I'm so sorry for upsetting you earlier. What can I do for you?"

"I need a favor."

"Yes?"

"I need the television studio to give me air time tonight for an interview. Can you make that happen? Aren't you buying lots of ad time? They would listen to you."

"I'm sorry. I don't understand. What is the nature of this interview?"

Johnnie had to think fast. Telling Jacque about the ghostly image in the lightning wouldn't work. "I want to help Robin get re-elected. You know, tell stories about our childhood and what an inspiration she has been to me. How she helped me after the accident. Real heart-warming stuff."

"That sounds wonderful! But what is the hurry?"

As long as he was lying, he went for it. "I…um…it needs to be a surprise for Robin… for her birthday tomorrow. She doesn't know I'm doing this."

"Johnnie, this is interesting. In fact, I think the timing could be perfect. Chief Tobias is being interviewed in a just a few minutes. I'm here at the studio to watch it…for some opponent research. Providing equal air time on Robin's behalf would be very advantageous. I'll speak with Ms. Halley."

"Thanks. Tell them I'll be there in fifteen minutes." He hung up.

Kemper took her phone back from him. "I'm calling Robin. She must be worried sick."

"Fuck no." He tried to steal the phone back.

She hit the brakes and the truck came to a stop in the middle of the road. "I'm just going to tell her you are okay and with me. Understand?"

He sighed. "Fine."

Kemper scrolled through her contacts and ran her finger along the screen. She held the phone to her ear. "Is this Robin?"

Johnnie couldn't hear Robin's side of the conversation.

"I have Johnnie with me. We are heading to the television studio. The storm looks really bad. You should get to the community shelter. We'll call you later." As Kemper brought the phone to eye-level, she cocked her head. "Huh."

"What did she say?"

"She didn't say anything. The call cut out."

He snorted. "Maybe I'll get lucky and the television studio will lose power…so I won't have to do the interview."

Kemper put her phone on the dash and patted his knee. "Don't be so defeatist. It will be fine. I believe in you." She resumed driving.

"That makes one of us." He chuckled to himself. He likely owed it to Kemper to lighten up and lose the snarky attitude. Although compared to Merv, Johnnie considered himself downright jolly. Kemper was being so nice, and it occurred to him he could reciprocate by giving her what he hoped would be a helpful warning. "Hey, Kemper?"

"Yes." She kept her eyes on the road.

"I think you should know something." Johnnie inhaled to brace himself, not knowing how she would take the news. "Um. Merv likes you."

"Ranger Hartley? What do you mean?"

"He, um, like…he wants to be your boyfriend. He asked me to keep it a secret. But sometimes secrets can bite you in the ass…know what I mean? Anyway, I just wanted to be honest with you."

Kemper seemed to stiffen. "Thanks. But I don't think this is…an appropriate conversation."

"Yeah. I get it."

They drove the rest of the way to the station without speaking. Johnnie looked out the side window at the streaks of water running diagonally from top to bottom. They appeared like several streams constantly changing course with their jagged lines. Somehow, it took his mind off his growing stage fright.

Despite the raging winds and the terrifying lightning, he felt an odd sense of calm and protection driving with Kemper. Like nothing could hurt him.

Another thought raced in. *Was Kemper his friend now?* Would they go hiking together or see a movie sometimes? Obviously, they wouldn't be dating. But it would be cool to have a woman friend. Someone nice who didn't act like a dick. Someone who actually listened who wasn't his therapist.

He smiled at her, although she didn't seem to notice. She had a death-grip on the steering wheel, her face forward, scanning the road for branches and rocks. Her terror was palpable.

Yes, he decided.

They could be friends.

* * *

Robin stared at her phone. What did Kemper mean she and Johnnie were going to the television studio?

Was Johnnie going to tell the world about their mom being alive? Was he so angry he would sink her career like this?

Fuck.

She put on her sneakers and grabbed her bottle of scotch. With her phone in her handbag, she exited her apartment and headed to the underground parking garage. Walking across the concrete ramp, a loud burp rose from her throat that echoed off the hard surfaces.

It was time to put an end to this nonsense. She fumbled with her key fob, opening and closing the car's locks with flashing tail lights. She tried the door. Locked. Pressing the fob a few more times, she eventually opened the door.

The car's seats were colder than penguin shit. The steering wheel, too. She shoved the scotch bottle into the crease of the passenger seat and pulled on her seat belt. "Johnnie, I won't let you get away with this."

Robin backed out of her spot, hitting the accelerator too hard. The car whipped back and hit the car directly behind hers. "Oh, shit." She pushed and pulled the gear knob back and forth until finally finding 'forward'.

She tapped the accelerator and inched toward the exit gate of the garage but misjudged the distance and hit the plastic bar with a loud clack. The broken plastic scraped across her front grill as it lifted; once in the air, the right-most portion split off and fell across her windshield.

Nothing she could do about that now. She accelerated and the car jerked forward. The street was dark; rain like a carwash pelted her windows and she pressed different levers on the steering wheel column until the wipers turned on.

She grabbed her phone. Hitting the microphone icon, she shouted, "Navigate to the television…place."

The phone chirped back in a haughty woman's voice. "Navigating to Tel Aviv, Israel. Calculating…"

"No bitch!" She pressed the button again. "The television station."

After a few more tries, the navigation app seemed to get the correct location.

Robin drove through the rain, not stopping at posted signs. She had to head off Johnnie to stop him from telling the world about mom. Make him forgive her and listen to reason. Even if it meant apologizing to the butthead.

She grabbed the bottle of scotch, twisted the cap off with her teeth, and spat the red aluminum onto the passenger seat. Another gulp burned the back of her throat and she gagged.

A few minutes later, at an intersection, a car behind her honked. How long has she been sitting there? She continued driving through the river of rain. Time seemed to slow and her lids grew heavy.

Only a couple more minutes, she thought.

Blinking to stay awake, her vision suddenly turned to black. A nice calm black like drifting in space. It only lasted a split second until a voice in her head screamed, "Wake up! Open your eyes!".

Heart racing, her eyes flew open. She was still driving, but her front left wheel was riding in a shallow ditch. Jerking the steering wheel, the car swerved to the right and back onto the pavement.

Whew.

Another half mile down the road, exhaustion returned, weighing down her head and shoulders. Blinking again, over and over, she summoned all her will to hold on to her vision and force back the relentless waves of drowsiness.

In her final thoughts, she whispered, "Johnnie, please don't".

Unable to fight anymore, she let go of the wheel and embraced the sweet, calm blackness beneath her eyelids.

Chapter 19

Chief Tobias checked his phone again to read the time. He was on in five minutes and needed to concentrate. Not usually phased by public speaking, he shifted in his chair, not relishing the personal questions the news producer might ask. Tobias inspected his tie, wondering if the stripes in red, white, and blue were too gimmicky. Although, his campaign button, with a boxing glove in the center, seemed to be popular with the public. Many constituents would come up to him on the street, their fists sparring the air, pretending to box with him. When groups of little kids did this, it caused him to chuckle; but more so, he was further convinced his lead over Robin Crosswell was secure.

A few minutes later, the producer, Ms. Halley, approached. "Are you ready, Chief? Follow me to the set." She wore a black suit jacket over her black T-shirt and what seemed to be a heavy slathering of foundation on her speckled nose and cheeks.

He followed her to a platform with two angled club chairs and a tiny round glass table with two bottled waters.

She gestured, "Please take a seat. Our technician will put a mic on you."

After a fussy stage hand got him wired up with a sound check, the lights behind the camera dimmed. The producer took the seat across from him.

A cameraman counted down: "5...4...3..." with the remaining countdown on his raised fingers. The camera's top light turned red.

Ms. Halley cleared her throat. "Good evening, St. John. We have a special guest tonight. Our own Chief of Police, Mr. Joseph Tobias. He is running for the office of Senator-At-Large against Senator Robin

Crosswell." She turned to him. "Good evening and welcome."

He nodded. "Thanks for having me. It is an honor to be here." He offered a friendly, toothy smile.

"Well, let's begin. Most people would agree that you've been an excellent chief of police for nearly a decade…seeming to enjoy your job. What prompted you to run for the Senate?"

Tobias had practiced this answer for weeks and had given it to the local papers several times. "Well, Ms. Halley, yes, I love serving the public in my current position. But when I see the lack of progress under Senator Crosswell, I can't stand by and let things get worse. How many jobs has she created for our local economy? None. What has she done to help our schools? I can't think of one thing."

"I see. So, you believe you would do a better job? What would be the first issues you would tackle if elected?"

He had practiced this part as well. So far, everything was going great. He eased his shoulders and smiled again. "Our island is severely lacking in manufacturing jobs and low-income housing. On day one, I would draft legislation to tax the richest properties to fund decent low-income housing. In that legislation, I would apply a portion of that tax revenue toward creating new trade schools on the island to train the next generation. I would also propose tax incentive programs for manufacturing businesses that wish to transfer to St. John from the mainland and eliminate the red tape for new small businesses."

Ms. Halley nodded, but with a pointed stare that made her seem unconvinced. "As Chief of Police, you enforced laws. But creating laws is not the same thing. How do you feel your experience in law enforcement qualifies you as our next senator?"

His breath caught in his throat. This was not the softball question he had hoped for. "Oh, well…" Tobias searched his brain for a worthy answer. "Senator Crosswell has been in the legislature for four years and has nothing to show for it. Honestly, anyone could do better. You don't have to be a lawyer with a fancy degree to fight for the people and know what they want and need." He nodded, feeling he had given an excellent answer despite the pressure.

The producer shuffled the note cards in her hands. "In your campaign, you call yourself a fighter."

"Yes."

"Most politicians find greater success through compromise and negotiation with their peers; more so than through what you might consider 'fighting'. Some wonder if you have the temperament for political life. Claiming you have the tendency for knee-jerk reactions, as with the wrongful arrest of Senator Crosswell's brother for the two murders last April."

Tobias exhaled slowly, forcing a vast volume of air through his wide nostrils. He couldn't touch the subject of Johnnie with a ten-foot pole—it wouldn't come off right. Thankfully, his practice included a great script to draw on. "Andréa, may I call you that? I chose public service because I care about the residents of this island. You know, I was born here...raised here by a single mom. When faced with the hard choice of protecting the public from a serial killer or waiting for additional evidence and letting more people die, yes, I'll choose to be safe than sorry. I think most people would agree with that approach. As a fighter for the good of our community, I won't apologize for that."

Andréa nodded, her face unreadable. "Chief Tobias, let's touch on a new subject. You mention being a son of a single mother. Tell us a bit about your upbringing and personal life."

He gave a wide grin. *This was an easy one.*

"My mother was my everything for as long as I can remember. She passed when I was just out of high school. We were poor, but I always felt loved. Everything I do, everything that I've become, is because of her. She cleaned people's houses for minimum wage. I learned the value of hard labor. She would always say—I remember it clear as day—'be the change you want to see in the world.' I still believe that. Which is why I'm running for the Senate."

He had made up this last part. In truth, his mom was a broken person, who voiced little hope for her life or enthusiasm for their future. Many nights he heard her groan with pain from the arthritis in her hands and knees, from hours of washing floors and scrubbing toilets. He vowed to make her proud—to have a position of status where he could make the rules instead of follow them. The day he became chief those nine years ago was monumental; he imagined her beaming at him from heaven.

The producer looked down at her notepad. "She sounds like a wonderful woman. And you never had children of your own?"

"I consider myself married to my work. But I love spending time with children. I coach the middle school baseball team and read stories to the first-grade class at the library every week." He maintained eye contact with the producer, trying to appear sincere. Although he knew it was cheesy, he added, "I believe children are our future."

Out of the corner of his eye, he spotted a strange-looking man wearing a mass of brightly colored feathers on his head. He couldn't help being distracted.

The camera-man waved to Andréa with a signal he didn't recognize.

Andréa said, "Thank you for coming in tonight, Chief Tobias. It's been a pleasure to speak with you."

Tobias grinned, happy the inquisition was over. "The pleasure has been all mine."

Andréa turned to the camera. "After a short break for our sponsors, we'll be back with the nightly news."

The camera light went off and a staff member approached to remove Tobias' microphone.

Andréa shook his hand. "Truly. Thanks for coming in. Best wishes to you in the election next week."

He rose, his gaze reaching past her. "Who is that…man with the feathers? And is that marijuana smoke in the air?"

Andréa rolled her eyes upward. "That's our meteorologist. We asked him to come in to talk about the cold snap. He asked if he could cleanse the set with burning sage before he went on. Something about asking Tempestas—the Roman goddess of sudden weather—to restore the natural order."

"Excuse me?"

"Don't ask. He's a handful. I refused at first, but he got very upset. Hell, if his chanting helps bring back warmer temps, I can live with that."

Tobias grunted. "He sounds like a looney to me."

"Don't get me started. I have to run. Benji will show you the way out." Andréa strode across the studio toward the control room.

He waited for his escort and checked his phone. Ms. Teller, the librarian, had texted him, saying he had done well. He sent a smile emoji back to her. The next text on his phone, issued over an hour ago, was a police alert on behalf of the local hospital, asking for information on a missing patient, a Mr. John Logan Crosswell.

What the hell?

Benji, the young man who had first greeted him at the television station, walked up. "Sir, Andréa asked me to give you this." He offered a black T-shirt, size extra-large, with the yellow WSTJ logo. "Please follow me."

As they moved past the cameras and toward the main hallway, Tobias spotted a man entering one of the side rooms. It was just a split second, but he knew without a doubt who it was. A thin man in a crisp suit and bowtie entered the same door behind him.

The Chief tapped Benji on the shoulder. "What is Crosswell doing here?"

"I really shouldn't say."

Tobias grabbed Benji's shoulder and brought him to a firm halt. He growled, "Is this some kind of sick joke? Some kind of set up?" His neck under his dress shirt collar prickled with anger, despite the cool indoor temperature.

Benji's eyes were wide, his mouth agape. "Sir? What do you mean?"

Whatever Johnnie was doing here had to be something stupid at best. At worst, perhaps Johnnie was going to humiliate him somehow. Or maybe the idiot was playing detective—looking for another beating from the same person who had jumped him earlier.

"Fine. I'll find out for myself." Tobias shoved Benji to the side and he strode toward the door that Crosswell entered.

He turned the knob, ready for a battle, and entered the room. Tobias boomed, "What in hell are you doing here, Crosswell?"

Tobias' jaw dropped at the sight before him.

Johnnie was in his underwear, exchanging clothes with the thin man in the green room. A dead iguana lay on its side on the dressing table. With both men showing way too much skin, Tobias abruptly backed out of the room and shut the door with a slam.

Benji looked at him questioningly. "Is everything all right?"

With a growing sense of dread, Tobias replied, "No. Probably not." He considered his options. Something his mom had actually said often was, 'if you don't know what to do, just take a breath, watch and listen'. She said this, knowing his preference for action at all times, which hadn't always served him well as a young boy.

This time he would listen to mom's advice. He pointed back toward the studio door. "If it's all the same to you, I'd like to stick around for a while."

Chapter 20

After the Chief exited the dressing room, Johnnie turned to Jacque. "Why is Tobias here?"

Jacque, busy pulling his legs through Johnnie's shorts, gave a smile. "Don't you recall? I mentioned this on the phone. Chief Tobias just finished up an interview. A rather uninspired one, in my opinion. You know, 'I'm a home town hero'…blah…blah. Have you decided on what you'll say? I really wish you would let me coach you for a few minutes."

Johnnie looked down at his feet. Jacque's dress shoes didn't fit, which meant he had to wear his high-top boots with the navy dress slacks. "We don't have time for that." He squinted at the wall clock through the cracked lens of his glasses. "It's almost ten o'clock."

The consultant, now wearing his white undershirt and Johnnie's still wet cargo shorts, blinked at him. "I don't follow. What is your fascination with the time?"

Johnnie checked his look in the mirror. "Hell, I look like a kid dressed as an accountant for Halloween." He adjusted his broken glasses on the bridge of his nose, saw no hope for them and threw them on the vanity table.

"I think you look very nice. Very nice. May I?" Jacque approached and fussed with the knot of Johnnie's bow tie. "There. Perfect. Now, are you going to tell me the real reason you are here?"

"What do you mean?"

"Your right eye is twitching. It's subtle. You should know I'm a master at reading people…well, most people. Now, tell me the truth."

Johnnie plopped in front of the dressing table and ran his hand across

Stumpy. The iguana was still stiff as a board. "I'm here to warn the island's residents to get to shelter. Cudlow's dead mom warned us in a dream that folks might die if they don't reach the shelter by midnight."

"Yes, when I met Mr. Loughton this morning, he mentioned his mother's ghost and the warning. This cold snap and storm were certainly unexpected. So, you aren't here to talk about Robin at all?"

"Nope. And it's a good thing too, because I hate her guts right now."

"I see. Well, I have one small request. That thing we talked about earlier today? The woman in Miami? Let's leave that subject be, if you don't mind."

"Sure."

Jacque clapped his hands. "Great." In a more somber tone, he added, "I'll have you know, I once received a warning from a ghost."

"Yeah?"

"Yes. It foretold my grandfather's death. Twenty days later, it came true."

Johnnie turned in his chair. "Wait. You aren't mad that I lied to you?"

"Heavens no. Is there anything I can do to help?"

With a laugh, Johnnie said, "When Tobias tries to arrest me—for whatever made up reason—could you post my bail and not tell Robin? I really don't want to see her tonight."

Jacque squeezed his shoulder. "It would be my pleasure."

Benji entered the dressing room. "Johnnie, come with me. You are on in ten minutes."

He followed Benji with Jacque trailing behind them.

Inside the blackened studio space, Benji brought them to a row of metal folding chairs along the back wall. Notably, Chief Tobias was on the far end of the row of six, sitting with his arms crossed and sporting a stone-like expression. Tobias gave a quick side-eye toward them, but then fixed his eyes forward.

Johnnie whispered to Benji, "Why is he still here?"

The front-desk clerk whispered back, "He wanted to stay. Is that a problem?"

Jacque intervened. "It's fine." He directed Johnnie to the furthest seat from Tobias, leaving three empty seats from the Chief.

Benji pointed. "That technician over there will get you mic'd up. Just relax. Eight minutes."

After a tense few moments, the station producer, Andréa, walked up. "Mr. Crosswell, nice to see you again. How are you feeling?"

He was feeling many things. Fear, dread, anxiety, anger. But he needed to keep it simple. "I'm fine."

"Wonderful. We are ready for you. Follow me."

In the span of two minutes, he was brought on the set, his microphone inserted under his suit jacket and affixed to the placket of his dress shirt, and a sound check was completed. Stage lights beamed on him; he appreciated their warmth but not the glare. Past the cameras, twenty feet away, he met eyes with Tobias, who gave a murderous stare. Johnnie looked over toward Jacque. The consultant gave him a thumbs up. None of this felt right.

Andréa took the seat across from him. "Are you ready? I'm going to introduce you, then ask some basic questions before discussing your sister's campaign and some other things." She flipped through a notepad. "Before we get started, some quick questions. Your age?"

"Forty-five."

"You've lived here on St. John for how long?"

"Five years."

"Your military service in the Marines…how many years?"

"Twenty. I think." Panic washed over him. Was that right? He couldn't remember. He wiped sweat from his brow and rubbed it on Jacque's suit pants. "Shit. I'm really not sure."

Andréa nodded. "It's all right. My research says twenty-two years. We'll go with that."

The lights in the studio dimmed except for the ones pointed to the stage. A camera person, a figure Johnnie couldn't discern, called out, "Counting down. Ten, nine…"

Suddenly sick to his stomach, he blanked on what he wanted to say about the storm.

Two figures walked up to the edge of the set behind the camera. Kemper and Merv. Merv was wearing Johnnie's blue plaid blanket as a cape. Kemper gave Johnnie a broad smile.

He smiled back.

"…three, two, one."

And the interview began.

* * *

When the background lights lowered, spots from the stage lights formed in front of Johnnie's eyes. Maybe they were real. Maybe a product of the intense fear causing a sort of blindness. Andréa's introduction echoed in his ears, like he was in a deep canyon, surrounded by high, smooth white walls.

He blinked a few times, trying to regain his senses.

Andréa turned to him. "Mr. Crosswell, thank you for joining us tonight. As Senator Crosswell's brother, I'm sure you are following the election coverage. Would you say that the two of you are close?"

He froze. "Close?"

"Yes. What is your relationship these days?"

The last thing he wanted to talk about. "She's an okay sister."

"Just okay?"

He wasn't here to put down Robin, even though his anger still raged. Deciding to be the bigger person, he took a deep breath and offered robotically, "She's super smart. Cares about people. Loves public service and...all that stuff."

Fortunately, Andréa seemed to pivot. "As I understand it, she stayed by your side through your first year of recovery after your near fatal injuries in Afghanistan. You received a purple heart for your heroism. According to accounts I've read, you single-handedly saved the lives of a visiting U.S. delegation from a mortar attack. Can you tell us a bit about that?"

Johnnie sighed. It was time to pull off the Band-Aid and just get on with it. "I'd rather not. I'm here to talk about something else."

Andréa looked down at her notes and then at the camera operator. "What would you like to talk about?"

"The storm outside. It's going to get much worse." He looked at the camera and rose from his seat. He stepped toward the camera, but his microphone cord tugged on him. Not knowing how to release it, he stood his ground. "People will die if they don't get to a storm shelter by midnight. They have to get to the community center or find a basement or...something. Now! Now damnit! Don't wait! Please, turn off your televisions and stay away from your windows!"

Andréa stiffened. "Please sit." She turned to the camera. "We'll be back in four minutes after a short commercial break."

The camera operator threw up his hands, shaking his head and mouthing something to Andréa that appeared to be a refusal.

Andréa rushed up to the camera and shut it off with the button on the side. "Stan, we have to go to a break." She held her earpiece to her head. "Run the commercials again from the last spot."

The studio lights came back on. She turned back to Johnnie, her eyes were angry slits. "We talked about this. The maps from NOAA don't confirm any of what you are saying. There is no hurricane. This interview is over."

"No. Look, sometimes weather maps and data are wrong." He turned to Kemper. "Boss, tell her. The lightning! Fuck, it's forty degrees and we've had rain, hail, strong winds and…frozen iguanas!"

Just then, Dougie approached, his hands balled into fists. Wearing a ridiculous feather headdress, he screamed, "You! You aren't *qualified* to know the weather. I'm the *expert* here. How dare you scare my fans! The goddess Tempestas spoke to me during my meditation. This is just a small upper atmospheric disturbance. I want you to apologize!"

Johnnie bared his teeth. "I'll do no such thing. You're a…fuckin' baby footed dick-munch weirdo."

"No, YOU are the weirdo, weirdo."

Tobias strode up. "Ha! I knew it. Idiot is off his meds again. Ms. Halley, I'd be happy to take Johnnie back to Cruz Bay and let him calm down in a nice, cold cell."

Merv joined the huddle, no longer wearing the blanket. "Hey, calm down roid-man. Johnnie here is just trying to help. I'll drive him home."

The Chief bristled, his nostrils flaring, "Ranger Merv Hartley! *What* did you call me?"

Dougie turned to Merv. "MERV? You're Merv? My girl Lilly told me you tried to hit on her earlier. Scumbag. I'm gonna kill you!" He swung at Merv and punched him in the jaw.

Merv tumbled to the ground. But he wiggled over and grabbed Dougie's legs, pulling him over as well. The pair wrestled on the ground, now tangled in several electrical cords crossing the floor. Feathers from Dougie's headgear fluttered in a spray of color, before his headgear rolled away from the melee.

Tobias tried to pry the two away from each other. "STOP! That is an order!"

Both men rose and dusted themselves off. Merv had a bloody cut on his lip. Dougie's flaxen long hair was a tangled poof and his tiny dress shoes had come off, revealing marijuana-themed socks. Tobias, Dougie and Merv faced each other in a tight circle, glaring at each other in a soup of testosterone and fury that meant round two of their battle would soon erupt.

Johnnie stood to the side, wondering how this three-man standoff was going to resolve itself. Glad he wasn't part of it, he glanced around. Andréa walked away, calling for security. Kemper waved for him to come leave with her, mouthing, "Let's go."

Leaving was tempting, but Johnnie also noticed one more thing. Stumpy, now mobile again, was climbing the television camera. Mesmerized, Johnnie just watched.

And a brilliant thing happened.

* * *

~Three Minutes Earlier~

Under the heat of the artificial lights, Stumpy savored the new feeling in his limbs and tail. But where was Johnnie? What was this place?

Still stiff from the chill, he crawled down from the padded ledge and sniffed the air. He needed more information. An exit opened to a long straight path with high walls. The sound of noises, including the voices of Johnnie and the man with the tall forehead, murmured in the distance.

He followed the sound.

His stomach churned with a longing for food. Perhaps a tasty snack to take the sting off his cold stomach.

He came upon a large space with many people, some angry, milling about. A human stepped back onto his short tail. It hurt.

Unable to scurry to safety, he climbed. Climb the metal frame to get away from further injury from the humans. Climb to safety...climb to get Johnnie's attention.

At the top, his claws sought secure footing on the metal and plastic. The perch was warm. Warmer than the surrounding air. As if sitting on his favorite flat rock at the beach under the midday sun.

He kept his eyes on Johnnie.

[Yum time?] he called out to his friend, raising a front leg in the air.

Johnnie turned to face him and smiled. His friend seemed to be pleased to see him.

Stumpy's other friend, the one called Merv, was in a confrontation with two other humans. Much like his own confrontations with his usual foe, Greentail. But they didn't appear to be fighting over snacks.

Basking in the heat from his perch and the overhead rays of light, Stumpy settled down to watch and stay out of the fray.

* * *

Merv noticed the thick band of gold on Dougie's wrist. Looked expensive. *If only…*

The stench of Tobias' breath poured down his face, as the Chief held him back from his opponent. But desperate times called for desperate measures. He stuck his tongue out at Dougie. "Ha! Whatcha gonna do now? You fight like a moron. Lilly needs a *real* man. Not some featherbrained loser with a tiny dick and a stupid perm."

The weatherman's face turned three shades redder. He threw another punch at Merv.

Tobias swung Merv out of harm's way; the chief received the full force of the blow on his chin.

Merv fell out of Tobias' grasp and onto the floor. In a crab position with arms and legs underneath him, he back-peddled to give Tobias room for the expected response.

Tobias didn't disappoint. The Chief faced Dougie like a pulsing volcano. He shed his suit jacket, throwing it to the ground, then rolled up his sleeves and loosened his tie.

Dougie's face turned ashen, his mouth open in dismay. "I'm sorry Officer. I didn't—"

Tobias slugged the weatherman in the stomach with such force, the long-haired meteorologist reeled backward and dropped several feet away. The chief yelled, "You, motherfucker, are under arrest!"

A security guard rushed towards them. "What happened?"

The Chief brushed blood from his lip with his thumb. "Your weatherman punched me. I'm arresting him for assault."

With glee, Merv got to his feet and walked over towards Dougie. The weatherman was holding his stomach, his hair in disarray covering his face. On his way over, Merv surreptitiously kicked his golden prize toward an unlit corner filled with electrical cables. Hovering over him, Merv said, "Ha. I guess I'll just have to check in on Lilly while you are wasting away in jail."

Tobias pushed Merv out of the way. "Shut the fuck up. You and Johnnie need to get the hell out of here before I arrest all three of you." He asked the security guard for some zip ties or duct tape. The guard said he would be right back.

Merv's eyes widened, noticing something remarkable off to his side. It was time for more fun. He moved slightly to his right and egged on Tobias. "Arrest us? What for? We were just minding our own business before you threatened to arrest Johnnie for no fucking reason and this weather freak went Rambo on me. Like I said before, you need to lay off the roids dude. They are messing with your brain." He knew he was on shaky ground, but there was no way he could lose. Still, he kept a good three paces away out of immediate reach from Tobias.

And it worked perfectly. Tobias shouted, "That does it! You, down on the ground now. Crosswell!" He yelled across the room. "You too. Get on the fucking floor now, hands behind your backs."

Merv glanced at Johnnie and nodded.

Johnnie's eyes darted toward Stumpy and then he nodded back to Merv.

Both men lay on the ground, chins on the polished concrete floor, arms crossed behind their back.

Tobias seemed to be waiting for the security guard to bring the zip ties or whatever. He kicked Johnnie in the ribs.

Johnnie screamed. "Ow! Shit!"

"I said, shut up!" Tobias made a hand-gesture like a gun pointed at Johnnie's head. The Chief muttered, "I should have smoked your lame ass this morning at the library. Save the world from your brain-dead stunts."

The security guard returned and Tobias walked a few steps away to receive a roll of duct tape.

Merv and Johnnie faced each other, still prone on the floor.

They exchanged guarded smiles.

Merv whispered, "Do you want to tell him?"

Johnnie whispered back, "No. But I can't wait to watch this later."

After a few seconds more, the producer, Andréa, jogged onto the set and turned off the main camera. The one that Stumpy had been warming himself on. "Who's fucking iguana is this?" Into her headset, she said, "Goddamn. Is it off now?... Good." She spoke to Tobias. "Sir, I'm afraid the last few minutes have been broadcast live. We just cut the feed."

Johnnie pushed himself off the ground and into a cross-legged sitting position. He pumped a fist in the air. "Way to go, Stumpy!"

Merv also came to a sitting position. He high-fived Johnnie. "Now that is what I call justice."

Tobias' jaw fell open, but his mouth seemed frozen, unable to speak.

Andréa took the Chief's arm and guided him a few feet away into a huddle. "Chief Tobias, our switchboard has been lighting up. Some calling to say very unkind things about you. But more importantly, most of the calls are about the storm. Viewers are reporting flooding, vehicle accidents, and roofs being torn off buildings. And a Detective Arturo Bell is trying to reach you...something about a fire near the dock."

The Chief sputtered an incoherent response. He turned slowly, eyeing the room in a 360-degree rotation. The technicians, staff, the security guard, Kemper and Andréa stood around him in a circle with disapproving looks.

Merv, still sitting on the floor, savored the moment and grinned. It was all so fucking fantastic. He scrambled to a stand and extended a hand to Johnnie to help him up, bro-style. They joined Tobias' circle of doom. No one spoke in the odd stand-off for several awkward seconds. Kemper broke the tension by approaching the camera and lifting Stumpy off the top. She transferred him to Johnnie's arms, like a mother giving her naughty child to its father.

Tobias announced, "I'll let this go...for now. I have important business back at the station." He dropped the roll of duct tape and broke through the circle to retrieve his suit jacket on the floor. After donning his jacket, he glanced quickly over his shoulder at the group, who still had their eyes trained on him. With a scowl, he announced, "Be safe everyone." Then he strode toward the exit and disappeared.

Dougie retrieved his shoes and high-stepped it in the opposite direction toward a quiet corner of the studio to make a phone call.

Andréa held her headset to her ear, then whispered something to Johnnie. Merv couldn't make it out, but it seemed like bad news, because Johnnie looked as if someone murdered his best friend. Johnnie left with Andréa toward the control booth.

The staff and the others began chatting and moving around the space. The camera operator was inspecting the main camera, using some tissues to wipe off iguana dung.

With everyone distracted, Merv strolled over casually to pick up his prize and slip it in the pocket of his shorts. He didn't dare inspect the item. Not yet. But from the heft of Dougie's gold watch, Merv was sure he wouldn't be losing his pinkie finger to Bisbee next week after all.

Chapter 21

Relieved that Tobias had left the television station, Johnnie held Stumpy close and stroked the iguana's dorsal crests. "Who's a good boy? Stumpy's a good boy!"

The station manager, Andréa, touched his shoulder. She whispered, "Johnnie, Dottie McPherson just called our public hotline. She said she tried you on your cell but couldn't reach you."

"What is it?"

"She didn't say. But it sounded like an emergency. Come with me. You can use the phone in my office to call her back."

Johnnie wrinkled his brow. "Thanks." He passed Stumpy back to Kemper.

Once in Andréa's office, she handed him a pre-printed slip of paper with the heading 'While you were out' with Dot's name and phone number. "I'll let you take this privately."

"Thank you." He watched Andréa leave and close the door behind her. He dialed Dottie; she answered on the first ring.

"Hey, Dot, what's up?"

"Johnnie, Robin just called me, drunk as a skunk and out of her mind. She was crying and talking nonsense. I think she's been in a car accident. The call got cut off and now she isn't answering. Johnnie, can you track her on your phone? You guys do that, right?"

His sister was never one to drive in bad weather and certainly not at night if it couldn't be helped. Robin was always so worried about hitting a donkey outside of town or being slammed by a car coming around a blind corner.

"Sorry Dottie, my phone is fried."

"But you can use the app online, right? Just log in. I do it all the time. I would ask Arturo to find her, but Robin insisted not to call him."

"For fuck's sake, Dottie, you mean Robin could be critically injured from drunk driving and all you care about is not telling Arturo or the police?"

There was a pause from Dottie, which he hadn't expected. Because Dottie never paused. She would deflect or laugh or tell you a gossipy story to avoid an uncomfortable subject, but never got quiet.

"Well?"

"Johnnie, this would *kill* her re-election. You understand?"

"Shit. I don't fucking care. If you only knew what an awful person she is…"

"Hey! Shame on you. She loves you. You know that's true. Robin can be grumpy and a handful—but she would do anything for you."

The office door opened and Kemper tiptoed in. She mouthed, "Is everything alright?"

Seeing Kemper's eyes, a sense of defeat overcame him. Her earlier words flooded back to him. *The Johnnie I know cares about people.* As much as he wanted to deny it, he did care about his sister. Even if she was fucking evil. He mouthed back to Kemper, "It's Dottie."

Directing his attention back to the phone, he softened his tone, but decided he wasn't backing down just yet. "I'll find her location and call you back. But that's it. She's your problem." He slammed down the receiver.

Kemper asked, "What happened?"

"I have to locate Robin. Do you have the Life 360 app on your phone? I need to login."

She tapped a few buttons and handed her phone over. "Anything I can help with?"

"No." He examined the open app and found the log in. Remembering his password was always a challenge for him. But after his shipwreck a few months back, he'd gotten a new phone and created a new password that he used for all his apps—'Stumpyrulz!'.

Quickly, he found Robin's location and, surprisingly, she was only a couple miles west of the television station along Centerline Road, as if she had been on her way to see him. "Found her. I'm calling Dottie." He closed the app.

A loud boom shook the building and the lights went out, leaving only pitch darkness.

"Whoa!" Kemper sidled up next to him and held his arm. "Oh no."

Johnnie didn't mind her holding on to him. "We're okay." He dialed Dottie back on Andréa's desk phone. After a moment, an electronic voice came on, "The number you have attempted to dial is out of service…" He ended the call and hit redial. Now only a steady beep indicating no service at all.

Kemper took the handset from him and held it to her ear. "No service?"

"Nope."

She took the note with Dottie's number and tried it on her cell. After a couple moments, she nodded. "Just beeping. Landlines seem to be out. So, tell me what's going on. Why did you have to locate Robin?"

He was too tired to maintain this secret and he trusted Kemper. Drawing in a long breath, Johnnie closed his eyes and let the truth be known. "She was drunk driving and got in an accident. But Dottie said I can't call the police. Can you believe this crap?"

"Oh, gosh! Come on, let's go get her." Kemper grabbed his hand and pulled him toward the exit.

He jerked her back, holding onto her hand. "I'm not going. She got herself into this. You saw it. It's fucking dangerous out there."

Kemper grunted, "I'll go." She pulled to escape his grasp like a stubborn Pitbull, but he didn't let go.

Johnnie shook his head. "Are you crazy? You can't go out there!"

She stuck two fingers into his chest. "Let go of me! What's wrong with you? She could die!"

He released her. "Oh, come on. Really? I bet she's fine."

Kemper hit some icons on her phone and held up the Life 360 map. "Got it. I'll go get her myself!"

With his eyes adjusting to the darkness with the aid of the red glowing exit sign above the office door, Johnnie made out Kemper's eerily defiant eyes. He couldn't take it anymore. "Stop! Jumping Johosephat…I know what you are doing. You think you can shame me into going to get her? Look, I warned the island about this dumb storm. What more do you want from me?"

Kemper shook her head. In a low weary voice, she said, "Maybe I don't know *who* you are." But instead of waiting for a response, she left the room and closed the door.

"Wait!" He threw open the door, but she was gone. Johnnie walked around Andréa's desk and slumped down in her office chair.

As he made a lazy circle in the chair, he considered his options. Be the bigger man and help his sister? One last time? Then be free from her forever with a clear conscience. Yet, his buttocks felt affixed to the chair with super glue.

He wondered what his mom would say about his hesitation. Her words in Miami still haunted his thoughts: *what matters is getting up every day and being there for others.* Johnnie couldn't imagine a life on the streets helping homeless people. Maybe his mom was just making up for all her wicked deeds, trying to assuage her conscience. Still, she must be lonely without family. He ought to go find her and make sure she is okay. After the storm, he'd make it his mission. He whispered, "Mom, I'm going to find you. I will."

A boom of thunder outside punctuated his promise. He chuckled. Maybe the weatherman was right about the goddess Tempestas. "Like that one, God lady?"

Yet, it occurred to him the best way to find his mom would be with Robin's help. Which meant he had to go save her sorry ass.

Fuck.

Johnnie leapt up and raced after Kemper, hoping she hadn't left yet. He called down the hall. "Wait! Boss! Don't go!"

* * *

The Reverend pulled up into Gertie's driveway, which was littered with branches and leaves. He leaned over, his face inches from hers. In a voice smooth like buttercream, he asked, "Did you have an enjoyable time? I sure would like to see you again."

Gertie could tell he expected a kiss. And not just a peck on the cheek. "Yes, it was great. See you at church on Sunday?" She offered a handshake.

Taking at least some of the hint, he eased back and took her hand, lifting the back of it to his lips. "You know, it isn't fit for man nor beast on these roads tonight."

This was certainly the truth. On their way back from the restaurant, they encountered mud flowing onto the road and a toppled tree, plus a light show greater than the Fourth of July. What should have been a thirty-minute drive took almost an hour and a half.

"Yes, you should hurry home. Before the roads get worse. Like you said, the big guy is looking out for you." She smiled sweetly, gleeful at using his own words against him.

"Let me walk you to the door." He pulled on the latch of the driver's side door.

Without intending to, she shouted a sharp, "No!" She took a cleansing breath. "No need for us both to get soaked." She whipped open her car door, her keys already in hand, and raced to the house, her feet splashing through puddles.

Once inside, she waved from the other side of the screen door. "Bye, drive safe!"

Gregory waved back from behind the steering wheel.

She shut the door and leaned against it. "Thank God that is over!" She kicked off her wet shoes.

As she turned toward the kitchen, she noticed her floors looked oddly clean, unlike the heaping trash pile she had left hours earlier. The oven was on with the door ajar.

A snore from the sofa alerted her to the culprit. *Cudlow?*

In a way, he seemed kind of cute sleeping there, wearing her pink robe. Waking him would be a pity, especially after he cleaned her floors.

Instead, Gertie turned off the oven, then went to her bedroom to don a sweater and yoga pants. She grabbed her laptop and set up on a comfy chair opposite him. There were so many things for her to plan. With the internet out, she could still type up her to-do list. First, research building codes for restaurants. Then, how to set up a corporation. And decide on a name for her bistro, devise a menu, develop a budget for new restaurant-quality cooking appliances because there was no way, on God's green earth, she would touch the ones already in that place. She added 'look up a good extermination company' to the list.

A few minutes later, a tremendous thunder crack shook the house. Gertie yelped.

Cudlow rolled over, apparently also startled by the noise. "My goodness. When did you get home?"

Gertie smiled. He seemed so disheveled, yet sweet. Like a sleepy kitten. Or maybe a very sleepy and still sexy Cudlow. Maybe she was juiced up from the excitement of her new endeavor. Maybe geared up from earlier expectations about her date, before she discovered the Reverend was as dull as dish soap. Whatever it was, she plunked her laptop on the floor and dove over to the sofa. She threw herself on top of Cud to nuzzle him. "Hey, kiss me."

"Stop it, Gertrude." His eyes were wide now. "I didn't come here for this."

"Oh, really?" She pulled herself up and straddled him instead. "I'm in such a great mood. Ask me why! Ask me why I'm in such a fantastic mood." She leaned over to kiss his neck.

"Stop! I mean it. Let me up."

She perceived both terror and seriousness in his tone. "Fine." Gertie moved off him and took a seat on the sofa arm. "Kill joy! Well, I decided to start a business. A pastry café. I found the best location. I could really use your help. You know so much about running a business. I don't know what paperwork I'll need—"

"We don't have time for this!" Cudlow got to his feet and ran his fingers through his hair, his eyes darting maniacally. "Go get a coat. We'll take your car."

Boom! Another thunderclap caused the ceiling fan to shudder, and the lights went out.

Gertie inched her way toward Cudlow. Finding his arm, she wrapped it around her. "I think the Lord is saying we should go have some fun in the dark." She unwrapped the front of his robe and tucked herself against him. "It isn't a night for man nor beast—"

He lifted her chin. "Gertrude. I need you to listen. We can't be here."

She ran her hands across his buttocks and murmured, "Yes, let's go to the bedroom and snuggle under the covers."

Cud backed away from her but tripped over her coffee table, landing on the hardwood floor. "Ow! Blast!"

Her eyes adjusted to the dim light from the night sky outside her picture window. "Oh, no! I'm sorry. Let me help you. I'll kiss it and make it better."

Cudlow scrambled upright and raced behind her armchair as a barrier. "Please. What can I do to make you come with me?"

"With you? Where?"

He hesitated, then let out a long breath. "To the community shelter. My mother says if you stay here, you will die at midnight."

Gertie shook her head. "Wait. Are you telling me that your mom's ghost told you this? Are you feeling okay?"

"I don't expect you to believe me. I hardly believe it myself. But if anything happened to you…"

"Ha! You *do* love me. Say it. Say you love me."

"Fine." He approached her and took her hand. "I will if you promise to come with me. Right now."

The weariness and resolve in his voice made her wince with guilt. "Cudlow. I was just kidding. You don't have to say that. I'm just…I mean…" What did she mean? A frolicking roll in the hay was one thing. Proclaiming love for each other was something completely different. After Cudlow's mental break with reality a few weeks ago, all this talk of love might send him into another downward spiral. She didn't want to hurt him. "I'm sorry. I'm just in a strange mood. It's been a weird day and I'm so excited I can't think straight."

With a softness in his voice, he said, "I understand. Now, can we go?" He gripped her hand tighter.

The rain was pouring outside her front window like a car wash. Lightning stretched across the sky in a spider's web. "Cudlow, I'm fine with being friends, but I'm *not* going back out in that. Not on the word of a ghost. It just isn't safe."

Cudlow released her and took a seat in the arm chair. "Mother! Please help me. Please tell Gertrude. Make her believe."

Gertie sniggered and crossed her arms, looking around the dark space. "Yes, Camille. Show me the error of my ways."

They waited, frozen in place, glancing around for a response.

After a long thirty seconds, Gertie chuckled, "Ha! See, I knew it."

BLAM! In an explosion of glass, the kitchen window shattered near the sink, a thick tree branch through the middle.

Gertie ducked and screamed. "Oh, dear God!"

A flower pot crashed through the front window, sending shards towards them. A sliver lodged in Gertie's arm. Wind and rain howled through the living room. Bracing herself against the wind, she ran her hands through her hair. More tiny rice-sized slivers stuck to her fingertips.

"Damn. Okay, Mrs. Loughton. You win!"

Cudlow grabbed her hand. "Get a rain coat and boots. Come on. I need you to drive."

A minute later, they were on the main road, heading north toward Centerline Road.

Gertie focused on the road and her breathing, trying to concentrate and trying not to have a heart attack. "Your mom does *not* fuck around."

Cudlow seemed to pluck something from her hair. "That's better." He held out a quarter-size chunk of wood from a broken window pane for her to see. "Mother has a way about her, doesn't she?"

"Well, at least I know one thing." She clenched the steering wheel, aiming for the center of the road to avoid a growing river of detritus.

"What's that?"

Gertie ran her hand through her hair. "I never met Camille, but I think I would have really liked her."

Chapter 22

Johnnie found Kemper in the lobby. She was zipping up what seemed to be a borrowed yellow men's rain coat from its gigantic size. "Boss, stop, I got this."

She looked up. After a blank stare, she said, "Do you?"

Kemper was rarely sarcastic, and even more rarely angry. Yet, she was clearly both, if he interpreted her tone correctly. "I'm sorry. Really. I'll get Robin."

She stuffed her hands in the deep pockets of the jacket. "Great. I'll come with."

"No. It's dangerous. Please stay here with Merv. Take care of Stumpy for me. Please?" He put a hand on her shoulder, which he hoped was a reassuring move, yet this contact made him feel like a phony. He pulled his hand away like it was on a hot stove and rubbed the back of his neck instead.

The tension around her eyes softened. "Are you sure?"

Even in the dim red light of the emergency exit sign above the door, he noticed the concern on her face.

"Yes."

"Alright. The station manager said we should all be safe here. We'll hunker down for the night. When you get Robin, bring her back here. Deal?" She removed her jacket and extracted a cell phone and phone charger from the pocket and handed them to him. "Take these. Call Merv's number when you find her."

"Thanks, boss. Whose coat is this?"

"Benji gave it to me. He found it in a prop closet. Plus, an extra phone charger. He's a sweetie."

Johnnie nodded and took off Jacque's suit jacket and handed it to Kemper. He put on the rain coat over the dress shirt and bow tie. Bracing himself for the cold and rain, Johnnie pushed the exit bar on the steel door and began running across the dark parking lot. Once behind the steering wheel with the engine on, he plugged in the phone. It came to life with a charging symbol. A good sign until...

Oops.

Damn.

He'd forgotten to ask for the passcode to unlock it. Without the code, the phone was almost useless. Dreading the idea of going back out in the deluge, he closed his eyes, filling his mind with self-hate.

A rapping on his window snapped him out of his fixation. Through the streaming water, a human figure stood next to his car.

It was Kemper, wearing Jacque's blazer, wet as a sewer rat, hair smattered on her cheeks. She yelled, "Zero, five, eight, four. The code!"

Flustered, Johnnie realized he would never remember this. "I need a pen." He checked the glove box.

Kemper hopped up and down, shivering. After a couple of moments, she pulled on the door latch to the rear seat and climbed inside. "Whew! Look, maybe I should just come with you."

He kept rummaging for a pen.

She held up a black marker and asked for his hand. "Here let me." Kemper wrote out the numbers on his palm.

Johnnie asked, "What is that, a birthday or something?"

"Something like that. Let's go."

He adjusted the rear-view mirror to view Kemper. "Boss, I'm thinking you don't trust me. You're being...well, just like Robin. I'm not trying to be a dick, but—"

"Shoot. No, you're right. I trust you. I'll look after Stumpy. Just promise to get her..."

"I will. Promise. I'll drop you back at the door."

After dropping her off, he consulted the app to confirm Robin's location. Her pin hadn't updated in the last forty-five minutes.

He put the wipers on their top speed and still had trouble seeing. He had left his glasses at the television studio. Broken, they would have been on little help. Was this a suicide mission? Probably. But his Jeep was relatively new, which meant good tires and brakes. Although good brakes meant nothing going over a cliff.

Ten minutes later, he located Robin's car. It was in a ditch on the upward slope of a hill. Which was lucky in a way, because he didn't bring any rope for rappelling.

The rain had lightened to just a drizzle for the moment. He parked behind her car, leaving the headlights on, and approached. The front of her car was smashed, including the windshield. The airbags had gone off but were now deflated. Robin's body, strapped in by her seatbelt, slumped toward the passenger seat. Johnnie noted a bloody slash on her forehead.

"Robin!" He pulled on the car door. It wouldn't budge. "Come on, wake up!"

He busted the remaining glass in the windshield to crawl through. As he shimmied across the slick surface, nuggets of glass scraped across metal hood, poking small holes through his rain jacket. He tugged on her arm. "Robin! Say something!"

She stirred. "Where am I?"

A flood of emotions gave him gooseflesh. Happy she was alive. Angry that he was happy about that. He swallowed hard and tried to focus. "We need to get you out of here. Take my hands."

She wept. "I'm sorry. Just let me die…"

"I'll remember you said that." He crawled further through the windshield, struggling on the slick metal. He spotted an empty alcohol bottle in the foot well. "Jumping Jackass." He stretched his body to reach it, picked it up, and tossed it behind him onto the grass. "Is anything broken?"

Robin shifted in her seat and unhitched the seatbelt. "I don't think so. My chest hurts."

After some negotiation of the steering wheel and glass, he pulled her out of the car. "Come on, we need to get you dry and look at that cut." He took off his rain jacket and draped it over Robin.

They got in his Jeep and he made a K-turn to head back in the direction of the television studio.

After a moment of silence, Robin said, "Did you do it? Did you tell the world about mom? Bastard…"

"What the hell is wrong with you? I didn't mean it. I just…oh, forget it."

"You hate me. What else is new?"

The rain picked up again, obscuring the road. "Let's just be quiet, okay? I'm freaking out."

Robin yelled, "Watch out!"

Johnnie slammed on the brakes. The road was completely washed out. The jeep skidded, fishtailing side to side. They stopped right on the precipice.

A set of headlights approached in front of them, on the other side of the washout.

"Shit!" Johnnie jumped out of the car and waved his arms furiously. Against the hard pelting rain, he ran up the hill across the mud toward the approaching sedan to warn them.

Squinting in the darkness, the vehicle looked very familiar. The car came to a safe stop about ten feet away from the chasm. The driver, a woman, rolled down her window.

"Johnnie, is that you?"

It was dark, but he recognized the voice.

"Gert, you need to turn around. Head back home. There is no way to drive past this."

A male passenger with an English accent wearing a soggy pink bathrobe exited and shouted. "Johnnie! We are trapped. Barely made it this far. The road was washing out behind us. But Gertie powered us through. A veritable Evel Knievel!"

Shit.

"Come on," Johnnie waved. "Get in our car. We'll figure it out."

He helped them trudge across the upside of the hill toward his Jeep. Once safely inside Johnnie's car, all wet as mops and shivering, the mood inside was somber. Lightning pierced the sky and the rain poured in buckets.

Cud interrupted the silence. From the backseat, he clapped Johnnie on the shoulder. "Johnnie! You did get my tarp! Wonderful! I'll make us all some ponchos." He held up his pocket knife. The rapid crinkle of plastic overtook the sounds of the rain outside.

Robin, more alert now, asked, "What do we do now? If more of the road washes away, we can't stay here."

Cud stopped cutting momentarily. "Wait! I know a place. There is a turnoff about a kilometer west. There will be a bit of walking, but we'll be safe there."

Johnnie wiped water from his forehead. "Yeah? Where exactly?" He backed up the Jeep to change direction.

Cud said, "You'll see. Trust me, son. It's our best option."

* * *

A few minutes later, Johnnie parked the car on the side of the road at Cud's instruction. There was nothing special about this location. No buildings, no turnout or discernable paths. What did Cud have in mind? All his white-haired friend said was, "We need to hike the rest of the way. Just a fifteen-minute jaunt."

Cud had divided the tarp into four equal pieces which they each used as extra rain and wind protection. A thin sheet of plastic would do nothing to protect them from a lightning strike on their trek, but Johnnie was thankful for the makeshift outerwear.

Hiking through the brush and mud in a downpour at night with no flashlight was a terrible idea. Really, the worst possible. Using the flashlight on Kemper's phone would have helped but would drain the battery or worse, the rain would cause it to short out.

Johnnie could clearly sense Cud's enthusiasm and his friend's quick pace could not be argued with. His energetic friend charged ahead, leaving Johnnie to hold on to Gertie and Robin, helping them navigate rocks and trying to steady them from falling.

After about ten minutes, Johnnie yelled up to Cud in the lead, "How much further?" He wondered if his voice would carry through the din of the rain.

Cud ignored him and continued on, pushing branches out of his way, clearly on a mission.

Robin, gripped Johnnie's hand tighter. In a broken voice, she said, "This is insane. Let's go back to the car."

Clearly Robin was scared. Which was unlike her. Johnnie chalked it up to the alcohol still in her system. But she had a point. Was Cud going to get them killed? In the dark, each foot plant was treacherous. Never mind the fact that there could be unseen rocky cliffs that would send them plummeting, breaking their skulls.

But Cud's plan was better than none.

Johnnie replied, "Don't worry. Cud knows what he's doing."

A few minutes later, the vegetation cleared, opening up to a level area with old stone walkways. A former sugar mill plantation ruin. He didn't know which one, not knowing which direction they had been walking.

Cud stopped and pointed to a large silo-shaped stone structure about fifty yards to his right. "Over there. Come!" He jogged up to them and took Robin's hand. "We'll be safe and dry there. Let's go."

This left Gertie with Johnnie. He asked, "Gertie, how are you doing?"

"I twisted my ankle aways back. But I can make it."

In short order, they entered through an archway into the stone building. The walls of the room were a mix of rock, brick and concrete, with a ceiling height of about seven feet. The key feature though was that it was dry. Johnnie listened. The space was also quieter than the driving rain outside.

He turned on the flashlight app on Kemper's phone and scanned the space. In one corner, a huddle of iguanas in a solid mass scared the shit out of him. Like seeing a pod of baby aliens from that movie. The largest one hissed at him with pure malice. Or it could be the iguana didn't appreciate the flashlight in its face. "Damn! Jumpin' Jesus. Look at those things."

Cud chuckled. "See? They know a good place to hide in a storm too!"

"Well, I'm going to sit over there, away from those things. They seem pissed."

"Rightfully so. You know, I stayed here during the hurricanes. They built these plantations to take a direct hit and then some. We'll be fine here until morning."

Johnnie replied, "Thanks, Cud. I thought we were goners." He took off his tarp and shook off the water.

Gertie eased down next to the wall to sit on the floor. She took off her left boot and rubbed her ankle. "I don't suppose anyone has any food? I had the worst dinner."

Cudlow sat beside her. "No, sorry dear. I had gotten us a few supplies, but in my haste, I forgot them at your house. I can go try to find some wild mangoes—"

She held his arm. "No, maybe in the morning. I just want to sleep." Gertie rested her head on Cud's shoulder.

Johnnie tapped Robin's shoulder. "Let's sit over there. Give them some space."

His sister was no longer crying but her face was sad. Her hair was soggy and she didn't have makeup. She was still wearing the oversized men's rain jacket, making her seem even smaller. In that moment, she resembled the image in his mind of Robin at twelve years old after being reprimanded by dad for spitting out her vegetables at the dinner table.

"Johnnie, I'm really sorry…"

He nodded. "Me, too. Let's get some sleep. We can talk in the morning."

They sat a respectful distance from Gertie and Cud. He wrapped the tarp back around himself to trap his body heat, just as the others had done.

Johnnie turned off the flashlight on the phone, then checked the time—just after midnight. Maybe Gertie survived Camille's curse. He shut off the phone to conserve power.

Johnnie, sitting shoulder to shoulder with Robin, whispered, "I swear, if those iguanas turn on us, I'm gonna offer you up as a human sacrifice."

She snorted and punched him in the shoulder. "Butthead."

With a chuckle, he closed his eyes. His rump hurt from the stone floor, radiating a dull ache up his spine. Adding to his misery, his soaked clothes clung to him uncomfortably. A memory flashed about his basic training days. Being cold, wet and exhausted was the norm every day back then. How had he survived that? Youth was definitely not on his side anymore. Yet a familiar sensation overtook him, where his brain and body desperately cried out to shut down and sleep.

As his mind settled, he considered what his therapist Lou would make of his current situation. She always ended their sessions asking what he was grateful for. After some thinking, it was clear. He was grateful that his sister, Gertie and Cudlow were alive. Plus, thrilled to be out of the fucking rain.

But more than anything, he appreciated that this goddamned shitshow of a day was finally coming to an end.

Mentally, he gave a middle finger to the goddess Tempestas.

Under a stupor of drowsiness, his thoughts drifted further. Were all goddesses such cold-ass bitches? He supposed male gods were also angry unreasonable assholes; drunk on unlimited power and acting much like Chief Tobias during his rages. Why would people pray to ancient gods and goddesses when they were such insane pricks? Nothing about religion made sense.

Johnnie's head tilted downward, resting his chin on his chest. Images swirled in his head about a tiny-footed feathered god with long hair and a red-tie. The bird god spoke to a flock of seagulls and chickens asking them to bring him some hairspray and to find his watch.

It made little sense.

But dreams never do.

Chapter 23

With the power out, the television studio was illuminated by several candles the producer had borrowed from the weatherman's dressing room.

Kemper searched for Merv. She followed an odd bashing sound and found him down a narrow dead-end hall. A red emergency exit sign illuminated the narrow space.

Merv pounded a vending machine and rocked it front to back.

"Hold on, Merv. Stop!"

As he turned, she noticed the outline of Stumpy on the floor a few feet to his side.

He grunted. "I'm starving. I used to break into these all the time in high school. My record was five seconds."

"Merv, this is stealing."

He shook his head. "Boss, I'll insert some quarters later. Promise." He beat on the side of the machine with his fist. Then with both hands, pulled the machine slightly forward, then side to side. "Motherfuck—" Merv looked at her. "Sorry. I didn't mean to curse in front of you."

"Just leave it alone."

"No! I almost got it." He walked around the side and ran a couple steps up to it, leaping and throwing his shoulder into the side.

BAM! The snack machine fell over, cracking the front glass and sending jagged pieces towards her. She jumped away. "Merv! What the…?"

He shook his head. "Hey, I didn't mean…whatever." He turned on his cell phone flashlight and dug through the broken glass front to pull out several bags of pretzels and corn chips. He handed one to her. "It worked, didn't it? Hey, do you think iguanas like strawberry Newtons? They count as vegetables, right?"

How could Merv act so nonchalant about damaging property and stealing? It was just a temporary power outage. Not the end of the world.

Kemper huffed. "I'm going to find a broom. This glass is dangerous."

He grabbed her arm gently. "Hey, look." Despite the dim light, she could see his expression had changed. He was no longer smirking like a teenager who stole his dad's car for a joyride. Instead, he looked…well, repentant. His tone was softer too. "I'm sorry. I'll clean this up and promise to pay the damages later. You go distribute all this to the others."

"I get it. You were trying to help."

Merv chuckled. "You know what they say about good intentions."

"No, what?"

"Intentions get you detention! That's what my grandpa used to say. The story of my life."

She laughed. "Okay, I'll hand these out, although I feel like an accessory to a crime."

"Crime, schmime." Merv donned a silly pleading voice, his wrists together as if in handcuffs, "I'm sooo sorry officer, I swear, the vending machine hit me first! It was self-defense. A bona fide… snack attack!"

She couldn't help but laugh, despite her inner sense of right and wrong. "Okay, stop."

Merv gathered all the bags of treats and piled them in her arms. "I'm saving two for me and Stumpy."

"Roger that."

He placed his hand along her jawline, his eyes piercing. "You know, Kemper. Hearing your laugh is the best part of my day."

Stunned, she blinked. Was this some sort of come-on? Swallowing hard, she didn't know how to respond. "I…um… I like you, too." Did she mean that? It just seemed the polite thing to say. In that moment, all she could do was retreat. She backed away like a scared mouse, spun and strode toward the television studio.

Behind her, she overheard Merv say with joy, "Stumpy, she said she likes us! Really likes us! Give us a high five, bro!"

As she handed out the snacks in the darkened studio, she explained Merv's 'accident' with the machine. No one disapproved. Many of the staff asked her to thank Merv. Even the producer, Andréa.

When she returned a few minutes later, she found Merv had righted the machine and had swept up the glass. He was sitting on the floor with Stumpy on his lap. It was hard to see, but it looked like Merv was dangling a potato chip in front of the iguana, who was aggressively chomping at it.

She sat on the floor opposite him. "Is salt good for him?"

"The ocean is full of salt. Can't hurt."

"Everyone said thank you...for the food."

In a self-deprecating tone, he said, "Yeah, I'm a hero."

"I'm sorry for giving you a tough time before. I can be a bit...judgmental. I've always been someone who follows rules."

"Well, I think you are just a good person. Probably the best person I know."

She sighed. "Sometimes it feels lonesome. That I'm no fun at all." She inhaled sharply, these words hitting hard. "You know, that's what he said...my fiancé. The last thing he said to me during our breakup is that I don't know how to live...how to enjoy things." A tear rolled down her cheek. In the dark, she hoped Merv wouldn't see it or notice the crack in her voice. She took a deep breath. "I think he's probably right."

Merv set Stumpy on the floor and scooted over to sit next to her shoulder to shoulder, although his shoulder was about four inches higher because of their height difference. "Here, have a potato chip. No one can stay sad eating chips."

She took the chip and chortled, but her voice whimpered, making her laugh sound more like a cry. "Ha. But no thank you." She tossed the chip to Stumpy. The iguana scurried to snap it up.

Merv patted her knee. "Look, cheer up. I know tons of bad jokes. Want to hear some?"

Kemper wiped her eyes, which instantly caused irritation from smearing chip salt in her right eye. "Ow!" She rubbed it, causing it hurt more.

"Are you okay?"

"Ugh. I'll be fine. I'm not really in the mood for jokes." Thunder rolled above them in a prolonged cacophony of booms. After a long silence, she asked, "Do you think Johnnie will be okay?"

Merv shook his head. "He'll be fine. He always is. Hey, I have to ask. What is the deal with you two? Are you in love with him or something?"

"What?" Kemper's eyes froze wide. What kind of question was that? A moment passed and with each micro-second, she realized she had to say something, or it might seem a tacit agreement. "No. Absolutely not! I care about him like any boss would." She met his gaze and heat burned her cheeks. Heat from embarrassment, maybe anger. Raising her voice, she added, "AND I'm your boss, too. Don't forget that."

Merv shifted away a few inches. "Look, I wasn't accusing you of anything. I just notice that you treat him better. As if he was some great guy and I'm a turd sandwich."

Still fuming, she retorted, "I don't treat him better!"

"You do. Maybe you don't see it. No, I get it. He was a war hero. I respect him for that. Anyway, just completely forget what I said. I'm sorry." He crossed his arms as if he was waiting for her to forgive him.

She wasn't sure what to say. In the dark, Stumpy was crunching on what sounded like a plastic snack wrapper. The iguana's noises would have been comical, if it weren't for Merv's tantrum.

A few seconds later, he pushed up from the floor. "I'll leave you alone. See, I always do this shit. I try to be a good guy. Shit. I *want* to *be* a good guy. But I aways do and say the wrong things. See you later."

She hadn't meant to upset Merv. He had hit a nerve and on reflection, he had a point. "No, Merv...wait."

He halted. "What?"

"You are right. I treat him different." In a more formal tone, the tone she used in annual performance reviews, she added, "Thank you for bringing this to my attention. I'll be more mindful of this in the future."

Merv joined her back on the floor, sitting beside her, bumping shoulders. "Boss, it's not like I'm filing a complaint. Ha! Lighten up, okay."

Kemper laughed. "Yeah, that's what *he* said..."

He laughed. "See, that was funny. You're funny! Screw your ex. He must be a complete tool."

No one had ever called her funny before, she thought. She brightened. "Thanks for saying that."

"You know, if you were my girl, I would never let you go. Hypothetically speaking, of course." He leaned over, his face just inches from hers, his gaze intense. The red light from the exit sign reflected in his eyes, just like in an old Polaroid picture. With a tilt of his head, his lips caressed her neck. His hot breath caused a primal sensation on her chilled skin.

Johnnie had warned her about Merv. In fact, she had seen Merv and another ranger, Taylor, 'doing it' behind the Yellow Parrot bar one evening.

"Stop. What are you doing?" She pulled away.

"Sorry. You just smell nice. And we don't have much else to do." He leaned into her. "I'm yours…if you want." He ran his fingers through her hair. "I won't tell, if Stumpy won't." Merv kissed her neck and unbuttoned her blouse.

In a way she hadn't expected, his kisses felt good, sending tingles down her back. She inhaled sharply as his hand slipped under her shirt. After her fiancé broke up with her, she had seriously wondered if she would end up alone for the rest of her life.

Crack! A surge of lightning filled the air with an instantaneous buzz of electricity, startling them.

Brought back to reality, she pulled away. She had no feelings for Merv. It wasn't right.

"No. Stop. I mean it." Kemper pushed him away, then rose from the floor and adjusted her bra. "I'll see you…bye."

"Sorry, I thought you wanted…look, don't be pissed. Wait! I need to tell you something. Sit down."

Hands on her hips, she whispered, "What? What do you have to tell me?"

Merv rose and took her hand. "Kemper, I'm serious. I need to tell you…that I love you. For months now, I've been in agony, my heart breaking every time I saw you. You're my boss. I know it's wrong. But you are the sweetest, prettiest, kindest person I've ever known. I didn't know how to tell you. Please. I probably don't deserve someone like you. But I love you. Damn. I actually said it."

He loved her? This had to be complete horse-hockey. She worked her hand free of his. "Merv, I'm sorry. I don't know what to say." Although she hadn't yet admitted it out loud, her recent heartbreak had driven her to reevaluate her life and she had decided a radical change was needed. Maybe this was the best time to come clean. "I wasn't going to mention anything until it became final, but I've applied for a few jobs on the mainland, in DC. I've decided I'm going to move away from St. John the first chance I get."

"Sure, no worries. I'll go with you."

She furrowed her brow. "No. That's not my point. I'm trying to say politely that I don't love you back. You CAN'T come with me."

"You don't have to love me. I can love you enough for the both of us."

This was madness, she thought. "Do you hear yourself?" Before she could utter a further rejection, the sound of footsteps down the hall caught their attention.

The studio assistant Benji approached. "Hey, any more cookies left in the vending machine?"

Kemper took this opportunity to excuse herself. "Um. Not sure. I'm going to check on the others." She strode past Benji toward the studio.

Shame burned her cheeks and she retreated to a small alcove on the news set away from the others

The station employees were mostly asleep, curled up on the set furniture; some had wrapped themselves in costumes or curtains as make-shift blankets.

The whole day was surreal.

One thing was clear.

Moving away from the island permanently, if given a new job opportunity, was her best option.

Chapter 24

Johnnie startled at the tickle of feathers on his arm. His eyes flew open. A chicken had been sleeping on his lap. "Shoo!" The bird fluttered its wings chaotically and it pecked him on his chin before racing off into the dark. "Ow. Dang. What is this, a zoo?"

Robin laughed. Although he heard her clearly, he didn't know where she was. Searching the darkness, he located her sitting about ten feet away, leaning against the opposite wall.

The other noise in the space was Cud snoring. Meaning, it was probably still the middle of the night.

Johnnie whispered, "That wasn't funny."

Robin's disembodied voice replied, "Ha! Little brother, I wish I had a video of that. I don't know what time it is. Probably a couple of hours before dawn. The rain has tapered off."

"Good. Because I have to pee. How long have you been awake?"

"Most of the night. When you get back, I think we should talk."

Johnnie sighed. Talking with Robin was usually a one-sided deal; as in, a lecture where Robin dictated his entire life. Defeated, he responded with sarcasm, "Great. Hold that thought." He stood and headed toward the exit.

Once outside, he noticed the rain had subsided to just a light drizzle. The air had warmed up appreciably—now in the mid-seventies, from his guess.

He didn't want to venture far to do his business. The dark, dense cloud cover from earlier had broken up, with some stars visible between the gaps. At their elevation, he should have been able to see the lights of Cruz Bay in the distance. Yet only a couple points of light were perceptible, meaning the power outage was likely widespread.

Upon his return, he sat shoulder to shoulder with Robin. He whispered, "Okay, what's so important?"

She whispered back. "I should have told you about mom. I'm sorry."

"Oh, just like that. One 'I'm sorry' and that makes up for lying to me for five years? And now drunk driving?"

"No. I just want you to understand. Mom put me in a difficult situation. I'm not perfect. But please, don't take your anger with me out on her. Don't turn her in."

"Oh, jumpin' Johosephat, I would never do that. I was just pissed."

Robin exhaled. "Good. You know, I haven't spoken with her or seen her in all these years. We only communicate using an intermediary. I had to call my contact to alert Mom to get out of town because of what you said. I may never find her again."

"Shit. I'm sorry."

"You didn't leave me any choice."

"You'll find her again. I mean, you have a system for everything. Don't you have a backup way to contact her?"

Robin shook her head. "No. I gave her the code word that cuts all ties. Damn. I was so furious with you. Hey, what were you doing at the television studio then?

He closed his eyes, feeling embarrassed by the entire ordeal. "Warning the residents about the storm. You know, because of the ghost."

"Huh? After that goddamned nonsense at the library this morning, you still think a ghost predicted the storm? Are you feeling alright?" She held her hand to his forehead as if reading his temperature.

Johnnie reflected on the last twenty-four hours. Was he alright? First the ghost dream, then nearly killed by the police chief, later seeing the murderer Thomas Smith and learning the call from Greta wasn't real. Topped off by discovering their criminal mom was still alive, then getting beaten up by the stupid weatherman, and lastly the fracas at the television studio. So he kept it simple.

"I know the part about Greta asking me to protect the library was…" he sighed, "a mistake." He paused, considering how to describe his reasoning. "And the news producer showed me the radar maps showing there wasn't a hurricane. Honestly, it was the fucking lightning. If you had seen it earlier…I know this sounds dumb, but I *just knew,* with all my being, that the ghost's warning to get residents to shelter before midnight *had* to be true. For fuck's sake, think about it. You could have died out there…"

He couldn't tell if Robin was buying all this. It was a lot to take in for anybody. It was best to leave it there. "Ugh, I have a lot more to tell you, but maybe another time."

She pulled on his arm. "You didn't tell Arturo about my drinking and car accident, did you?"

"Jesus, Robin. No. I'm not a rat fink."

She snorted. "Damn. I think my political life is over anyway."

"Ha! Not after what happened earlier tonight. Chief Tobias really shit himself on television."

"What do you mean?"

"I'm sure they will re-air it or you can find it on the internet. Man, he really screwed himself."

"Sorry to hear that."

"Ha! Come on, you love it. Tobias is a complete dick."

"He's actually a decent man. Although, I honestly don't know why he hates you so much."

Johnnie wondered as well. Probably the 'naked on the ferry' incident. "Yeah, me neither. You never asked Arturo?"

"I leave Arturo out of our family business. Hey, now that you know about mom, tell me how it went in Miami. What did you two discuss? How is her health? Did she seem happy?"

"She seemed fine. We had sort of talked about family. Shit. I had no idea…I wish I knew it was her at the time. I would have asked her about lots of other stuff."

"What stuff?"

"Like, what was I was like growing up? Or later. Both you and Darla said I was an asshole. Is it true? Give it to me straight."

Robin yawned. "Let's get some sleep. I promise we'll talk about this another time. But what matters is, you are a halfway decent brother most of the time. Even though you are a pain in the neck and a butthead, you are definitely not an asshole."

"Ha. A ringing testimonial…"

"Johnnie, don't push it." She tousled his hair and kissed him on the cheek.

"Okay, sis. Sweet dreams." Johnnie left her and moved to his previous spot. He swished some chicken feathers aside, curled into a ball on the floor, and fervently wished for daybreak to come.

Cud's snoring continued, echoing off the curved ceiling.

Everyone was safe and sound. And he was talking with Robin again. Things could have gone so much worse last night. He expected the morning would be full of new challenges, with massive infrastructure damage and extensive road closures. It was best to conserve his energy, get some sleep, and enjoy the relative peace in the meantime.

And maybe, if he was lucky, Cud's ghost mom would never bother them again.

* * *

Cud woke to the sound of Gertie singing outside. The sun was up. Both Johnnie and Robin were still asleep. He brushed back his tangled hair and headed in the direction of Gertie's angelic voice.

As he emerged, she turned. "Hey there, sleepy head."

Gertie was weaving some palm fronds, sitting on a stone wall. Her aura was pale blue and she gave off a cheerful energy. But what struck him the most was her glowing skin. Gertie was always beautiful in his eyes. Yet in this particular morning light, she was transcendent.

The surrounding area was full of twigs, leaves and other scattered organic matter. Swaths of eroded soil revealed where the rain water had converged and carved new channels in the earth.

Cud asked, "What are you making?"

Gertie beamed. "I didn't know what to do with myself, so I thought I'd make us some hats. The sun is pretty strong. We'll probably need to hike our way out of here. I'm almost done with the last one." She pointed towards the West. "Look over there, a rainbow."

Towards Cruz Bay, an enormous rainbow arched over the entire horizon. It was stunning.

"Gertie, I need to tell you something."

She continued her weaving. "Do you want to help? I can teach you—"

"No. I mean, that would be lovely. But I owe you an explanation."

"Explanation for what?" Her busy fingers kept moving.

Cudlow wondered if this was a bad time. Yet, he wasn't sure he would get the chance again. "I haven't been honest with you."

"About?"

"Can you put that down? This is difficult."

She put down the palm leaves. "You know, I still want to pick your brain about my new business. I have so many questions about taxes and how to incorporate. I was thinking a sole-proprietorship, but might need employees—"

He sat beside her. "Please. Listen."

She rolled her head as if working out some kinks. Then looked him squarely in the eyes. "Yes. Go ahead."

"I've been avoiding you these past couple of weeks...as I'm sure you've suspected. And I want to apologize. I was scared. Perhaps I'm still scared. Our relationship has been...not the easiest. Mostly because of my errors in judgement and emotional issues. I wasn't ready. But I loved you so much, I thought I could..."

"Please, Cudlow, you don't have to explain. Like I said, I want us to be friends. I shouldn't have flirted with you last night..."

"What I'm trying to say is, I *still* love you. Will *always* love you. I don't want to be *friends*. But I need more time."

Gertie blinked. "Sure. Yes. We have lots of time."

"Really?"

"I was thinking of traveling a bit. Get inspiration for my new business. I wanted to go back to France...maybe see my cousin in Spain. So, don't fret about it. We can talk about 'us' when I get back." She gave him a warm smile and the look in her eyes showed pure love. Yet, the next moment she picked up the palm frond and continued working on it without looking up.

"I would like that." Cud couldn't quite read Gertie's intentions. He had hoped she would have reciprocated a declaration of love or, at a minimum, perhaps leaned in to share a romantic kiss. But instead, her manner was so matter-of-fact and business-like about their situation. Not that she came off cold, but perhaps more indifferent.

A strange realization hit him. Is this how he had come across to his first wife? Fully distracted by thoughts of business...insensitive, callous? But no, Gertie could *never be* like his former self. Not remotely.

He thought it best to let her be. "Um, ah, I'll go see if Johnnie and Robin are awake."

Gertie didn't look up, but resumed singing as she worked. "Somewhere, over the rainbow…"

Such a fitting song. Cud hummed the tune to himself as he walked back to the plantation structure.

He found Johnnie and Robin awake. "Are you ready? We should go into town."

Johnnie was holding a cellphone. "We just spoke with Dottie. She heard from one of Gertie's neighbors that her roof blew off. Good thing you guys got out of there."

"Hmm. Good indeed."

Robin said, "I need to get to the office right away. Arturo said that if we can hike down to North Shore Road near Cinnamon Cay, he can pick us up."

Cud grinned. "I know a trail. If we are lucky, we might come across some good fruit for breakfast." He patted the knife sheath on his belt.

Robin put her arm around Johnnie's shoulder. "Where's Gertie?"

Cud motioned to the outside. "Weaving us hats. Come, you need to see the rainbow."

The three walked outside and gazed at the sight.

Gertie shuffling with a small limp, joined them and put her arm around Cud's waist.

Cud asked, "How is your ankle? Do you think you can walk?"

She nodded. "It's just sprained. I'll be fine."

He bent to unlace his boots. "Please, take these. They may be large on you, but they have excellent ankle support. I must say, these boots made me feel invincible. Perhaps you'll feel the same."

Gertie laughed. "What will you wear?"

Cudlow stripped off the socks. "I walked this island barefoot for ten years. I'll be fine."

He handed her his footwear. She sat back on the low rock wall, trading her rain boots for his leather ankle boots.

Gertie gazed at the rainbow. "Looks just like a postcard."

Cud had seen many rainbows, but at this moment, Gertie seemed more beautiful than any refraction of light through atmospheric moisture. He mentally thanked the Lord for Gertie's safety. But more so, he mouthed a thank you to his mom, wherever she was. While Gertie was lacing the boots, he gathered the palm hats and distributed them to Johnnie and Robin.

Robin frowned as she tried on the woven cone-shaped bonnet. "I bet I look ridiculous in this."

Gertie looked up from her laces toward Robin. "Not as ridiculous as a second-degree sunburn."

Johnnie stood there, arms crossed, face rather sullen, like a boy who had just lost his puppy.

Cud, wanting to cheer up the crew, took this cue to don his hat and take center stage. "Robin, pardon me for disagreeing, but simply wearing a hat is *not* ridiculous. Let me demonstrate. Ahem." He launched into an Irish Jig. Not that he was Irish, but he'd taken part in many jigs at the pub during his time at university.

He bounced up and down, knees high, slapping his ankles. "Now THIS! This is ridiculous!" He twirled around, making funny faces and sang, "We all live in a yellow submarine—come on, Johnnie, join in! You know the words!"

Johnnie shook his head, his expression tight with disapproval. "Cud, come on. Save your energy for the hike."

"Oh, smile Johnnie! This is a glorious day." He shifted to a hula style dance. "Can't you sense it in your bones?"

"What's so glorious? We almost died last night. With the roads messed up, we might not get home for days."

Cud stopped dancing and beamed. "Johnnie, don't you realize? Home is where your loved ones are. Look around." He waved his arms in a circle. "See, we're *already* home."

Chapter 25

By the time they hiked down the hillside to North Shore Road, the rainbow had vanished and the sun blazed overhead. Arturo was waiting for them as promised.

Johnnie called dibs on the passenger seat of Arturo's police car, leaving Cud, Gertie, and Robin in the back seat. After the previous evening's hardships, Johnnie felt his mood lift significantly as it felt awesome *not* to be the one in the backseat behind the steel wire cage for once.

During the ride, Robin, using Arturo's phone, chatted at rapid fire pace with Dottie. Johnnie couldn't make out most of it, but didn't care to. With the day's heat, Johnnie busied himself by cutting Jacque's dress pants into shorts with the aid of Cud's pocket knife and rolling up his dress shirt sleeves.

Arturo drove them toward Cruz Bay. Residents at Estate Lindholm sat under trees, fanning themselves. It was clear the power was out. Electric lines along the side streets made squiggles on the pavement. As they passed Mongoose Junction on the north edge of Cruz Bay, they saw a jeep on its side. A mud line along the worn wooden houses showed a foot-tall high-water-mark but the water had since subsided.

Johnnie asked Arturo, "What's the plan? What can I do to help?"

"They could use some volunteers at the Yellow Parrot. It was struck by lightning and caught on fire last night. Mandy asked for help to clear up the debris and shovel out mud. Or you can join the church groups going door to door to check on folks. They have a makeshift command center at the firehouse."

Johnnie chose to work at the Parrot. When they arrived, Robin switched places with him to take the front seat. "Johnnie, meet me at my office around lunchtime. Hopefully, I'll have an update on the roads and how you can get home."

He nodded.

The streets were littered with broken shutters, window glass, and twisted metal. A perfect recipe for tetanus. Thankful he still had his work boots on, he navigated his way toward the waterfront.

His favorite bar, the Yellow Parrot, was in shambles. Half the roof gone. The other half blackened with warped steel panels. The bartop and shelves of liquor were obliterated, just splinters and shattered bottles. Support posts had snapped and he feared the remaining roof could fall at any moment. Several young men and a white-haired guy were taking a break under the shady part, drinking beers from a cooler. In the middle of the space, Mandy, the barkeep, with her hair in long dark braids and wearing her signature Mets cap, was dragging a broken table top to a newly formed trash heap.

"Hey, Mandy." He waved.

"Johnnie! You come to help?" She dropped the heavy wood top. "Whew." She wiped her perspiring brow with a bandana. "I could use some of that cool breeze from last night. Ain't it always the way? Cool when you don't want it, but boiling hot when you have work to do."

He chuckled. "Hey, take a breather. I'll take that. You want it over there?" He pointed to the pile.

"Yes! By the way, I want to thank you."

He hefted the table top to get a good grip. It was surprisingly heavy and he felt embarrassed struggling to lift it. "Thank me for what?" He set the end of the table down.

"Your warning on the news. I closed the bar right after. You would think the cold and rain would make these folks see reason and go home...but no, they were partying like there was no tomorrow. Something about a storm brings out the worst in people."

"You closed the bar because of my warning? Hell, I wasn't even sure I believed the storm would get this bad." He tried to lift the table again, but couldn't quite manage.

Mandy picked up the other end of the table top and they carried it together to the pile. "Johnnie, you come in here and hardly ever say a word.

So I said to myself, if this man goes on live television to give a warning, I pay attention. And wouldn't you know it…" In unison, they swung the table top back for momentum to heave it up on the pile. "Not ten minutes later, after the last customer left and I closed out the till, BOOM! A direct hit. Sparks and fire. Half the roof cracks off in a crazy gust and flies toward the bay."

She touched his shoulder. "Folks would have died if you hadn't done what you did. Like a miracle, no other explanation."

Johnnie had always admired Mandy. It was easy to be around her because of her inner confidence. Receiving praise from her made him stand a little straighter. "Well, I'm glad you were all safe."

"Ha! Look at this mess. Been trying to call the insurance company. They don't pick up."

"I don't know." He grinned. "Some paint, a little cleanup, maybe a bulldozer…this place will be good to go in no time."

She smiled. "I appreciate you helping. Oh! Go grab that piece of plywood over there. Take a good look at it."

He squinted at the object situated about five yards away from the bar's property by the ferry dock. "That one?"

"Yes. Turn it over."

Johnnie strode over to it. The large plywood sheet was cracked in the middle, but still intact. He turned it over and grinned.

"Did you see who did this?" he asked.

"Everyone who's walked by it this morning has beat on it, spit on it, spray-painted bad words on it, or worse."

Mandy was being polite in her assessment. Someone had spray painted a big penis on Tobias' election billboard. And it clearly reeked of urine.

Johnnie dropped it back in its original spot facing down, wiped his hands on his cut-off pants, and returned to Mandy. "Is this because…?"

She nodded. "Folks saw him on television last night. People around here don't tolerate bullies with a badge. You remember Jupiter? From the ferry? Thankfully he flipped it over to stop the parade of public urination."

Robin is going to love this, he thought. "I should show my sister."

Mandy fished her cell phone from her back pocket. "No need. It's all over social media." She scrolled Instagram to show him the images. "Some guy named Jacque reposted it a few dozen times. Same guy made a hilarious

TikTok of the Chief from the television footage. It had over 100,000 views in three hours."

Johnnie chuckled. Tobias's hopes to unseat his sister were toast. He muttered to himself, "Maybe there is justice in the world after all…"

Mandy strode over to the men drinking beer and clapped her hands loudly. "This place won't clean up on its own. Let's go, break is over."

For the rest of the morning, while Johnnie helped clean up at the bar, random people walking by stopped to come up to him, to say they saw him on TV, as if he were a celebrity.

Later on, preoccupied with sweeping, he heard Mandy say, "Hey, Johnnie, you have a visitor."

Hot, sweaty and tired, Johnnie heard a car horn and looked up.

He recognized the driver immediately, plus her little green friend.

* * *

Kemper waved to him from behind her Park Service truck windshield. Stumpy was on the dashboard. "There you are!"

Johnnie dusted off his hands and waved back. "How did you get through? I thought all the roads across the island were closed."

"Just Centerline Road. But it still took two hours to get here around the debris."

He waved to Stumpy. "Hey, fella. How'd it go last night?" Awkwardly, he realized he should ask Kemper that question instead of the iguana. "Um. Kemper, how did it go last night? Was everyone safe?"

"Yes, we were fine."

"Where's Merv?"

"At the visitor center. I need to call everyone to see who can come in this afternoon. We're doing a damage assessment and working up plans on what to repair first."

"What about the government shut-down?"

"We're being considered 'essential' workers in light of the storm damage. Hey, do you still have my phone?"

He'd completely forgotten he had borrowed her phone. Checking both pockets, he discovered the only possessions on him were his Jeep keys, a torn-off paper medical wristband, and his still soggy wallet. No phone.

"Damn. I'm sorry. I must have left it at the place where we camped out at last night."

"Johnnie, I really need my phone!"

"Shit. See? This is why I'd be a lousy assistant. I don't even know where we were. Some old plantation ruins. Cud probably knows the name."

"Don't worry about it. I'll check with Mr. Loughton."

He wrung his hands. "No, boss. It's my fault. I'll get it back to you. Today. Promise."

"Thanks. Hey, Dottie told me Robin got into the office at eight this morning. Just a minor cut on her head. I guess things went alright with you two?"

"Yeah. I think I forgive her. Mostly."

"I'm glad."

"Hey, Kemper…I really appreciate you…being there for me yesterday." Not wanting this declaration to seem too touching, he added, "And being there for Stumpy, too."

Kemper rolled her eyes. She picked up Stumpy and exited the car. Handing the iguana to Johnnie, she had a serious expression. "Johnnie, I will always be there for you. But I've been applying for jobs on the mainland. I'm planning on leaving St. John at the first opportunity."

He arranged Stumpy on his shoulder. "Well, I wish you would stay."

"You do?" Her eyes brightened.

"Well, yeah. I need at least one *normal* person in my life…"

Kemper's shoulders sank. "What about Greta? She's got a good head on her shoulders, from what I hear."

"I *love* Greta. That's different. Besides, I don't know if she's ever coming back."

"I see. Well, I'll give it some consideration."

"Cool."

Kemper returned to her vehicle. "Be safe, Johnnie. See you later!"

After she departed, Johnnie wondered how he was going to find Cud and then get transportation to locate Kemper's cell phone. It was mid-day and time for lunch. He headed to the Legislative Annex, hoping Robin might help.

He grunted with pain as he walked, his legs and back aching from the previous night's hiking, sleeping on a stone floor, and all the manual labor at the Yellow Parrot.

A sense of defeat came over him with the plain and devastating irony of his situation.

You can't go one day without my help, his sister had said just yesterday. And he hated her guts for that.

Only it was so true.

So goddamn true.

❋ ❋ ❋

Dear Diary,

It's been four days since the storm, and life is slowly getting back to normal.

Cud and I moved back to my place, which was completely undamaged except for some water that came into the bathroom window. Go figure.

Gertie won't be able to return to her house until the roof and windows are replaced, so she headed to Paris for a month to attend a fancy pastry school. Cud secretly enlisted the Goddess to redesign Gertie's house, including a surprise kitchen remodel.

The biggest news is that an anonymous rich person donated ten million dollars to repair the roads and I know it wasn't Cud or Jackson because I asked. Dottie said a man wearing a sequin tank top walked into Robin's office unannounced and dropped off a cashier's check. So I think the money came from Thomas Smith. But maybe we'll never know.

Work has been hard. We're pulling twelve-hour shifts with all the repairs and I'm exhausted when I get home, especially navigating all the road detours. Cud is still singing all the time and drinking all the milk, but somehow, I don't care anymore. I'm just glad we have power for the refrigerator, considering many areas still don't have electricity.

The election is coming up in two days. Tobias has left the island on a 'family emergency' but that is probably bullshit. In the meantime, Arturo is acting police chief and doing a great job. Robin is so proud of him, but now she's complaining he doesn't have time for her. Karma can be a bitch.

Stumpy is back at Hawksnest. Since the storm, the number of chickens on the beaches has quadrupled, or maybe more. I can tell he is pissed. I watched him trying to chase them off the beach but they aren't scared of him. Poor Stumpy.

Dottie said Jupiter saw the freaky weather dude on the ferry carrying a bunch of suitcases. Which means maybe the Goddess broke up with him. I asked Cud to see if he could find out. Not that I'm still infatuated with the Goddess, just curious. All he said is, "You know, she doesn't have an aura," and walked away. Like, what the fuck does that mean?

I spoke with my therapist Dr. Lou last night and told her the whole ghost dream saga. She said that dreaming and remembering dreams are usually good signs that perhaps my brain is continuing to heal. I hope she is right. Last night I had a nightmare about being chased in the woods by a group of evil house cats before falling into a deep dark hole. So maybe I was happier when I didn't remember dreams.

Lou asked me about Greta. I said I didn't want to talk about her. Mostly because I don't have a clue about when she will return or where we stand.

Sweet dreams Diary.

Love, Johnnie

It was only seven at night. Since the storm, he and Cud usually ate dinner early and went to sleep before eight due to their long days of physical labor.

Cud was currently snoring on the sofa. Yet, Johnnie felt wide awake for another reason. He closed the diary and glanced over at his new replacement phone. Dottie had transferred all his old contacts into it from the cloud earlier that morning. Somehow, all the photos on his old phone didn't transfer. It was as if his entire time with Greta had been erased.

His short-lived romance with Greta had felt magical. He especially enjoyed her laughter and the sensation of her long red hair caressing his face. Yet, he also recalled their conversation about having kids. It was a theoretical conversation given their early courtship. Without a doubt, Greta would be an amazing mom. However, at the time, he told her he didn't want kids.

A sense of guilt weighed on him about how selfish it would be to ask her to give up motherhood should their relationship continue. Johnnie inwardly vowed that if she were willing to take him back, he would do everything in his power to overcome his fear of parenthood and reconsider.

He slunk down under the covers, staring at the dark ceiling trying to picture Greta's face. The image in his mind was fuzzy. He recalled the small clover-shaped birthmark on her neck. What color were her eyes? Green? Blue? Grayish?

The more he tried to piece together memories of their time as a couple, the more the memories faded and he wondered if there was any true love in the world. But maybe if he heard her voice, the pieces might come flooding back to him.

He picked up his phone and dialed. She answered on the third ring. "Johnnie? Hi, how are you? I saw the news about a storm."

Johnnie moved the phone to his good ear. "Hi. Yeah. The storm was pretty bad. Lots of damage. Some power outages."

"Oh! That's horrible. How is Gertie? Robin? I saw the fight televised at the news station. I can't believe Joseph said that to you. What happened?"

Discussing the events leading up to the brawl would take too long.

"It doesn't matter. I called because…" He paused. Why exactly did he call? "Um, how are things with your dad?"

"Dad got more scans done yesterday. His chemo will take months. Doesn't look good. I talked with Ms. Teller a few minutes ago. I have to quit my job. Wouldn't be fair of her to not backfill my position for months."

"Sorry to hear about your dad. But…you are coming back, though… eventually?"

There was a heavy silence. "No. I'm moving back here permanently."

Johnnie's eyes watered and his jaw trembled. "I…I understand."

"Look, I'm in the middle of making Dad dinner. Can I call you tomorrow?"

"No. I'm good. We're good. I just…"

"Shoot. Ow! Sorry, I just burned myself…hold on."

He heard a series of metallic clatter noises and her voice trailed off before the line went dead.

And that was it. Johnnie chose not to call her back. It was, to say the least, an awkward ending to their relationship. Definitely not providing the sense of closure he needed.

Maybe his infatuation with Greta wasn't actual love, he wondered. She was the first woman to take an interest in him since his accident. Perhaps his deep attachment to her was just his excessive longing to feel accepted.

If he was facing facts, it made no sense that Greta, the smartest, nicest woman on the island would want anything to do with his damaged brain. So perhaps their parting was inevitable. Still, his insides hurt, like someone had carved him up like a Halloween pumpkin, scooping out his heart, leaving pathetic globs of seeds, mush and sorrow in his otherwise hollow core.

Yet, he decided it wasn't officially over between them until he saw her in person. He needed to have a real conversation with her, face-to-face, to understand if what they had was real.

However long that would take, he could wait and hope.

About the Author

DS Whitaker is a Virginia author who loves quirky, contemporary stories with oddball twists. Johnnie and the Tempest is the fourth book of the Johnnie Series.

Her debut novel, Antigenesis, was a finalist in the 2020 National Indie Excellence Awards. Book one of the Johnnie series, Johnnie Finds a Dead Body, was a 2021 NIEA Finalist for comedy.

Follow her on X at @ds_whitaker. To get updates about the next books in the Johnnie series or her other writing projects, visit her website and subscribe to her mailing list at www.dswhitaker.com.

Other works by DS Whitaker available on Amazon:
        Antigenesis
        Planet of the Creeps
        Shower of Lies

        Johnnie Finds a Dead Body (Book 1)
        Johnnie the Pirate King (Book 2)
        Johnnie in Miami (Book 3)

She plans to release the next book in the series, tentatively titled *Johnnie and the Warrior Camp*, in early 2025.

Dear Reader!

While I have your attention,
please consider leaving a book
review on Amazon or Goodreads!

Thank You!

www.ingramcontent.com/pod-product-compliance
Lightning Source LLC
Chambersburg PA
CBHW051950220626
47052CB00004B/888